The Escape Plan

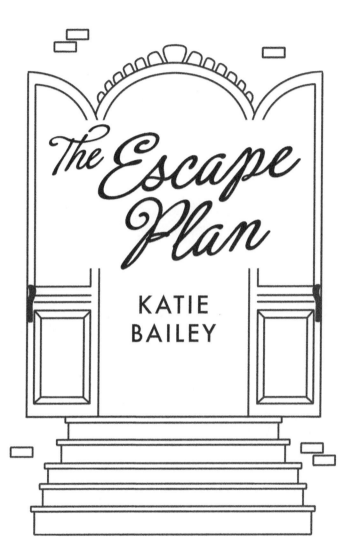

The Escape Plan

KATIE BAILEY

Book cover design and illustration by Melody Jeffries

One for sorrow,
Two for joy,
Three for a girl,
Four for a boy,
Five for silver,
Six for gold,
Seven for a secret never to be told.

- Popular modern version of an eighteenth-century nursery rhyme based on an old superstition about counting magpies to predict good or bad luck.

Irish Name Pronunciation & Dialect Guide

Aoife - *Ee-fah*, girl's name
Eoin - *Ow-en*, boy's name
Niamh - *Nee-ve,* girl's name
Roisin - *Ro-sheen*, girl's name

Aye - Yes
Barry's - The best tea in Ireland, objectively speaking
Bookies - Slang for bookmakers, a place you can make bets on sporting events
Claddagh - *Clah-dah* - a popular Irish symbol symbolizing love and friendship
Class - Excellent, amazing
Craic - *Cra-ck* - fun; a good time
Dose - Annoying person, used as an insult
Eejit - Idiot
Fair play - A compliment meaning "well done" or "good job"
Grand - Good/fine
Halfwit - Stupid

Number plate - License plate
Rock the Boat - A popular Irish wedding dance where guests form a row on the dance floor and mimic rowing a boat
Sláinte - *Slon-che* - the Irish word for health, used to say "cheers!"

Prologue
Beckett

YOU KNOW how some people feel like a specific thing? Like, how a loved one feels like home, a romantic interest feels like falling, or a friend feels like laughter?

Well, to me, my grandmother always felt like magic.

Growing up, she told my siblings and me countless stories about Irish folklore. She taught us to salute lone magpies to avoid sadness and to never disrupt faerie trees for fear of bringing bad luck.

She also loved stories about love itself. She often told one about a boy she'd once loved but ended up losing because the fates determined different paths for them both.

To this day, I'm still not sure how much of what she told us was true, but I do know that when Gran was around, nothing was ever dull or boring. She weaved a golden thread through our childhood, and many of my memories center around that specific feeling of magic she brought to the smallest of everyday situations.

A lack of ingredients in the fridge to make dinner turned into barefoot dance parties in the kitchen as Gran made pancakes shaped like stars and crescent moons.

My inability to concentrate in school, humming tunes to myself in the back of the classroom—and, as a result, being berated by my teacher for being "thick" and "an eejit"—led to the appearance of my first guitar in my bedroom, as if by magic.

It was an ancient, battered instrument, and I cherished it because *finally*, I'd found something I was good at.

I knew Gran was behind the gift, but when I asked her about it, she smiled, tapped her nose, and said, "What's for you won't pass you, Beckett. So if music's what's for you, make sure you hold on to it. Never give up on it."

Like any good Irishwoman worth her salt, she had many sayings, but "What's for you won't pass you" was Gran's favorite. She loved the idea that we don't get to control our own fates, that life has its own funny way of working things out. That if something is meant to be, it will be.

And that's how we lived, with her at the helm of our family ship. Chalking our circumstances up to fate and waiting for fortune to hopefully favor us. Times were often tough in our home, but when the going got really tough, Gran's magic was always enough to make me believe in something better.

Believe that there was always a little magic to be had, if you just looked in the right places.

Last year, when Gran passed away peacefully in her sleep, her loss hit me hard.

And for a long while, it felt like the magic died with her...

Until I found myself in Serendipity Springs.

Chapter One
Beckett

"DID you get one of those wee square hamburger thingies yet, Becks?" asks Eoin from the phone screen in front of me. He pokes his glasses farther up his nose and leans forward curiously.

"Don't be an eejit, Eoin," Callan says as he gives him an elbow to the ribs. "Haven't you seen *Supersize Me?* There's nothing 'wee' about any of the food in America. Everything is massive there. Even the cars. Speaking of, have you seen many pickup trucks yet, Beckett?"

"I'm still inside the airport," I say, a little tired, already feeling the pinch of jet lag. "So no, I haven't spotted any trucks yet."

"Crying shame, that." Callan clicks his tongue.

"What about the Statue of Liberty? Have you seen that, Beckett?" Aoife asks.

"Like I just mentioned, I'm still inside the airport. In Boston. And as the Statue of Liberty happens to be in New York—"

"What about Oprah?" Niamh interrupts me, clapping her

3

hands so all her bracelets jangle. "Do you think you'll get to see her? Do you think she'd write me an autograph?"

"Well, America's a big country, and I imagine she lives in Los Angeles, which is at the other end. So I'd say the probability of me running into her is pretty slim."

"Aw, come on Becks," Niamh says with a pout. "I think getting me an autograph is the least you could do, considering you're off gallivanting in America all summer, leaving us behind in rainy Ireland."

My sigh in response is good-natured. I love my siblings to death, but most conversations with them feel like running a marathon. And with the added novelty of them all being crowded around Callan's phone on FaceTime from roughly three thousand miles away, this particular conversation feels like running in circles more than most. "Tell you what, Niamh. If Oprah Winfrey happens to pay a visit to the small central Massachusetts town of Serendipity Springs in the next few weeks, I'll do my best to get you an autograph, okay?"

"Brilliant." Niamh smiles. "Cheers, Beckett."

"Don't mention it," I say dryly. "And on that note, I have my bags now, so I should probably get going."

"Text the family group chat when you get there," Aoife instructs.

"Aye, and take photos of some trucks for me," Callan adds.

"Will do," I say. Easier than reminding Callan that he's twenty-three years old and perfectly capable of googling pictures of whatever specific truck it is that he wants to see.

After about seventeen rounds of goodbyes and a parting piece of advice from Aoife to "see if I can find myself a local Dallas Cowboys cheerleader to date," I hang up feeling equal parts despair for my siblings' appalling geography knowledge, excitement for my adventure ahead, and homesickness for my family.

Or, more accurately, guilt about being here.

Ireland suddenly feels very far away.

I've never left them before. Not like this.

But they're all grown up now and busy with their own lives —Aoife's married with a baby on the way, Callan's finished his apprenticeship and is working as an electrician, Eoin's happy as can be working at a local animal rescue, and Niamh's in college training to be a midwife.

Everyone is fine.

Nobody needs me in any kind of urgent way.

And as Mam told me a few weeks ago before she set off on her honeymoon in Greece with her new husband Paul, it was about time I stopped looking after everyone else and started worrying about myself.

She told me I should take a holiday, go see the world. Do something *I* wanted for a change.

To which I replied that I was absolutely fine, thank you very much. Of course, this opened the entire McCarthy family floodgates of *opinions*.

So. Many. Opinions.

Since Gran died and my long-term girlfriend Roisin left me, I'd been feeling a bit aimless. Like I was living a kind of Groundhog Day of work, eat, sleep, repeat, with no real end in sight. No real purpose.

I didn't think it was a huge problem, to be honest. But between my siblings, Mam, Paul (who gets a family opinion now that their nuptials are complete), and Eoin's one-eyed dog, Enya (who Eoin firmly considers a voting member of the McCarthy clan), a consensus from my family soon formed: *they just want to see me happy.*

And currently, I'm apparently not happy enough for their liking.

So, here I am. Off on an apparent pursuit of happiness— AKA, on holiday in America for the rest of the summer.

Because I didn't have the heart to tell them that a change

in my location would do nothing to change the way I feel. Or didn't feel, more like.

I step outside the airport and am greeted with the type of glorious, blazing sunshine that is about a once-a-year occurrence back home.

Standing still, I close my eyes and tilt my head upwards, letting the early morning rays dance over my skin, warming it.

I'm snapped out of my celestial-adjacent moment all too soon, though, as a man dressed in a suit and carrying a briefcase barrels into the back of me, almost knocking us both over.

"Move it, moron!" he yells in a nasally voice, his thick Boston accent making him sound extra angry.

Which makes me smile.

"Top of the morning to you, too," I respond brightly. We don't actually say this to each other back home but I felt like leaning into a stereotype for this rude man's benefit.

However, the man simply rolls his eyes at me before hurrying on his way, and I chuckle to myself over my first real encounter with a member of the American population.

Mr. Bernard Prenchenko, who I am house sitting for this summer, warned me that Bostonians can err on the side of rude. But once I hit the road and drive the one-and-a-half hours west to his apartment in Serendipity Springs, he says I will be likely to find nothing but hospitality, kindness, and a warm welcome from the locals.

I pick up my guitar case in one hand and my suitcase in the other and head towards short-term parking, where Mr. Prenchenko has parked his vehicle in area 4C and left the keys sitting in the left front wheel well, trusting fella that he seems to be.

When I find the correct number plate, I have to laugh as I discover that Prenchenko drives a Ford F150 truck.

I take a picture and send it to Callan, who responds in seconds with one word: "Lethal."

Which, in Ireland, is common slang for *great!* Or, as the Americans say, *awesome!*

I can only hope that my drive in the truck to Serendipity Springs complies with the slang meaning of the word rather than the literal outcome.

After an hour and a half spent sitting in the driver's seat of a vehicle twice the size of what I'm used to, navigating six-lane highways filled with drivers as impatient and angry as Mr. Move-it-Moron at the airport (and on the wrong side of the road at that), I somewhat miraculously make it to Serendipity Springs in one piece.

Thankfully, the roads here aren't quite as hectic as those in the greater Boston area. They're actually a bit more reminiscent of the winding country roads you'd find back home in Ireland.

I steer the truck into a multi-story parking structure on a quaint, tree-lined street in a town that's set to be my home for the rest of the summer and exit the behemoth vehicle on slightly shaky legs. Honestly, I feel more grateful to have my feet back on solid ground right now than I felt after eight hours on a transatlantic plane ride.

It takes me almost no time at all to collect my relatively small bags from the spacious truck bed, lock up the vehicle, and walk around to the front steps of The Serendipity apartment building. I drop my luggage on the sidewalk and dig around in my jacket pocket for my phone so I can pull up the instructions Prenchenko emailed me to access my new apartment.

Leaving truck keys with his truck at the airport was

apparently acceptable, but leaving a house key with said truck keys was apparently not.

While I'm house sitting for him, Prenchenko is staying in my hometown of Castlebar in County Mayo, Ireland, teaching a Social Anthropology summer session at the fancy private school where I work during the school year.

I happened to mention to a colleague that I had a desire to go on a trip, and she told me about the soon-visiting lecturer from an American college who would have a vacant apartment Stateside while he was in Mayo and was looking for someone to watch it for him.

That's another thing about the Irish—someone always has a friend of a friend of a friend to hook you up with anything you might want.

What I wanted was a temporary escape from my life. A holiday that would keep my family off my back.

This house sitting gig seemed, well, serendipitous.

And, when I found out what college said lecturer was visiting from, I almost fainted in shock: Spring Brook College, in Serendipity Springs, Massachusetts.

Where my beloved Gran attended school over half a century ago. Not that any of us knew this information until recently.

Serendipitous, indeed.

I'm hoping that not only will my time here be a getaway from my regular routine, but that it will also allow me to feel close to her. To learn something about her life back in her youth, before she was *Gran.*

I scan Mr. Prenchenko's email, then glance up at the neat brick building in front of me, and my heart picks up the pace a little. "Home sweet home," I mutter to myself.

The Serendipity is rather charming—four stories high with intricate stone detailing and old-fashioned wrought-iron balconies, all adorned with creeping vines of ivy.

Nothing like the ugly blocks of flats we have on every street corner in Ireland. A few steps lead to the grand double front doors flanked by old-timey lights. And atop one of those lights sits a little magpie, its head tilted to one side as it... studies me.

Well, not studies me. Obviously.

It's a bird.

A bird which is simply looking in my general direction.

I look around to see if I can spot a pair for the magpie. But when I realize that there's only one in the vicinity, I swiftly lift my index and middle fingers to my forehead and give it a salute, just like my Gran taught me when I was knee-high to a grasshopper.

We Irish are a superstitious bunch, and if you're brought up knowing anything at all, you'll know to always salute a single magpie.

One for sorrow.

"Hello." I give the magpie a nod for good measure, and then almost stumble backwards when I swear I see it wink.

My abject shock lasts for all of the millisecond it takes for my brain to catch up with my idiocy, and I remember that birds don't wink, just as they don't study people.

Must've been a trick of the afternoon sunlight.

That, and the jet lag.

I really need to sleep.

"You talking to yourself, or to me?" a man grumbles from behind me, and I turn to see a bearded guy giving me a funny look. He's wearing dirty jeans and is holding a toolbox in one hand. He also has a phone pressed to his ear, but he's definitely addressing me, not whoever might be on the other end of the line.

"Uh, myself, I guess," I admit with a wry smile.

The guy raises a dark brow, then takes a step away from me. Which is totally understandable. Although not quite in

9

the vein of the small-town friendliness Mr. Prenchenko promised me.

I glance at the magpie one more time, then watch as another one comes to perch on the railing nearby.

Two for joy.

That'll do nicely. Two magpies together definitely bode for a good start at my new residence. So much so that I grin... and then promptly rearrange my face to neutral as the handyman gives me another wary look.

Before he can try to have me committed or something, I grab my guitar case, suitcase, and backpack and make a beeline for the stairs, checking the instructions on my phone again.

Mr. Prenchenko's email says he left two keys in his mailbox for me: one for the front door of his apartment, and one for the front door of the building.

And said mailbox is... inside the building. In the lobby. Of course.

Kind of an important detail to overlook there, Prenchenko.

I sigh as I read the instructions again and see that a building manager, Steve, is mentioned. Maybe I can knock on the front door and hope this Steve guy will let me in.

I'm about to do just that, but I give the door a little push first—just in case.

To my surprise, it opens.

I walk right in.

The heavy door shuts behind me with an unceremonious bang, and I take a moment to assess my surroundings.

This place is... *insane.* In a good way. The lobby is large, with an old-fashioned wooden front desk that sits unoccupied and shiny hardwood floors. To the right, there's a sweeping grand staircase.

Not quite what I was expecting—for some reason, I imagined more the tall and modern apartment building from

Friends. But this place has a super cool vintage-y vibe so far. Or, as Callan would say, *lethal.*

I quickly locate the wall of mailboxes by the staircase and scan them until I find one labeled "Prenchenko." It's got a combination lock, and I enter the code he wrote out for me in his email. Pull the knob.

Nothing.

I enter the code again.

Still nothing.

I rattle the little knob, but the box stays firmly shut.

Maybe I'll need to summon Steve the building manager after all. I scan Prenchenko's email once more, but there's no mention of where Steve's office is, nor a number for him.

Details are apparently not Prenchenko's forte.

The email does, however, mention that the owner of the building lives on the fourth floor. Hopefully they can help me?

Not like I have another choice, so I guess I'll go find out.

With a shrug, I head for the elevator.

Chapter Two

Keeley

"TODAY IS GOING to be a good day," I tell my steam-obscured reflection in the bathroom mirror.

I tuck the towel tighter around my chest, then lean forward and run a hand over the fogged-up mirror, my fingertips trailing through the condensation as I peer into my own blue eyes.

"You hear me, Keeley?" I squint at myself in a vain attempt to make my apple-cheeked, round face look stern. "Good days only from now on."

I nod at myself in agreement, then begin to drag a brush through my long black tangles, reveling in the fact that I feel human again after my shower.

Forget Andrew.

Forget about him needing "space."

Today *is* a good day.

I *will* it to be.

Three weeks ago, Andrew—my boyfriend of five years—completely blindsided me when he announced out of nowhere that we should "go on a break."

Three days ago, I managed to be completely unprepared

and caught off guard *again* when he told me he thought that break should be permanent.

So really not a break at all, but a break*up*.

It was clear to me from the moment he said it that he had already made up his mind, and I wasn't about to grovel if he didn't want to be with me anymore. I watched my mom plead with my dad to take her back during their divorce more than a few times, and it was heartbreaking to watch her get rejected because Dad had "moved on."

Even more heartbreaking was what happened after the divorce was finalized.

So, when Andrew suddenly "moved on" from me, I was hurt and confused... but I wasn't going to follow in my mom's footsteps. So, I gave myself these past three days to eat entire pints of Ben & Jerry's while watching *The Notebook* on repeat.

Wine may have also been involved.

Three days was more than enough, because honestly, by the time I woke up this morning, I was kind of sick of my own moping. And given that this is the week my air conditioning decided to completely give up in the midst of scorching summer heat, I'm also just generally sick from rotting in my furnace-hot apartment while sustaining myself on sugar, dairy, and fermented grapes.

Nevermind the fact that *I* was beginning to smell fermented, too.

The glorious everything-shower I've just stepped out of marks the beginning of a new era: it's time to stop crying and get my head back in the game.

I haven't heard his footsteps upstairs over the last few days, so I'm going to go ahead and assume that he's packed up and gone camping or something. That he's taken some time, alone, to reflect and process our breakup.

I've done the same. And now, I have no choice but to continue as normal. Which means getting dressed in actual clothes and heading to the town library to get some writing done… right after Craig comes to fix my air conditioning.

As if on cue, my phone vibrates on the vanity.

I drop my brush and press my phone to my ear. "Hello?"

"Keeley! This is the fifth time I've called!" My second cousin's shouty voice is so loud and booming, it echoes through the bathroom.

"Sorry, sorry, I was in the shower," I tell him. "Just need to get dressed. I'll be down in five minutes to let you in."

Craig clicks his tongue impatiently. "Can I just come up?"

"The front door will be locked," I reply, patiently. My cousin is notoriously grumpy at the best of times—he's known around Serendipity Springs as "The Scowling Handy-man." But I don't want him to leave without taking a look at my AC unit. The apartment building I live in, The Serendip-ity, has air conditioning throughout, but for some reason, my apartment hasn't been cooling off lately.

The building manager, Steve, insists there's nothing wrong with my AC—or anyone else's—and while he's point-blank wrong about this, he's also stubborn as a mule that he's right.

So I called in scowly backup in the form of Craig because I could really do without another sweltering late July night of non-sleep.

"I just saw some guy walk in without using a key," Craig says, and I let out an audible sigh of relief.

"Oh, perfect. Yes, come on up."

"On my way," he replies.

I'm about to hang up when I hear some banging, followed by a lot of swearing.

"It's locked," Craig grunts.

"But didn't you say you just saw someone walk in without a key?" I ask. Stupidly. Because my question serves as a red flag to a bull.

"You'd better be down here in one minute, Keeley, or I'm

14

leaving!" Craig practically shouts. "I have better things to do than wait around outside your apartment building."

I want to point out that he told me he would be here sometime between nine and ten this morning and that it's only 8:58 right now, but I know that will just make him leave faster.

So, instead I say, "Coming now!" and run.

It's only when I fly out of my apartment and into the hallway that I realize I'm barefoot and still wrapped in a bath towel.

"Noooo," I moan.

I stop for a moment, weighing up my options, before ultimately deciding that running around my building practically naked is a safer option than sleeping in burning heat for another night. Most of my neighbors have surely already left for the day to go to work, and I'm unlikely to bump into poor old Mr. Prenchenko next door and give him a heart attack because he usually doesn't take his morning walk until around ten.

Plus, if I take the elevator rather than the stairs, I have less chance of exposing myself to any unlucky souls who may be lingering in the lobby.

A quick dash down to let Craig in, and I'll be back in my apartment and fully dressed before anybody will be the wiser.

And I'll get my AC fixed. *Win, win.*

I run to the elevator at the end of the hall and jam my finger on the button, and luck must finally be on my side— see, told you today was going to be a good day—because the bell pings and the doors fly open right away. Which is unusual, at best, for our creaky old elevator.

Without a moment's hesitation, I launch myself inside and promptly stub my toe on something hard.

"Ouch!" I exclaim as I trip, tumbling forward. The feeling of falling makes me weightless for a moment before—

15

"Easy there," comes a smooth, deep voice with a lilting, melodic accent. The sound of the voice is accompanied by the sensation of rough, sure hands on my upper arms.

The hands steady me, preventing my fall, and I look up into a pair of glinting eyes that are the prettiest shade of hazel-green I've ever seen. A pair of eyes that belong to the person with the deep voice and the sure hands. Which, I realize, make up three very attractive parts of a very attractive man who is currently holding me upright. In an elevator.

While I'm wearing only a towel.

Alarm bells ring in my head and I stumble back, only to almost trip again over what I now see is a guitar case.

The handsome stranger's eyes follow mine to the large, black case on the floor. He smiles a little sheepishly. "Ah, sorry about my guitar."

Only, with his accent—which I now identify as Irish—it sounds more like "sahrry aboot me geetaer."

I suddenly feel a little giggly. Although that could have more to do with the general hysteria of meeting a handsome Irishman in an elevator while unclothed than his pretty accent.

"Oh, no, no, that's okay," I say as I back away, both hands tightening around the top of my towel. AKA, clinging to it for dear life. "I should be the one to say sorry about my, uh"— I look down at my body, then back up at the stranger—"general state of undress."

The stranger's smile turns amused, his eyes full of laughter as he runs a hand through his short, messy light brown hair. "Ah, I hadn't noticed until you mentioned it."

I look up at him to gauge the extent of his sarcasm, and when I see his lips twitch, I realize he's speaking it fluently.

The Serendipity is a relatively small apartment building with a tight-knit community feel. I know most of the residents, if not by name, then by face.

So at least I can confirm this isn't one of my neighbors. Hopefully he's a one-time visitor to the building whom I'll never, ever see again.

This is the shred of dignity I cling to as I hurriedly reply, "Yes, well, goodbye," then turn to flee the elevator, deciding I'll take my chances with the stairs.

The elevator doors close in my face.

Swearing under my breath, I hit the "open door" button, but the doors stay firmly closed.

Guess this is happening, then. I'm taking the elevator. With an Irish stranger who smells not unlike Irish Spring soap. And who may or may not be laughing at me.

"Not quite goodbye," he says, his eyes twinkling as he watches me, a smirk playing on his lips.

Yeah, scratch that. He's *definitely* laughing at me.

"Guess we're stuck together," he adds. "At least, until we get to the next floor."

I slump against the wall in defeat, trying to ignore my unfortunate elevator buddy.

"Why are we not moving yet?" I mutter, more to myself than to my new Irish elevator buddy.

Craig is bound to be grumpy as all heck. In fact, he's probably getting in his truck and leaving as I speak, which means that by the time we get to the lobby, I'll be faced with the dilemma of slinking back to my apartment to bake like a Thanksgiving turkey for another day, or chasing The Scowling Handyman down the street like a crazy woman.

I'm not sure which option is worse.

"I think it might be stuck." Irish Stranger smiles, totally unfazed. "It's probably because of the number of times you pressed the buttons. Maybe you confused it."

"I don't know what goes on where you're from, but elevators don't get confused here in the USA," I retort. It's this guy's stupid guitar's fault that we're stuck, when you think

17

about it. It was the root cause of all my panicked button-pressing.

"Mayo," he says.

"Excuse me?" I turn to look the guy full in his face.

And my, what a pretty face it is. He's got a strong, angular bone structure that contrasts with his full lips and mischievous eyes.

"Mayo," he says again in his lilted accent, and I'm now faced with the additional concern that I'm stuck in an elevator with a psychopath who wants to put me in a sandwich.

"I have no idea why on earth we are talking about condiments, but I'm more of a Miracle Whip girl, thank you very much."

His brows fly up. "What in the name of arse is Miracle Whip?"

"It's like mayonnaise, but better."

He starts to laugh. It's a nice laugh. "Ah, no, no, no. I'm *from* Mayo. As in, County Mayo, Ireland. Although, now, I am very intrigued about this Miracle Whip you speak of. Can I buy it at the shops here?"

"Oh," I reply, my cheeks reddening. "Yeah, it's in every grocery store. On the shelf right next to the—"

"Mayo?" he finishes with a lopsided smile, a dimple popping in his right cheek.

"I was going to say 'mustard.'" I can't help but smile back, forgetting for a moment the peril of my current situation. Probably due to that admittedly very-much-not-unattractive dimple on show.

Just for a moment, though. Because as we share a smile, he seems to remember that he's smiling at a woman in a towel and abruptly looks away, his cheekbones flushing. He presses another button, uselessly. We're still not moving.

18

"Do you really think the elevator's stuck?" I ask the obvious.

He pauses for a moment. "I do."

I slump farther against the wall. Craig will be long gone by now, my dreams of sleeping in a cool room tonight up in smoke.

"I've lived here for three years, and the elevator's never gotten stuck, as far as I'm aware," I can't help but grumble.

"Today's your lucky day, then," Irish Stranger says.

"Ha," I bite out, then assess the elevator panel. The thing is ancient, and I don't see a button to call for help. I also, of course, don't have my phone on me in my towel-clad state. "So what do you folks do in Ireland during emergencies?"

"Dial 999," he says immediately.

"Congratulations, we're both dead," I reply with a sigh.

"112?"

"What on earth is that?"

He gives me a look. "The other emergency number."

"The *other* one? You have two different emergency numbers in your country?"

"We do."

He offers no further explanation, and I continue to stare at him. "*Why?*"

He blinks, like he's never considered this to be strange, then shrugs. "Guess we Irish like to have choices when facing mortal peril. What do you do here?"

"Call 911. But I don't think a stuck elevator constitutes a real emergency."

Although, it should. Especially when you're stuck with someone this good looking.

"Maybe we could call the building management," the man suggests, looking at me expectantly.

I raise a brow at him. "I do not have a phone in my current possession."

"Ah." Irish Stranger smiles. "I wasn't going to ask but... any particular reason you decided to take an elevator ride unclothed this morning?"

"Because today was going to be a good day," I say, which earns me a baffled look.

"I see," he replies slowly, and I have a sudden feeling that now *he's* the one wondering if he's trapped with someone deemed a danger to society.

Suddenly, the elevator lurches, and I do a little cheer. Silently, in my head, of course. Because this man already thinks I'm cuckoo for Cocoa Puffs.

Nevertheless, I'm delighted. Maybe my luck is turning and I'll catch Craig before he leaves after all!

My cheeriness, however, is short-lived when I realize the elevator is going up, and not down.

Ping!

The doors slide open at the third floor, and before I can throw myself out of the elevator and make my escape, I instead freeze to the spot.

Because standing in front of me is Andrew. My boyfriend.

Ex-boyfriend.

And he's holding hands with Lisa. His best friend.

Though they look a whole lot more than *just friends* at this moment.

Chapter Three
Beckett

WHILE MY GRAN'S favorite saying was "what's for you won't pass you," she had many more in her repertoire.

When it came to the conversation of love, Gran's opinion was "there's a lid for every pot." Which pretty much translates to *there's someone out there for everyone.* AKA—no matter how quirky or odd or different you are, there will always be someone to match you.

"You'll catch your death going out like that" was offered up anytime anyone went outside without a coat on. Didn't matter how many times I told her colds come from germs, not the weather, she was adamant that she was right.

But for some reason, my grandmother's inaccurate saying is the first thing that pops into my mind as I stand in the elevator watching the beautiful, raven-haired, towel-clad woman's arms break out into a million goosebumps.

Goosebumps that I'm pretty sure have nothing to do with the current temperature and everything to do with the man and woman we've just come face to face with.

I have an immediate instinct to take off my coat and wrap

it around the woman protectively, sheltering her from... whatever this is.

Because right now, she looks even more like she wants to die of mortification than she did when she practically nosedived into my arms a few minutes ago. The expression on her face makes my heart twist in a way I can't explain.

But it's July, and I don't have a coat or even a sweatshirt, so I just stand here. Uselessly.

Meanwhile, the woman blinks at the couple a few times before she exclaims, "Andrew! Lisa! Fancy seeing you both here."

The man—Andrew, I assume—balks at the sight of us, while the woman named Lisa goes as white as a ghost.

"Keeley!" she squeaks, nervously tugging on a strand of her blond hair.

Keeley. Pretty name.

The thought is fleeting, though, because Keeley's spine suddenly straightens, like she's being pulled with a string. She stands to attention at the mention of her own name as she levels her deep blue eyes on the couple.

"What's going on here?" she asks, but her voice sounds completely different to how it did a few minutes ago. It's quieter and has taken on a throaty, almost achy, quality.

And while I don't know Keeley—or Andrew or Lisa—I know enough about humankind to know this situation is not good.

Andrew appears to recover quickly and furrows his brow deeply as he assesses Keeley. His eyes dart to me, though I know his next words are not meant for me. "I could ask you the same." Keeley looks beyond flustered at this point, but Andrew is apparently unaware as he presses. "Did you just go for a swim or something?"

His question makes her startle, and she glances down at

herself, like she's just remembered her current state of undress.

"Uh... yes!" Keeley says haltingly. "A swim. That's a really, um, reasonable explanation for this."

Andrew squints at her. "Isn't Mrs. Benson's seniors' aquarobics class on Saturday mornings?"

Keeley's jaw ticks. "I... joined in."

"You *joined in?*" Andrew parrots, his dark eyes mocking.

"Um, yes."

"So, you're telling me you woke up this morning, took part in an aquarobics class for the elderly, and then proceeded to ride the elevator to my floor afterwards?"

"Not entirely," she backpedals. "I was trying to let Craig in, and then I got stuck in the elevator with..." She gestures towards me vaguely.

"Beckett," I supply.

"Beckett." She nods gratefully. "And the doors just opened here, on your floor, by themselves."

"Sure they did." Andrew's tone drips with condescension, and he looks at me for a moment before his gaze swings to Keeley and then back to me.

"I'm not in the habit of lying." Keeley stares at Andrew coldly, her arms crossed across her chest. "Unlike some people."

"Drew, can we just go?" Lisa asks quietly, shifting on her feet and looking down at the hardwood floor. "Serendipi-Tea is going to be packed if we wait much longer."

"You're going to Serendipi-Tea together?" Keeley's head jerks back like she's been physically struck.

Andrew shrugs, a sudden guilty look passing over his features. "They have the best breakfast sandwich in town."

Keeley seems frozen in place, her eyes round and her mouth downturned.

Despite my grandmother being a prime gossipmonger her

entire life, I personally prefer to stay out of other people's business. But something about the woman next to me is making me rethink my norms.

Before I can think twice, I smile at the couple broadly as my fingers hover over the "doors close" button.

"I hope you don't mind taking the stairs, Andrew, because Keeley and I were actually in the middle of something here. Enjoy your breakfast sandwiches."

Before he can respond, I press the button, and the elevator doors shut in the guy's face.

For a split second, I'm happy to no longer be seeing that chump, but then, I catch the thunderous look on Keeley's face as the elevator chugs upwards to the fourth floor.

"What did you do that for?" she demands.

"What's a breakfast sandwich?" I ask, ducking her question.

"Exactly how far away is Ireland?" She sighs impatiently, screwing up her nose. "It's a bagel or an English muffin with eggs and bacon or sausage, and maybe cheese, and... wait, no. Don't distract me. Why did you do that?"

"Ah. We call that a breakfast roll back home." I nod and then shrug. "And I did that because you looked like you could use a hand with that guy. He your ex or something?"

Her cheeks redden as she glares at me. "I was totally fine handling that myself."

"You were?" I stare at her. "Because if I recall correctly, you announced that you took a geriatric aerobics class this morning."

"AQUArobics."

I arch a brow. "I'm not exactly sure how that's any better."

"It's not!" Keeley exclaims. The doors pop open on the fourth floor, and she peeks out to check that the coast is clear before stepping into the hallway. "But seriously, *Beckett*"—she says my name like it tastes bad—"I don't need your help, or anybody else's. I'm fine." She pauses, her eyes screwing up as she adds, "*I'm fine*" a second time, almost under her breath. Almost like she's trying to reassure herself of this statement.

And with that, she turns on her heel and marches towards the stairs.

I watch her go until she disappears around the corner and the elevator doors threaten to close again. Perhaps beyond my better judgment, I'm utterly intrigued by this beautiful, feisty woman.

And still none the wiser as to why she was dressed in a towel.

Chapter Four
Keeley

"Aw, DARLIN' you're a sight for sore eyes, aintcha?"

I look into the heavily-made-up eyes of Sissy Mayhew—a former Miss Texas, circa 1966—who currently reigns as the Spring View Library's overlord... *ahem*, head librarian.

She's got to be in her eighties at this point, but she's still here working every day, except Sunday, when the library is closed, and Wednesday, which is her day off... and which she spends at the beauty salon every single week.

In all the years I've been coming here, I've never seen her in anything other than a full face of makeup, a big, poufy blowout, and a lot of rhinestone jewelry.

"I guess I am," I say with a self-deprecating smile. I have no idea if her question was rhetorical but either way, I'm sure she's correct in her assessment of me. I'm wearing cut-off denim shorts and an oversized t-shirt that reads "Fries Before Guys" across the front. I had no time to blow-dry my hair so it's pulled back in a sloppy bun, and I didn't even attempt eyeliner on my ridiculously puffy red eyes.

"Oh, Keeley," Sissy tuts as she swats the air with one mani-cured hand, chuckling like I've just said something hilarious.

Her shrewd gaze moves over my face. "My offer's still on the table to show you some of the latest Mary Kay products—I have an eye cream that will do wonders for you!"

Oh, yeah. When Sissy's not stacking shelves full of books, she peddles multicolored makeup palettes and "miracle anti-aging creams" as her side hustle.

"I'm fine, thank you," I reply with as much cheer as I can muster. "I've still got half a jar of the last eye stuff I bought from you."

Which is a lie. The jar's still full.

"Suit yourself, darlin'," Sissy says skeptically. She shakes her head like I've deeply disappointed her, and I take this as my cue to scamper past the front desk and head upstairs.

The Spring View library is in a stone building on the edge of Oldford Park, where I spent a great deal of my childhood feeding the packs of rather aggressive and entitled ducks in the pond.

My grandfather and I had a standing Saturday morning routine back then. After my parents' divorce, Dad had a pretty hectic schedule between his busy job and having full custody of two kids. So Grandpa was my designated babysitter on Saturdays when my dad took my older brother to soccer practice.

Which I was happy about. The two of us would go to Dough Re Mi, a local bakery that sold—and still sells—the best Boston creme donut you will ever have the pleasure of eating. We'd buy a half dozen—three Boston creme, three plain unglazed. Then, we'd stroll to the park and sit on a bench by the pond, feeding the greedy ducks crumbles of the plain donuts, while each eating a Boston creme before splitting the third.

It was our belief that one point five donuts each was the Goldilocks amount. Two made me feel sick after, and one wasn't enough to fully satisfy my sweet tooth.

After we'd eaten our treats, we'd walk through the rest of the park until we reached the library. After greeting Sissy—who's been part of the furniture here for as long as I can remember—my grandfather would browse the mystery and thriller sections while I perused the middle grade books with even more hunger than I'd had for my donuts.

I inhaled everything, from *The Babysitter's Club* and *Warrior Cats* series to *Anne of Green Gables* and *Little Women*.

Grandpa and I would sit in the back corner on the second floor of the library for hours, reading our books in the big comfy chairs.

Those perfect Saturdays are one of my favorite childhood memories. They're what made me want to pursue writing... although I didn't quite envision my current job when I dreamed of being a writer back then.

To this day, Grandpa is a voracious reader, although he favors audiobooks now as his eyes are failing. Last time I chatted with Amanda, one of the lovely nurses at his assisted living facility, she told me he listened to ten books in the past week.

As for me, I'm still a regular at the library—even on Saturdays. And today, of all days, I can't think of anywhere better to hide.

For one, the library is blissfully air conditioned. For two, no way am I risking running into Andrew and Lisa again as they skip home together after their *breakfast sandwich date*.

Barf me a river.

My cheeks flare red in a particularly potent combination of rejection and humiliation as I select a squashy-looking orange beanbag in lieu of a real chair. I sit crisscross-applesauce and open my laptop.

I pull up a rather boring article I've been working on about a change in local traffic laws. But I'm not focused in the least, my head still swirling in a mess of Andrew and Lisa.

They've been best friends forever, and I was always accepting of this. Did my best to strike up a friendship with Lisa too and never let myself slip into the role of "jealous girl-friend" by wondering if the two of them had ever thought about being something more to each other.

I didn't want to be that person, but apparently, I was naïve not to be.

Before I can stop myself, I'm closing my tab and opening social media, typing Andrew's name into the search bar, and scouring his profile—trying not to wince at the picture of him smiling into the camera, his brown eyes kind, his dirty blond hair tousled from the wind.

I took that picture. We were on a hike outside of town, and the wind picked up so crazily that we almost blew away. It was a fun day.

In a Relationship with Lisa Stanson.

I feel idiotic. Dimwitted. Stupid as can be.

How long has this been going on between them? Was it happening behind my back?

I moan audibly, clapping a hand to my forehead. This earns me a disapproving "Shh!" from the elderly man reading a book on Chernobyl at a nearby table.

Which actually sounds like a pretty nice destination to escape to, given the circumstances. Right now, I'd take pretty much anywhere on planet earth. Or Mars, potentially.

I'm still half-daydreaming about buying a one-way ticket to Italy (not Chernobyl) and doing a bit of an eat-pray-love thing to "find" myself (minus the love part, of course, because screw love) when my laptop starts chiming with a Zoom call.

I whisper an apology to the frowny man as I stand from the beanbag, digging in my backpack for my headphones.

"Hi, Freya!" I answer the call as I duck into one of the private study rooms along the wall to avoid further scorn from the grump.

29

"Keeley," my editor says warmly, her eyes crinkling at the corners as her smiling face fills my computer screen. "How are you?"

"Good, yes, great," I lie clumsily as I set my laptop on a desk and perch on the edge of a chair.

Freya frowns a little as she takes in my puffy, makeup-less face, but unlike Sissy, she thinks better of mentioning it. "Wonderful. Sorry to call on a Saturday, but I just popped into the office to do a little weekend work and saw you were online, so I thought I'd try you."

"Sure," I say with a wry smile. Freya works in Boston at OneWorldMedia's huge, shiny headquarters. And while she loves to make it sound like her "popping into the office" on the weekend is a rarity, I am totally convinced that she's a workaholic and would sleep at her office if she was able to.

Freya taps a pen against her cheek as she smiles at me. "So how's that traffic violation report coming along?"

OneWorld is a huge media conglomerate with a ton of cool stuff under their umbrella. They also have a ton of way less cool stuff, including the management of several municipal websites in this area. I got a job with them right out of college as a remote content writer for the Serendipity Springs town website.

And even though writing about local bylaws and town council meetings to determine stop sign placement is all very exciting (*not*) you have to start somewhere. I'm grateful to have a job with such a reputable company, with a fantastic boss overseeing my progress.

"It's scintillating," I joke.

"You know, I could hook you up with much more interesting work in a heartbeat if you really wanted," she says teasingly, dangling proverbial bait in front of me, as she often likes to do.

Over my two years working here, Freya's become somewhat of a mentor and friend to me, and she's been super candid with me about my future as a writer. Especially after I let it slip that I was a massive fan of Evoke, a lifestyle website OneWorld also owns.

Evoke is kind of like BuzzFeed, but with less quizzes about what food you'd be, and more interesting, thought-provoking pieces on culture and current events in the Boston area, all aimed at women in their twenties—like me.

I'd love to write the kind of op-eds Evoke publishes and leave local traffic laws far in my career past, and Freya has made it clear that she could easily get me started in an intern position.

Problem is, Evoke's staff all work in-office at HQ, so I'd have to move to Boston.

"I know you could," I tell her warmly. "And I appreciate it, I really do. But—"

"Yeah, yeah." Freya swats a hand good-naturedly. "You won't leave Serendipity Springs."

I nod. It's not that I have anything against Boston, but I'm a lifelong Serendipity Springs resident, born and raised. My dad's side of the family has been here since before my great-grandparents.

Even after I graduated from one of the local high schools, I went to Spring Brook college at the edge of town to study journalism and creative writing. I met Andrew there. Sophomore year, he lived in the dorm next to mine, and we soon became a couple.

Fast forward to today, when I'm freshly single and hypothetically ready to mingle—with no obligation to stay here for the sake of my relationship—and leaving town still doesn't feel like a logical option.

For one, I cannot be a twenty-five-year-old intern living in the city. How would I pay rent? I wouldn't even be able to afford a car so I could come home and visit my Gramps and my brother, which is a non-negotiable for me.

"You know I can't afford to live in Boston as an unpaid intern, so I guess I'm stuck with traffic reports for now."

"Traffic reports... and let's not forget the star signs," Freya says, and I snort with laughter. I don't believe in star signs any more than I believe in pigs flying, but every week, Freya gives me the task of writing random advice for people born under every moon of the year.

Filler content, she calls it.

The highlight of my week, I call it. Which might sound a little sad, but Sissy Mayhew is a great believer in star signs, and this comes in very handy from time to time.

"Although, speaking of written in the stars," Freya starts, her voice totally casual, though her dark eyes glint in a way that makes me think she's testing the waters for something she has stuffed up her sleeve. "What if I told you there may soon be a full-time *paid* writing position available at Evoke?"

My breath catches and I'm sure I misheard. "Excuse me?"

Freya's smile widens. "I was chatting with Nisha, Evoke's editor, earlier this week, and they're about to hire a new permanent staff writer. I told her I knew someone perfect for the job."

"Really?" I bite out, trying to ignore the way my stomach flutters.

"Really," Freya confirms. "Of course, it is an in-house position, so you *would* have to move... but you'd be on salary. Not to mention the position comes with full benefits."

"It does?"

She names a number.

"Wow," I can't help but say.

It's more than I make now. Enough to rent a room in Boston *and* buy myself a secondhand vehicle.

But as much as my heart is racing at the thought of an

opportunity like this, I find myself still wrestling with the feeling that I can't, or shouldn't, leave.

"Like I said, it's a rare opportunity," she says with a twinkling smile, though I already know this as well as my own name.

"Thank you for considering me," I tell her, and I mean it —because the fact that this is happening at the same time my relationship has fallen apart seems almost... well, *serendipitous.* As much as I don't believe in that kind of thing.

Though I don't mention this to Freya—I once tried telling her that my boyfriend lives here in Serendipity Springs and this was one of the reasons I couldn't take a Boston internship. In response, she just snorted and muttered something about there being plenty more manfish in the sea.

In hindsight, she might have been correct about that one.

Not that I care about any man, fish or otherwise, right now.

"Excellent." Freya leans back in her chair, looking triumphant. "To interview, all you have to do is submit a sample article, so if—when—you choose to move forward with this, we can brainstorm ideas." Her eyes sparkle. "Although I think I already have the *perfect* topic for you."

This makes me smile. Once Freya gets this excited about an idea, there's no stopping her. "What's that?"

"During my conversation with Nisha, she mentioned that she went to Spring Brook College in Serendipity Springs."

"Yes! Same place I went to school," I say with a smile. As one of the head honchos at Evoke, Nisha is automatically an idol of mine, and I have shamelessly googled her. I figured this little tidbit of trivia could be useful should I ever get the chance to meet her.

"Funny, that." Freya's voice is carefully calm, and I definitely get the sense that she's working an angle, true journalist that she is. "Nisha mentioned something interesting about your town that I hadn't heard before. Apparently, there's a kind of urban legend about a building there. I can't remember the name of it, but it's an old apartment block, and as the story goes, the building has something to do with helping people find love?"

I laugh, trying (and failing) to make the sound seem sweet instead of bitter. "You're talking about The Serendipity."

"Yes! That's the one! Do you know anything about it?"

I snort. "I live in it."

"You do?" Freya's eyes get wide. "Anything... legendary about it?"

I smile the smile of a woman scorned, thinking how funny it is that if Freya had asked me this question just one week ago, I might have had something completely different to say. As a fifth generation Serendipitian, I'm all too aware of the lore about the town, and more specifically, about The Serendipity apartment building being a place where you might get lucky in love.

Hah.

"The urban legend is exactly that: an urban legend," I say fervently. "It's just a regular old building."

"Pity." Freya looks disappointed. "That sounded like it had some juicy potential as a feature article for Evoke. A light-hearted look at finding love on your doorstep."

For some bizarre reason, instead of thinking of Andrew and all the dinner dates and pool swims and movie nights on the couch we shared in The Serendipity, my thoughts turn right away to the Irish stranger—*Beckett*—in the elevator this morning. How he caught me with strong, sure arms after I tripped on his guitar case.

If anything has juicy potential for a story, it's that: a hilariously embarrassing meet-cute with a handsome, mysterious man.

If I believed in meet-cutes. Which I don't.

Plus, he was a little smug, a little too pleased with himself. A little too *pretty*. And I guess, in turn, I was a little unnecessarily sharp with him when he tried to help me. Which wasn't really fair. I was just reeling from the revelation of Andrew and Lisa together, of the fact that I hadn't just been broken up with... I'd been *left*.

I shove away the memories of twinkling hazel-green eyes and lilting accents, deciding that if I ever *do* see Irish Stranger again, I will just have to pretend I have amnesia and therefore have zero recollection of our elevator *non*-meet-cute.

With that problem sorted, I turn my attention back to the matter at hand and to Freya, who is grinning on the screen.

"Why don't you take the weekend to think about it—the job and the article you might want to submit for it?"

I'm sure I already know my answer; I want to apply. I want this job. I'm definitely going to need a different article topic, but I have plenty of time to brainstorm *better* ideas.

And if nothing more comes of it, it will at least give me something else to think about besides Andrew and Lisa.

"Deal," I say.

Freya smiles.

Chapter Five
Beckett

AS IT TURNS OUT, the fourth floor is not the place to find help with Prenchenko's mailbox. After a bit of door-knocking and a less than excellent impression left on my new landlord —who's the buttoned-up, suity type—I locate the building operator's office. Which, incidentally, was steps from the front door where I first walked inside. Go figure. Steve shows me how to work the most convoluted combination lock on the planet, and I'm finally able to retrieve my apartment key from the mailbox.

Now, as I set my bags down in my new digs on the second floor, I feel much more relaxed.

Mr. Prenchenko's apartment is more than I could have hoped for. Spacious, yet cozy. And while the multiple framed paintings of wild boar are an interesting touch, I'm extra pleased that the huge windows along the back wall overlook a grassy area.

After a bit of light furniture rearranging, I've pushed a couch up against that wall, so I can look out the window when I'm playing guitar.

I have a feeling I'll be doing a lot of that over the next few weeks.

Before I left Dublin, I was filled with a renewed vigor, a fresh purpose. I was going to go to America, visit the same town where my grandmother once lived, and work out what on earth I'm meant to do with my life.

Now that I'm here, it feels... daunting. I don't know if it's because I'm overtired and need a nap, or because I started my short tenancy here with the most unusual of elevator encounters, but I feel jumbled. Tangled like a piece of string.

I also know, in my bones, that if I fall asleep now, I'll be up all night. So instead of lying down, I shower and change into a white t-shirt, shorts, and sneakers.

It's a beautiful day, and I might as well explore this town. Find out what it has to offer...

Starting with coffee. Being Irish and all that, I'm usually a tea drinker. But today, I think I'm going to need something a little more caffeinated.

I manage to leave The Serendipity without any more awkward elevator encounters, though I do find myself wondering where the towel-clad woman with deep blue eyes—*Keeley*—ended up today. Still, I push those thoughts aside as I slip my sunglasses on and make my way down the street with the intention of seeing where I end up, no planning necessary.

When I come across a cluster of shops and restaurants, I stop to secure a coffee—an Americano, of course, because when in America...

And that's when I stumble upon a little music store.

Blue Notes, say the swirling letters on the sign above the slightly tattered blue-and-white-striped awning. There's a display of electric and acoustic guitars in the window and a poster advertising a local Indie Music Night.

Unable to help myself, I go inside.

"Hey, there." I'm greeted by a friendly guy about my age with black hair shaved so short, he's almost bald. He has intense blue eyes that look vaguely—impossibly—familiar, two full arm-sleeves of tattoos, and a huge smile that puts me at ease. "How can I help you today?"

"Hiya," I reply. "I was just out for a walk and spotted your shop, so I thought I'd come in for a browse."

"Shop," he parrots me, his tone delighted. "You're not from 'round these parts, are you?"

"Arrived here just an hour ago. From Ireland."

"Ireland," he says almost wistfully. "Home of U2. Van Morrison. The Cranberries. The Pogues. Thin Lizzy."

"Some of the best," I say, liking this guy already. "You a musician yourself...?"

"Ezra," he offers, sticking his hand out. "Ezra Roberts."

"Beckett McCarthy." I shake his hand.

"And yes, sure am." He smiles. "Drums are my first instrument, but I've been playing guitar all my life. You?"

"I'm a music teacher back home in Ireland," I say. "I teach music theory."

I don't mention that the school where I work is a stuffy, overpriced private school, and that most of my students are learning an instrument because a parental figure has forced them to rather than out of interest.

On the side, I give free guitar and piano lessons at a community center in my town. I love to teach kids that *want* to be there, want to learn.

Don't get me wrong, I'm grateful for my job at the school —it pays well, has good career security, and I get summers off. But a part of me has always wondered what it would be like to have a full-time gig teaching guitar lessons to kids who are passionate about music.

Kids who *need* music, like I did.

"Cool," Ezra says. "Do you make music, too?"

His question gives me pause, and I finally settle on: "I used to."

Luckily, he doesn't press me, and we continue to casually chat about music. After a while, he asks, "What brings you here to Serendipity Springs? You on vacation?"

"Yeah, a kind of extended vacation. I'm house sitting for someone for the remainder of the summer, living in an apartment building a few blocks over. The Serendipity?"

Ezra smiles. "I know it. My si—"

He's interrupted by the sound of chimes above the door as a woman bursts into the store at full speed.

"Ez, you would not believe the morning I've had. I got—"

The woman's words dry on her tongue as she takes me in, and I have to smile even as her expression takes on a familiar, scowling quality.

"Oh. It's you." Her deep blue eyes flare in a way that completely contradicts her flat tone.

I grin at the small raven-haired woman in front of me for the second time today. "Keeley, hi. Hardly recognized you with your clothes on."

Ezra's dark eyebrows fly up. "Excuse me?"

His tone is menacing, and when I look at him, I suddenly realize why his eyes looked so familiar.

He has the exact same eyes as her. Which means...

"Not like that," I backtrack quickly, holding up my hands as if to show her brother that I'm innocent. "We met in the elevator this morning."

"And my sister was naked at the time?!" His deep voice goes up an octave, almost comically squeaky.

"Toweled," I correct.

"What?" Ezra spits, and I'm surprised he doesn't crack his knuckles.

"Relax, big bro. It was all a big misunderstanding." Keeley rolls her eyes and crosses her arms.

39

Now that she's actually wearing clothes, I don't feel the need to keep my eyes away from her, and I notice details I missed earlier. Like how long her eyelashes are. How her lips are full and dark pink in color, and her nose is pierced and sports a small silver hoop. I also note that her t-shirt reads "Fries Before Guys," which I hope is a motto she is currently embracing if that fool in the elevator really was her ex.

And then, my eyes zero in on the silver ring glinting on her middle finger. It's an Irish Claddagh ring depicting a heart held by two hands, with a crown atop it. Symbols for love, friendship, and loyalty.

Claddagh rings are super common back home, sometimes used as wedding or engagement rings, but more often worn to signify a connection to a family member or loved one.

I have one given to me by my grandmother hanging around my neck on a chain, but I didn't think they'd be as popular here in America.

"I was wrapped in a towel, very much *not* naked, and Beckett and I got stuck in the elevator together," Keeley explains to her brother, but her mouth suddenly twists. "Then, we bumped into Andrew."

"I hate that guy," Ezra mutters.

"I can't say I was a fan, either," I say under my breath before I can stop myself. Unfortunately, I don't say it quietly enough, and Keeley shoots me a look.

I almost think she's going to snap at me, but instead, she glumly mutters, "That makes three of us."

The sight of her looking so downtrodden pulls at something within me.

It also serves as a reminder of why I don't date. Not anymore, at least.

After Roisin walked out of my life last year, I took a break from all things relationship.

We dated for such a long time, I thought it was a given that we loved each other. But after my Gran died, something fundamentally shifted between us. I wasn't making time for her as I picked up the pieces of my family and tried to be the glue that held the McCarthy clan together in Gran's absence. I could feel myself pulling away from her. Could feel the wedge between us growing wider and wider. But I couldn't stop it.

And so, she left me. I don't blame her for leaving me.

I was closed off.

Distant.

Not good boyfriend material.

When she broke up with me, I think she wanted me to fight for our relationship. But I couldn't rise to the occasion. She called me a selfish dope and a spineless eejit and much, much worse. I hated to see her in pain, hated to see how my actions—or lack thereof—were affecting her. Though I wanted to have her by my side, deep down, I knew she deserved much more, much better, than what I was able to give her at the time.

I'd done the right thing by her, letting her go. I imagined Gran looking down from heaven with a wry smile and a word of advice: "Sure there's a lid for every pot, Beckett. And Roisin? She wasn't your lid."

Since then, I've not had much desire to pursue another relationship. I've also decided that I'd rather be alone than be an unfit partner to someone.

"I should get going," I say, sensing that it's time I make my exit and give Keeley time and space alone to talk to her brother. "Nice to meet you, Ezra." I nod at him, then can't help but give Keeley a little wink. "And Keeley, a pleasure, as always."

"Meeting someone twice does not constitute the use of 'always,'" she replies, her tone still a little tart, but I swear I

41

see her lips twitch. Like she might possibly *enjoy* a little verbal sparring.

Glad that I might have brightened her mood even just a little, I head out the door of Blue Notes. It's only when I'm outside that I remember my Americano, sitting untouched on a shelf inside the store.

I don't want to interrupt Keeley and her brother, so I cut my losses, and instead of continuing my walk, head back in the direction of The Serendipity.

Maybe I could go for a swim. Because if the conversation about geriatric aquarobics earlier is anything to go by, apparently there's a swimming pool in my new apartment complex.

Imagine that, back in Ireland. Unheard of. If you want to get wet back home, just go for a walk because it's always raining.

A swim in the sunshine sounds like exactly the sort of thing I should be doing during my time here.

But by the time I'm back in my apartment, the thought of going for a swim is exhausting. The jet lag is weighing heavy on me, and I didn't get to consume the necessary caffeine I purchased. And so, against my better judgment, I find myself curling up on the couch under the window and letting myself be pulled into a deep, dreamless sleep.

Chapter Six
Keeley

FOOTSTEPS.

So many footsteps.

Two sets of them. Andrew's heavier thudding tread, and Lisa's lighter, clicking steps, like she's donned a pair of heels and is putting on a catwalk show in Andrew's living room.

The thuds and clicks have been on an endless loop for what feels like hours. And with each step, the sound seems to grow louder, echoing through my mind in a plodding pattern that taunts, "Her and him. Him and her. Them, up there, together."

A thud, then a bang. A giggle. A tap-tap-tap. Another thud.

Seriously. What are they doing up there, herding elephants? Moving furniture? Dancing the tarantella?

"Ughhhhh," I grumble as I roll over in bed, shoving the thin sheet off me as I go.

No, Craig never came back to look at my AC, and yes, it's still a million and one degrees in here.

I check my phone and discover that it's one o'clock in the morning. So much for crawling into bed early to get some so-called "beauty sleep" after this trainwreck of a day. Sleeping has been an entirely fruitless activity so far. After I went to bed, I spent an hour scouring the Evoke website, reading all the new content I could find, before turning off my light so I could lie awake and listen to the racket upstairs.

"So thoughtful of you both," I address the ceiling as I remove myself from my sticky-hot bed. I strip out of my oversized pajama shirt and change into a purple tank top, then plod to the bathroom.

Sissy was right, I decide as I look in the mirror. I'm a hot mess right now. Literally.

I scrape my hair into a bun on the top of my head, then root around in the drawer until I find one of those sheet masks that Mae, Ezra's wife, brought back for me on her last trip to Korea.

I smooth the serum-soaked white sheet over my face, reveling in the cool feeling against my skin. Then, I climb onto my makeshift desk in the living room, open the window, and duck out onto the fire escape.

My apartment doesn't have a balcony, but The Serendipity has one of those metal fire escapes that runs the length of the building. It's become one of my favorite places to sit when I can't sleep.

Tonight, though, it feels like more than just a nice place to sit. It's a total godsend. A necessary escape from the parade of elephants on my ceiling, taunting me.

I sink to a seat on the metal, pressing my back against the red brick of the building. It's quiet here and cooler than inside my place.

Below, the streets are calm and dark and quiet. Above, there's a sprinkling of stars in the velvet black sky.

I smile up at them, silently thanking them for being here with me in this moment.

This morning feels like an eternity ago, and at that point

—when I was reeling from the shock of finding Andrew and Lisa together—I didn't really consider the fact that she'd be here at The Serendipity a lot. I also didn't consider that I'm living right underneath the *brand-new happy couple*, so I'd know about it every time she's here.

Talking to Ezra about it was nice, but he didn't have much advice for me short of, "You're better off without that fool."

My brother never liked my ex. He has also become Handsome Irish Stranger's number one fan in the five freaking minutes the man has been in town, because he went on to recommend that I try dating *him* instead because he has "great taste in music."

A top priority in my choice of a life partner, apparently.

I went on to remind him that his wife, Mae, only listens to K-pop, which he despises—he's more into melodramatic sad-boy-guitar-clashing type of music, my dear brother.

That shut him up pretty fast.

I was a little nervous to tell him about the conversation I'd had with Freya about the opportunity at Evoke in Boston; that niggling feeling that I shouldn't leave was brewing in me again.

But Ezra kind of surprised me by being pumped. Immediately said that I should go for it. It's a dream opportunity.

He said that I'm single now, the world is my oyster, I'm twenty-five years old... I should be going after what *I* want in life. He reminded me that Boston's close enough for an easy day trip to Serendipity Springs—just over an hour each way— and that he'll help me look for a car. I could still easily visit my family. Every week, if I wanted to.

I'm not leaving, I'm growing my career.

Beep!

The sound of a car unlocking on the street below momentarily pulls my attention from my thoughts. I peer down in

45

front of my building just in time to see Andrew walking Lisa to her vehicle.

It compounds everything I've been thinking about—my life might be in Serendipity Springs right now, but so is my ex.

It really is the perfect time to grow elsewhere, to focus on my career and escape for a while, knowing that I can—*and will*—always come back for the people I love when they need me.

And more than that, with the reassurance that the people who love *me* know this too.

All of a sudden, the little flutter that danced in my stomach earlier is back. Now, it's tangoing up a storm, *Dancing with the Stars* style.

I'm going to submit an article that blows Nisha's socks off, and get myself my dream job!

With something that feels akin to peace, I watch Lisa drive off. Things are looking up. It's even cooled down since I've been out here, and I'm glad I left my window open. Hopefully, some of that cooler air has made its way inside.

I stand, stretch, and pivot around...

The window's closed.

"Could've sworn I left that open," I mutter with a frown.

I reach for the handle at the bottom of the window and pull... and keep pulling.

"What the?" I try—and fail—to pull it open again.

I swear under my breath as I try a third time...

The window remains firmly stuck.

I take a step back, my heart leaping in my chest.

I'm on the fire escape, in the middle of the night, dressed only in a tank top and pajama shorts. My options are bleak, at best. I could climb down the fire escape to the ground floor, but I don't have my key to get back into the building. I could also climb up the escape, but that would take me to Andrew's apartment, and if I know one thing for certain, it's that I'm not asking *him* for help.

No way.

Ez and Mae have a spare key to my place, but they also have a toddler, and I know that sleep is a precious commodity. I don't want to call them unless I absolutely have to. Which leaves old Mr. Prenchenko from next door. He's a wonderful neighbor and a fountain of knowledge about different cultures... but he's also hard of hearing, and wears hearing aids that I'm sure he takes off to sleep. But I guess I could tap on his window and hope that he'll wake up and let me inside.

And then... well, in all honesty, I don't have a clue what my next move would be, but one step at a time.

I take a deep breath, crawl over to what I think is Mr. Prenchenko's living room window, and tap on the glass.

Chapter Seven
Beckett

TAP, tap, tap.

The tapping noise in my dream gets louder and louder. And then, with a huge gasping breath, I'm jolted awake from the depths of sleep.

I open my eyes and sit straight up in bed...

No, not bed.

I look around the darkened room, and after a moment of discombobulation, still suspended in that dreamlike space between fantasy and reality, I notice how sore my back muscles are.

I'm still on Mr. Prenchenko's couch—the one I shoved under the living room window this morning, and then drifted to sleep on this afternoon. At some point in the past several hours, I've managed to lose my shirt and gain two throw pillows to stuff behind my head.

"Becks, you eejit," I reprimand myself sleepily. Now, the jet lag is going to take way longer to adjust to. Not to mention that I'm super uncomfortable and I could have been dozing in a comfy bed this entire time.

I'm summoning up the energy to get up and move when the noise comes again.

Tap, tap, tap.

This time, I know it was most definitely not in my dream.

Tap, tap, tap.

It's coming from the window. *What on earth?*

"Hello?" I say stupidly as I sit up on the couch.

I turn to look outside and come face to face with... the banshee.

"Ahhhh!" the banshee screams, her ghostly white face and equally ghostly wail sending a chill to my very bones.

"Ahhhh!" the exact same sound leaves my own mouth as my eyes lock onto the bright white face and tangle of black hair crouching before me.

The banshee is famous in Irish mythology. She comes to people at night and screams and wails to warn them of the impending death of a loved one. She's one of the country's most famous legends, though I believed it to be a story told to scare children, mostly. And although Callan swore up and down that he heard the banshee screaming the night before Gran died, I was pretty sure that what he actually heard was Aoife screaming at the television because her favorite singer on *The Voice* had just been eliminated from the competition.

Now, I'm not so sure.

I involuntarily jerk backwards and, of course, promptly fall off the couch.

Sprawled on the floor, my heart pounding, I scramble around blindly for my phone. And that's when I hear... *laughter?*

Yup. Definitely laughter.

Raucous, side-splitting laughter, in fact.

In none of the spooky stories I've been told over the years has the banshee laughed.

I sit up slowly, heart still racing like I'm competing in the

Irish Derby, just in time to see the horrendous evil spirit cackling away, doubled over and clutching her stomach.

Only then do I see that she's wearing a purple tank top.

Not quite the ghostly black robes I was expecting...

She then reaches for her chin, grabs the side of her face, and peels off what I now realize is a white mask, revealing none other than Keeley Roberts.

Laughing her pretty face off.

In the blink of an eye, I go from being absolutely terrified to mildly enraged. Which is not a common emotion for me, but the adrenaline coursing through my body is doing all the talking at the moment.

I climb onto the couch and yank the window open.

"What in the name of all that is holy do you think you're doing?" I demand as I poke my head outside.

"Sorry, I didn't mean to laugh. It was just so funny when you screamed and fell off the couch," she responds, still giggly.

Meanwhile, I'm still livid. "You scared me half to death. I thought you were the banshee!"

She tilts her head, her sloppy black topknot drooping as she does so. "The what?"

"A ghost," I clarify.

"Don't be silly, Beckett. Ghosts aren't real," she chastises.

"So why were you dressed as one?"

"I had a Korean face mask on," she says like this explains everything. Which it absolutely does not, because I have no idea what on God's green earth a Korean face mask is. She gestures vaguely at the ground. "I got stuck on the fire escape so I was hoping Mr. Prenchenko could let me back inside. Totally forgot I had this thing on... my bad."

She at least has the decency to look a little abashed as she looks down at the crumpled white sheet in her hand. Some kind of fluid drips from it.

I have about a million questions regarding her explanation —and about the disgusting drippy thing she's holding—but I settle for a simple, "Right."

Because the jury's still out for me on whether Keeley Roberts might be a little—a *lot*—unhinged.

"What are you doing in Mr. Prenchenko's apartment anyway, sleeping on his couch?" she asks curiously. "Are you staying with him or something?"

"I'm house sitting for him for the rest of the summer. You know him?"

"He's my next-door neighbor," she explains. Her eyes widen momentarily before narrowing to slits. "Which means that apparently *you're* my next-door neighbor now."

"I love how you say it like *I'm* the one engaging in questionable behavior right now."

She looks like she's about to retort, mouth open defiantly. But then she sighs, and the sound is almost agreeable. "Look. I really am sorry for scaring you, but I'm not making it up. I'm stuck out here on the fire escape. I climbed out because I couldn't sleep, but then, my window got stuck, and I can't get back into my apartment."

"You seem to find yourself getting stuck in bizarre places often, don't you?" I ask. I'm placated, almost smiling, because those big blue eyes look genuinely remorseful. And now that I'm not about to pee myself in fear of my imminent death or dismemberment, I do see the humor in the situation.

Plus, she looks, well... *hot* in her tight purple tank and silky black pajama shorts. Unhinged or not, the woman is undeniably pretty.

Not that I should be going down that train of thought...

Keeley wrinkles her nose. "Just today," she says. "For some reason."

"Want me to see if I can open it?" I offer.

She considers this for a moment, then nods. "Please."

51

I push the window open further, but still practically have to fold myself in two to climb out. I shimmy out onto the fire escape as gracefully as I can, and then stand to my full height, looking down at her in front of me.

The metal platform we stand on suddenly feels too small for us both as I become uncomfortably aware of the fact that I'm not wearing a shirt, and she is, once again, wearing next to nothing.

Keeley also seems to be aware of this as her eyes dart over my shoulders, pecs, and torso, before averting hurriedly. "Uh, you have a ring like mine," she says, her voice a little thick.

I look down at my chest, and my hand closes around the silver ring strung on the chain around my neck. "They're called Claddagh rings," I explain. "My grandmother gave me mine."

Shortly before she died, Gran gifted me this ring. A men's ring, oddly. On the inner rim, the words "*Maireann croí éadrom a bhfad*" are engraved. Like the majority of people in Ireland of my generation, I don't speak Gaelic, but a quick google search gave the translation to be "a light heart lives a long life."

I know the ring didn't belong to my late grandfather, because I'd never seen it until that moment. But when I asked Gran where she got it and if it had significance, she tapped her nose and gave her famous "what's for you won't pass you" line. In this case, she meant that if I was supposed to find out, I would.

Now, I wear the ring around my neck instead of on my finger, because that way, I keep the words—and Gran—close to my heart.

"Really?" Keeley's eyes are suddenly on me again, sparking bright under the starlight. "That's weird. My grandfather gave me mine." She twirls the little silver ring around her finger, her nails adorned with chipped black polish.

"Is your grandpa Irish?"

"No." She shrugs. "My family have been in Serendipity Springs for generations."

"Maybe he visited Ireland and bought it there," I suggest, and she nods.

"I'm not sure if he's ever been there. But that would make sense."

I take a step forward, carefully moving around her on the narrow fire escape. "Let's take a look at this window of yours."

She gestures to the white-rimmed window directly next to the window I just climbed through—she's right, we're well and truly next-door neighbors. I put my hands under the edge of the window and pull upwards with as much force as I can.

I almost lose my balance when it immediately slides open.

I turn to raise a brow at her. "Stuck, you say?"

Her cheekbones redden as she stares, goggle-eyed, at the wide-open window into her apartment. "Wha—I swear it was!"

Almost laughing, I hold up a hand to count on my fingers. "First, you accost me naked in an elevator. Then, you turn up in the same shop I happen to be visiting. And now, you come to my window in the middle of the night with tales of being trapped by a stuck window that seems more mythological than the ghost you were just posing as." I give her a crooked grin. "Are you stalking me, Keeley Roberts? Should I be fearing for my life?"

My teasing makes her face turn a bright shade of red that clashes with her purple shirt. "Why would I waste my time stalking you?"

"Because I'm handsome as can be," I tell her laughingly. "And funny. And exceedingly charming."

"As if."

"I could charm the skin off a snake, if I ever took the notion."

She snorts, but her cheeks are a deeper red than ever. "That's not even a real saying."

I let my eyes purposefully dip down to her bare legs as I say, "Well, I *would* have said that I could charm the pants off you, but you already appear to be missing your pants. Again." I grin at her, pleased with my American use of the word 'pants'—in Ireland, we say 'trousers'—but her eyes narrow so quickly that I add, "Plus, I like my appendages intact."

A burst of laughter leaps from her, and she claps her hand over her mouth as if trying to contain it. I like making her laugh.

"Now that I've come to your rescue for the second time in one day, I'll be on my way." I lift my chin in a nod. "Goodnight, neighbor."

"Goodnight, *Beckett*," she says pointedly.

I wait until she's safely inside her apartment, then climb back through Mr. Prenchenko's living room window and head straight to the bedroom.

My last coherent thought as I drift back to sleep is that I'm going to like being Keeley Roberts' neighbor.

I sleep like a baby for the rest of the night.

Chapter Eight
Keeley

ANDREW AND LISA can take my sleep, but they cannot take my breakfast sandwiches.

I'm going to have to take the risk of running into them this morning. I introduced Andrew to Serendipi-Tea, and we came here often together. But Sunday mornings? Those were always *my* domain. And I need a Serendipi-Tea breakfast sandwich in my life. Stat.

Because nothing is a better cure-all for a bad night's sleep than a bagel with eggs, cheese, bacon, ketchup, and extra bacon.

Serendipi-Tea is beloved by the residents of Serendipity Springs for very good reason. It's in an old two-story converted Victorian home about two miles from The Serendipity, and though there are cafes closer to my apartment, I particularly love this one.

The second you step inside, you're accosted by the delicious smells of sugar, coffee, and chai. Its decor is cool and quirky, and there are plants everywhere. I'm utterly charmed by the place.

And Andrew and Lisa can't—and won't—take it from me.

Or so I tell myself staunchly as I walk down the street towards the cafe, my Converse smacking the sidewalk as I go.

It's a beautiful morning, early enough that it's not deathly hot out yet, and the world is just starting to come alive. A trickle of people walk down the street in search of much-needed caffeine. Cafe owners put out sandwich boards advertising their daily specials. Mavis Pinkman is rolling up the shutters on her trinket store, Persnicketies.

I wave at her as I duck into Serendipi-Tea.

"Morning," I greet Nori, my friend and the cafe's new owner. She also happens to live on the third floor of my building, a few doors down from Andrew.

"Morning, Keeley." Nori's kind eyes move over me. "You look—"

"Tired," I finish for her, and she nods, her cheeks pinkening.

"I didn't know whether to say that or not," she admits, and I laugh. After finally falling asleep at 3am following the most bizarre and embarrassing middle-of-the-night encounter with Beckett McCarthy (AKA my new neighbor, horror of horrors), I was woken up at 8am by said new-neighbor's guitar playing (which, admittedly, was a more preferable way to be soothed awake than my "WAKE UP!" alarm clock).

But I know I must look a little worse for wear today. Again.

"Hey, you're way more tactful than Sissy was. She tried to sell me under-eye cream when she saw me yesterday."

"Typical." Nori laughs as she rings up my usual order on the till. Perks of being friends with the owner of your favorite cafe—she knows your Sunday order by heart.

I lean against the counter and do a quick scan of the cafe, but I don't see Andrew and Lisa anywhere, thank goodness.

"So, why so tired?" Nori asks in her usual, gentle way.

"Did you happen to see Andrew come in here with another girl yesterday?"

"No, I was off yesterday." Nori's mouth falls open. "You're not saying—?"

And I don't know if it's the fatigue or the need to talk to someone who's first reaction isn't "Why not date the Irish dude instead" (AKA my brother), but as Nori hands me my coffee with two pumps of caramel syrup and a splash of heavy cream, I find myself pouring out yesterday's saga from start to finish.

The only detail I leave out is the one where Beckett was shirtless and looking oh-so-sexy when I tapped on his window in the middle of night.

That particular little morsel I keep stuffed in my pocket. For me to think about, and me only.

Or, you know, not think about. Ever.

Because the way my cheeks heat every time I remember the skim of his gaze on my bare legs is not ideal. Not ideal at all. The man is clearly a terrible flirt, and I am clearly terribly stupid for letting his flirting work on me.

Plus, the smug look on his face when my window easily slid open will haunt me 'til the day I die.

I swear it was stuck before he tried it.

By the time I'm done with my story, Nori looks stunned. Her brow furrows as she pushes a stray lock of dark brown hair behind her ear. "That's unbelievable, Keeley. I'm sorry about Andrew."

"Thanks," I say appreciatively, smiling across the counter at her.

Nori and I have been friends for a while, and the usually warm feeling I have towards her only compounds as she adds, "You could have texted me when you got stuck on the fire escape. I would've come and helped you." Her eyes crinkle mischievously. "No wait, I take that back because then the hot Irishman wouldn't have come to your rescue."

"Hot *insufferable* Irishman," I correct her, glowering at the memory of his comment about me losing my pants. "The man's been here all of five minutes, and he's a rogue and... and... an incorrigible flirt!"

"Incorrigible, huh?" Nori descends into giggles.

"Yes," I say, pointing a finger at my friend. "In fact, you'd better warn Cash about him. I'm sure Beckett will flirt his face off with you too, and Cash won't be best pleased."

Cash is Nori's boyfriend, a retired baseball player who also lives on the third floor of my building. They started dating a couple months back, and they seem blissfully happy together.

"Cash has nothing to worry about." Nori waves a dismissive hand. "Chris Hemsworth could move into the building, but I'd still only have eyes for him."

"You guys are gross," I tell her, but I'm grinning. Cash looks at Nori like she hung the moon.

Andrew never looked at me like that.

Not even close.

I flinch away from the thought just as Nori hands me a large, warm brown paper bag. "One regular, two with extra bacon, one with tomatoes," she says, then winks. "And a chocolate chip muffin, of course."

"Thanks, girl!" I tell her as I tap my card on the reader, making sure to tip well. "You all set for the first Indie Music Night? It's coming up soon here."

When Nori bought Serendipi-Tea after the previous owner retired, Indie Music Night was one of her ideas to bring more business to the cafe. I'm excited to see that she's already putting her initiatives in motion, and I can't wait to support her when the first one kicks off.

Nori flushes with pleasure. "Yes! We have quite a few sign-ups and just need one or two more to have a complete roster. It's mostly thanks to your brother—his posters in Blue Notes advertising it have really helped spread the word."

"It's going to be a huge hit," I say with confidence.

"Thanks, Keels." She smiles. "Tell your Grandpa I say hi."

"Will do." I give her a wave, and then, bag of sandwiches in hand, I make my way down the street to Silver Springs retirement community. Ahead, Ezra and Mae are already parked and getting Everett out of his car seat.

"Keeley!" Mae presses me into a big hug, and I squeeze my petite sister-in-law back—she always makes me feel tall even though I'm barely five-foot-four. Then, I set down the sandwich bag and swoop to pick up three-year-old Everett from the sidewalk.

"Hey, li'l man. What's happening?"

Everett shrieks with laughter and lovingly places a chubby (sticky) hand on each of my cheeks. "Kiwi!" he greets me, which makes me grin. My nephew not being able to say his "l's" has earned me a very cute nickname.

"You ready to visit Grandpa Great and eat a chocolate chip muffin?" I ask, scooting him around so he's on my hip.

My parents are Grandma and Grandpa to him, so my Grandpa—my father's father—has the moniker "Grandpa Great" for Everett.

"Yay!" he cheers.

"You spoil him." Mae smiles as she hitches her backpack onto her back and picks up the sandwich bag. "I'll carry the food if you carry the child?"

"Deal," I say readily.

Ezra grabs a grocery bag of Gramps's favorite snack foods from the trunk and slams it shut. "Morning, li'l sister. You have a good Saturday night?"

"It was perfect. Just me, my book, an entire sausage and mushroom pizza from Domino's, and a Korean face mask."

"Sounds like a wild night," Ez says, practically dripping sarcasm.

Little does he know how accurate his summary is, thanks to shirtless-middle-of-the-night Beckett on the fire escape. I'm not exactly an expert in bare-chested men, but Beckett's body seemed to be comprised of a pretty wowing combination of broad shoulders and long, lean, ropy muscle.

Which I'm absolutely not going to tell Ezra about, for obvious reasons.

"An absolute rager," I reply as we walk into Silver Springs together. We say hi to Lainey at reception, and she waves us right in. My dad and his wife usually visit on Saturday mornings, while Ezra, Mae, and I keep Gramps company on Sundays.

This has been our tradition ever since Grandpa moved into Silver Springs. And when I (fingers crossed) manage to score this job at Evoke in Boston—which I emailed Freya about first thing this morning—I'll be sure to drive down here as many Sundays as I possibly can to keep this tradition going. Just like I talked about with Ezra yesterday when he encouraged me to apply.

We head straight to the sunny back porch that overlooks a beautifully maintained garden with beds full of black-eyed Susans, petunias, and asters. This space serves as a visiting area on the weekends for friends and family to spend time with the residents.

Gramps is already settled in a rocking chair, looking almost comical in his over-the-ear Beats by Dre headphones that Ezra and I gifted him for his birthday. In order to hear his audiobooks better, of course.

When he sees us, he smiles, and his wrinkled face lights up.

Everett squirms out of my arms and runs over to him, arms outstretched. "Grandpa Great!"

"Try not to break the old man, my dude," Ez mutters as Everett practically leaps onto his great-grandfather.

But Gramps just laughs good-naturedly and ruffles Everett's hair before he slips off his headphones.

We all take it in turns to greet him, and Grandpa smiles at each of us before turning adoring eyes back on Everett, who is now on the floor, playing with Grandpa's shoelaces.

"Very nice boy you've got there," he tells Ezra, his eyes going a little misty. "I once knew a boy like that, a long time ago."

I smile gently. Everett has a similar aura to Ezra's when he was a little boy, and I wonder if Gramps means Ezra—or even my dad, his only son—when he says this.

"Thanks. We're super proud of him." Ezra beams at his boy.

"As you should be. He's going to be a strapping young man, Ben."

Ezra and I both stiffen slightly and exchange a look. Then, Ez gently pats Grandpa's shoulder. "I'm Ezra, Gramps. Ben's your son, my dad."

"Oh." He blinks up at Ezra, his eyes unfocused for a moment. "That's right."

My brother pastes on a smile. "Are you hungry? Keeley brought us breakfast sandwiches."

Gramps nods. "I haven't eaten since last night. Pork chops and green beans."

"Sounds delicious," I say with my very own pasted-on smile. I know for a fact that Grandpa would have been served coffee and oatmeal this morning, as well as a post-dinner snack of muffins and fruit last night.

Gramps has dementia. He was diagnosed a couple of years ago, and his forgetfulness has been growing slowly but steadily worse. And while he's still his wonderful old self in so many ways, I miss the relationship we had in my younger years, when he just *got* me.

During the early stages of the illness, my dad worked with him to get his affairs in order while he could still clearly dictate what he wanted. He updated his will and picked out Silver Springs as the place he wanted to eventually live.

And then, one day, Gramps took me for a walk in Oldford Park. On this walk, he slipped a little black velvet bag out of his pocket and placed it into my hand with a squeeze.

"This is for you, Keeley," he said, eyes shining with what looked like tears. "Remember, my sweet girl, a light heart gives a long life, and in order to keep your heart light and free of burdens and baggage, remember to listen to it when it speaks. Don't let circumstances dictate what your heart wants, but rather, let your heart shape your circumstances."

I had no idea what any of this meant, but I hugged him tight, and when I got home, I opened the pouch to find a ring that featured a heart and a crown, with strange engraved writing in a foreign language inside.

It was a woman's ring, and it fit me perfectly.

The obvious explanation was that it had once belonged to my grandmother, who had passed away before I was born. But for some reason, I didn't think that was the case.

The ring felt like a secret Gramps was somehow sharing with me. A secret written in code that he hoped I would one day decipher.

I'd never met anyone else who had one like it... until last night.

I look down at it now, glinting on my middle finger, and spin it around.

Claddagh rings, Beckett called them. I vaguely knew the name of my ring, but never really thought about it, or the fact that it would've come from Ireland.

I make a mental note to look them up at some point and

turn my attention back to the table, where Mae is telling Grandpa about the trip they took to Korea a few months ago.

I'm about to take a bite of my bagel when my phone rings, buzzing on the table in front of me.

Freya, the display reads.

Of course she's working on a Sunday.

"'Scuse me a second," I say as I stand from the table, bagel in one hand and my phone in the other.

"Hello?" I answer, pacing away from the table and walking towards the garden.

"Eek!" comes the squeal in response.

I grin. "Got my text, then?"

"Sure did! I already texted Nisha to let her know that you'll be applying. She's super excited to get your article submission. You should start looking at rentals on Zillow; I recommend Malden Center or Oak Grove as starting points."

"I haven't gotten the job yet, Freya," I remind her.

"You're a shoo-in."

"I'm glad one of us is so confident," I say with a laugh, but my heart is beating fast. "This means I can start coming up with article topics for my interview..." I start listing off a couple ideas I've had already, none of which have anything to do with The Serendipity or my town's lore.

Nope. These article ideas are all interesting, of the moment, and based in *fact*.

"Actually," Freya interrupts me gently, and I can practically hear her huge smile. "I know exactly what she wants."

Phew. Probably safe from the article topic that can't be named, at least.

"Oh, yeah?" I ask, a tad distracted because a glob of cheese has escaped my breakfast sandwich and is trickling down my hand.

I clumsily attempt to lick it off.

"The Serendipity!" Freya announces.

My stomach drops. "What about it?" I say feebly, grasping at straws. As though we didn't talk about this just *yesterday*.

"You remember." Freya tuts. "We spoke about that supposed 'urban legend' about the building bringing people together, making them lucky in love?"

"Oh, yes. That one."

Freya goes on excitedly. "When I told Nisha this morning that you were going to apply for the staff writer position—and that you *live* in that building—she specifically requested that you write about the whole legend surrounding the place."

My stomach churns, and I laugh as casually as possible. AKA, not casually at all. "I figured I could write something factual, something based in reality. And as I mentioned, it's just some daft old story that holds no truth. Small town lore."

I'm flailing.

"That's exactly what she loves about this idea!" Freya croons in delight. "She wants whimsy. Stars aligning. Something that winks at bending the rules of science we so often use in today's swipe-happy dating world, with all the algorithms matching people up. She wants a fresh story with a fresh angle. Around three thousand words. Make it fun. Playful. Sexy."

My hand involuntarily tightens around my breakfast sandwich like it's a stress ball, which sends a river of ketchup and hot cheese squirting down my arm and splattering over my shirt.

Sexy, indeed.

From the table on the porch, Ezra is shooting me weird looks.

"Is there any way I could possibly write something—anything—else for her?" I panic-hiss into the phone. "Because I really do have a whole slew of other ideas..."

"Nope," Freya says cheerfully. "This is your best shot for landing this job, Keeley. And you're perfectly positioned, right on the ground there, to do the research and really hit it home with this article. I have full faith in you. And remember, my reputation is on the line too, because I recommended you. So do me proud, Keels."

With that, she hangs up.

I wipe my arm on my already fully ketchup-ed shirt, and I sigh as I launch my breakfast sandwich into the nearest trash can.

Suddenly, I'm no longer hungry.

Chapter Nine
Keeley

THERE'S a little less spring in my step when I trudge home around lunchtime, my pale skin beginning to redden as the sun climbs higher in the bright blue sky.

I'm so lost in thought about my phone conversation with Freya that when I fling open the front door of my apartment building, I don't notice Archibald the Bernese Mountain dog hurtling towards me at full speed until it's too late.

His owner, Sara, is about ten steps behind, yelling his name as he flings himself up and almost knocks me over. Somehow, I miraculously stay upright as Archie happily licks ketchup from my shirt before moving on to maul my face with ketchup-y kisses.

Despite myself, I have to laugh.

"Hey, cutie," I say as I pet his massive black head.

"Sorry!" Sara pants as she struggles to take control of her pet's leash. "Down, Archibald. Get down!"

"I think he's grown even bigger." I'm not sure what floor Sara lives on, but everyone in the building knows her. Mostly because they've been greeted by Archibald at some point or another.

"I know," she says, half in despair and half in utter infatuation with her sweet dog. "We're headed for a walk to burn off some of his energy. Later, Keeley."

I watch Sara walk Archie outside—or rather, watch Archie walk Sara outside—before making my way upstairs to my apartment. *Stairs* being the operative word, because I'm definitely not up for another stuck-elevator incident.

My apartment is still about a billion degrees, so as I clean my slobbery face with a hand towel, I decide there's no time like the present to get some laundry done. The laundry room is in the basement of the building, so logic dictates it's got to be at least a few degrees cooler down there.

Plus, it's unlikely that anyone else will be doing their laundry on a gorgeous Sunday. I can skulk in my dungeon in peace and begin to wrap my head around the fact that I have to write an article I'd happily trade for a hundred more pieces on traffic laws.

Huffing, I grab my (very full) laundry basket and begin my trudge to the basement.

Which, I am happy to confirm, is a *lot* cooler than my place.

I shoot off a text to Craig, asking (begging) to see if he can look at my AC this afternoon, and then get to work loading all my dirty clothes into a washer.

I'm adding soap when I realize I'm still wearing a shirt covered in ketchup. And I didn't bring a clean one to change into.

Glancing at the door, I quickly decide that there's little chance of anyone else coming in here. On top of that, I'm wearing a sports bra underneath my shirt, so if anyone *did* swing by, I could simply pretend I just got back from a run.

Which would, at least, explain how sticky and sweaty I am at the moment.

I'm whipping off my shirt when the door opens.

Because of course it does.

And because the universe hates me and is clearly out to get me, the person who has just walked into the room is none other than *Beckett freaking McCarthy*.

He's already three steps inside the room when he spots me. The second he does, a crooked grin moves over his face as he assesses me, shirt in hand, blush blazing on my cheeks.

"Keeley, we can't keep meeting like this." His lilting voice is almost mocking, and that darned dimple in his cheek is back.

"Hello, Beckett." Cool as a cucumber (yeah, more like hot as a chili pepper), I check my watch.

"It's after noon. I figured you would have located the nearest Irish pub by now."

His forehead creases, his grin disappearing. "That's an extremely rude—and, frankly, offensive—stereotype of the Irish people, Keeley."

His tone sounds a little injured, and I feel like I've just kicked a puppy or something. "Oh, my gosh, I'm sorry," I say, backpedalling furiously. "I was totally joking. I didn't mean to offend you..."

I trail off as I realize he's laughing.

The jerk is laughing at me.

Again.

I cross my arms and level him with my gaze. "So, you're not actually offended, then?"

"You couldn't offend me if you tried, Roberts."

"Oh, believe me, I try," I snap back, and he grins crookedly.

"Well, let it be known your efforts are commendable." He takes a couple of steps back, raises two fingers to his forehead and salutes me. "Now, I'd best be on my way and continue with my tour of the building. I'll leave you here to your stripping."

"Thank goodness. I thought you'd never leave," I reply evenly.

Beckett smirks before he puts his hand on the doorknob and pulls.

Nothing happens.

He pulls again.

The door doesn't budge.

"Are you serious?" Beckett mutters, and this makes me feel preemptively triumphant. Because I know there's a little trick with the laundry room door—you have to push the door in slightly before pulling—and I'm already mentally picturing how I'm going to march over there and fling it open for him. That'll make us even after he opened my "stuck" window last night.

"Need some help?" I ask in a sing-song voice.

Beckett—clearly without the same get-even vitriol pumping in his veins—shrugs and gestures to the door. "Be my guest."

I march right over. Place my hand on the door handle with a flourish.

Do the little trick where I push the door in slightly... and then, I pull.

Pull again.

Pull once more, with two hands this time.

Sigh in defeat.

"You're right, it's stuck," I concede.

"Weird, weird place, this," Beckett murmurs, his brow furrowed as he jiggles the door again.

The reality hits me that, for the third time in two days, I am trapped somewhere with Beckett in some kind of state of undress. It's beyond what feels like a regular coincidence at this point. It's almost... freaky.

And I must put an end to it. Now.

I wrap one arm around my stomach self-consciously and use the other to pound on the door. "Hello? Anyone?"

Of course, there's no response. There's only one apartment down here in the basement, where a really nice woman named Scarlett lives—but if she's home right now, she can't hear us.

"I'd call someone, but I don't have my phone with me. Again." I groan, more to myself than to him.

"Same," he says. "I guess we're stuck here. Again."

"Lucky us," I say sarcastically. It comes out harsher than I mean for it to.

He studies me for a moment, and then in one swift motion, he shrugs off the sweatshirt he's wearing and hands it to me almost hesitantly. "If you want it."

I hesitate, too, but come to my senses pretty quickly.

"Thanks," I say gratefully, pulling it on only to almost instantly regret my decision.

The sweatshirt is big and soft and fleecy inside, and it smells... well, it smells incredible. Woodsy and clean and masculine and delicious. It's all I can do not to breathe in deeply as I roll up the sleeves, which are comically long on me.

I thought there could be nothing worse than being trapped down here with Beckett while wearing only a sports bra. But I have to say, being practically bathed in his unfairly good smell might be worse. It's probably going to smell like ketchup and dog saliva when I give it back. Which is just one more item to add to "Keeley's Embarrassing Moments of the Weekend."

"Can't believe you're even wearing a sweatshirt in this heat," I tell him as I hoist myself up to sit on one of the dryers.

Beckett laughs good-naturedly and sits a couple of dryers over, his long legs dangling over the side. He's wearing shorts, and I can't help but notice what nice legs he has. Muscular, like he played a lot of soccer growing up.

"Mr. Prenchenko keeps his apartment at sub-arctic temperatures, and I haven't figured out how to change the thermostat yet," he confesses, and I laugh.

"He likes to be reminded of the winter he once spent in Yellowknife, studying Inuit culture."

Beckett smiles in amusement. "He'll be right at home in Ireland, then. It's been cold and rainy every day this summer so far."

"Um, on that," I hedge slowly. "I'm sorry about making a joke about the Irish drinking culture. Offended or not, it wasn't super polite of me."

"Unfortunately, the stereotype is often true. The Irish are big drinkers." He grins. "Not me, mind. I'm a desperate light-weight. But in general, I guess we are famous for drinking like fish. And for manufacturing Botox."

"Botox?" I blink.

"Yes," he says mock-proudly. "Ninety percent of the world's Botox is made in my very own County Mayo."

I snort, wondering if Sissy—a huge Botox fan—knows this little tidbit. "Fascinating."

"It's a real cultural hub, where I come from."

"What else is Mayo famous for?"

That flirtatious smile is back on his face. "We're known to be great craic."

My eyebrows fly up. "Ex-squeeze me?"

"Ya know, good craic. A grand old time. Life of the party. Et cetera, et cetera."

Man, just as I was warming to him, I find out he's on crack.

"I don't know how they do things back in Ireland, but crack is something upstanding citizens of the community generally avoid in this country."

"How boring," he says, eyes glittering.

"A little boredom never killed nobody," I mutter as I look at Beckett. He doesn't look like he's on crack, but then again, my only experience with such things is from watching those shoot-em-up movies with lots of bad guys and explosions. My eyes move desperately to the door. "Shall we bang on the door again? Shout a little louder for someone to rescue us?"

"It means fun, Keeley."

"Huh?"

"Craic. C-R-A-I-C. It's the Irish word for a good time."

"Oh." Abject relief washes over me.

Beckett grins wickedly. "I was informed that it means something entirely different to you Americans, but I needed to test that theory first to see if it was true. Turns out it is."

"You're the worst, Beckett," I tell him.

His smile grows. "My friends call me Becks."

Chapter Ten
Beckett

"FRIENDS, HUH?" Keeley—who is currently drowning in my sweater and looking very cute doing so—tilts her head at me, her long black hair waterfalling over one shoulder.

"Well, I figured that if we're going to be living next door to each other for the rest of the summer, it might be better to just be friends," I reply with a grin. "Then maybe you'll start keeping your clothes on around me."

Her blue eyes flare and I hold in a laugh. Teasing her is just too fun.

This morning when I woke up (at the crack of dawn, thanks to the jet lag), I lay in bed for a while replaying our conversation on the fire escape.

There's got to be at least fifty apartments in this building, and I can't believe that we've ended up being next door neighbors. I also can't believe we are somehow trapped in a small space together again.

But honestly? I can't say I'm disappointed.

I'm having more fun than I thought I would when I decided to walk around the building and explore its amenities.

Keeley glowers at me. "Maybe we'll just keep our relationship defined as strangers and leave it at that."

"Oh no, we are way beyond the point of me being a stranger to you, Keeley Roberts. I know your last name. I've met your brother. I also possess the knowledge of what kind of pajamas you wear, what brand of laundry detergent you use, and what color your bath towels are."

What I don't mention is that I'm also painfully aware that underneath that sweatshirt of mine she's wearing there's a small constellation of three freckles on the left side of her belly button. Which is pierced, to match her nose ring.

A fact I'm definitely *not* going to dwell on.

Because although Keeley's pretty and I enjoy her fun, feisty personality, I'm not here in Serendipity Springs to meet women.

Or *woman*, singular.

Oh, and I also don't want to sound like a total creep, being her next-door neighbor.

So, there's that.

"Fine, we can go with creepy stranger," she says with a smirk. *So much for not trying to appear like a creep.*

"How about Good Samaritan neighbor who rescued you from spending a night sleeping on the fire escape?" I counter.

"Hmm." She purses her lips as if in serious thought. "I'll meet you halfway with creepy neighbor."

"Handsome neighbor."

She laughs. "Neighbor."

It's my turn to smirk. "Or, circling back for a moment... friends."

"Fine!" She sighs. "You're right. I think we might be past the point of not being friends." She rolls her eyes. "Which is very unfortunate."

"Lucky, you mean," I counter with a grin. "For you, of course."

"I beg to differ. You clearly know so much about me because you're so obsessed with me."

"Guilty as charged," I say blithely.

"So maybe the more important question would be what *don't* you know about me?"

"Umm," I say, making a big show of tapping my chin like I'm deep in thought. "I don't know what age you are."

"I'm twenty-five," she says. "You?"

"Twenty-six."

She smirks cheekily. "I must say, I expected a much less boring question from you, Becks."

I like it when she calls me Becks, I decide as I smirk back at her, leaning forward to peer into her eyes. "Well, *Keels*, because you called my question boring, I'll have you know that my question was originally going to be about how you ended up with ketchup on your cheek. But I didn't want to be rude."

Her hand flies to her cheek, where a thin red line of crusty sauce is lurking. "Oh my gosh, I'm a mess," she mutters as she scratches it off. Then, she lets out a sigh. "If you must know, I squeezed my breakfast sandwich too hard, and a bunch of ketchup shot out of it."

This is possibly the last answer I'm expecting, and a laugh slips out of my mouth. "Again with these famous breakfast sandwiches I keep hearing about. But why would you use one as a squeeze toy?"

"It's a long story."

I nod at the locked door in front of us. "Judging by our current predicament, I can confidently say I have nothing but time."

Keeley sighs again, heavily this time. "Okay, we should probably start at the beginning. Do you know much about the history of Serendipity Springs?"

"Not really."

"Let me enlighten you..." Keeley then goes on to tell me a very colorful, very detailed story about the origins of Serendipity Springs.

Years and years ago, weary travelers stopped here to rest on a long journey and wound up drinking from the springs in the ground. After they drank the spring water, they found they had good luck—sick people were healed, the weather improved, good fortune seemed to follow them. And so, instead of moving onwards, the travelers stayed. Established the town while celebrating the good luck and fortune they'd fallen upon by drinking from the spring.

She finishes the tale and her face creases briefly. "Or, so the legend goes. It's pretty well-known lore around these parts, but in all honesty, it was probably just a good location. There's a microclimate of temperate weather here, good soil, free-flowing clean water..."

"Huh," is all I can manage.

This is the exact type of story my Gran used to tell me, about lore and luck and mysterious happenings in the world, and Keeley's words—the magic in the tale—are settling over me like a blanket steeped in nostalgia.

I've missed this feeling.

"So, what's this legend got to do with your breakfast?" I ask, eager for her to go on with the story. Eager to keep this feeling close.

"According to a popular story around here, this building— the one we're sitting in—is supplied with water from that spring. The very one the original settlers of the town drank from." Keeley frowns down at her hands. "So, some of the more hardcore believers think that The Serendipity has a divine ability to grant its tenants luck. Particularly luck in love."

"That's wild," I say. "It sounds like a lot of the old Irish folklore stories I got told growing up. Do you believe it?"

"Not at all." She turns her face away for a moment, and when she spins back around, her expression is almost defiant. "But this morning, while I was in the middle of eating my delicious breakfast sandwich, I learned that, in order to get my dream job at my dream publication, I have to write an article on this stupid legend." She winces. "The last thing I want to think or talk or write about is *love*."

I instantly recall Andrew and Lisa outside the elevator. How Keeley's face fell when she saw them together...

"Because living in the building has done the opposite of giving you luck in love?" I guess gently.

"Exactly." She barks a laugh.

"That sucks," I tell her. It's a stupid thing to say, but it's true.

"Love sucks," she emphasizes.

This gives me a thought. "So what if you *didn't* write about love? What if you take a different angle—explore your belief that these old stories about the building *aren't* true?"

She blinks slowly. "That's... not the worst idea in the world."

I arch a brow, somehow more amused as her face creases in deep thought. "You're welcome."

She glances at me, then rolls her eyes. "Thank you, Beckett," she sing-songs like a five-year-old whose mother just reminded her to be polite, but she's clearly hiding a smile.

I have to laugh. "It's really cool you're a writer."

"What do you do for work?"

"I teach music theory, but I give guitar lessons on the side."

"Explains why you and Ezra hit it off right away." She lifts her eyes heavenward. "And the guitar case in the elevator."

"Never leave home without it," I say cheerfully.

She tilts her head at me. "Do you ever perform?"

"Ah, I used to," I say with a dry smile. "There was a time I loved performing at the pub in my town. But not so much anymore."

"Well, if you're up for it, my friend Nori is hosting an Indie Music Night at Serendipi-Tea in a couple of weeks."

"I remember seeing the poster for that in Ezra's shop."

"Yeah, he's doing all the sound stuff for the night."

"And it's at Serendipi-Tea? Isn't that the home of those famous breakfast sandwiches you're always on about?"

"One and the same. Nori needs one more performer, and I'm sure she'd love to have you. It would be a huge favor to her to have the roster rounded out."

Keeley's leaning towards me eagerly, the expression on her face open and excited. And although I haven't performed anywhere, for anyone, for a while now, I find myself saying, "I'll think about it."

As soon as the words leave my mouth, there's a clicking noise, and the door to the laundry room swings open.

Andrew's standing on the other side, a basket heaped high with laundry clutched in his hands.

"What's going on here?" he sputters as he takes us in, sitting side-by-side on the dryers. Keeley goes a little pale.

"Just hanging out," I reply coolly. "Waiting for Keeley's washing to be done."

"You'll be here a while, in that case." He snorts, casting an eye over the washing machine, which still has the lid up. The drum is full of clothes, and I guess that, distracted by our lock-in and our conversation, Keeley forgot to actually turn the thing on.

She begins to slide off the dryer, but I hold up a hand and smile at her.

"Allow me, *friend*," I say grandly and, fully for Andrew's benefit, I walk to the washing machine, pour in detergent and fabric softener, and start the cycle before turning to wink at Andrew conspiratorially. "Guess Keeley here was so charmed by my scintillating conversational skills that the task at hand was temporarily forgotten."

"Becks! Enough with the charm thing," Keeley groans, but she's laughing, and I'm happy to note that the color has returned to her cheeks.

Andrew studies me like he's trying to work me out. Almost as if he's evaluating if I'm a worthy opponent...

Eejit.

In turn, I look at him like he's a bug that I'm deciding whether or not to flick out of the way.

Apparently, Keeley brings out my protective side.

"I don't think we've officially met," Andrew says coldly. "I'm Andrew. Becks, was it?"

"You can call me Beckett," I say pleasantly, and Keeley snorts with sudden laughter. She claps a hand over her mouth, like she's trying to force the outburst back in.

Andrew's mouth falls open momentarily before he regains his composure. "I'll leave you two to your *washing*. I have a date to get ready for." He shoots Keeley a pointed look, then turns around and flounces off, full basket of dirty laundry in hand.

We watch his retreating back through the now-open door. But instead of feeling relieved that we are now free from our imprisonment in the laundry room, I just feel irrationally irritated that Andrew interrupted our conversation.

"What an absolute dose," I say plainly.

Keeley raises a brow. "Dose?"

"A popular term of non-endearment."

"How delightful."

"Glad to be of service."

"Boy, does he seem to *hate* you, though."

"He was jealous," I inform her.

"Doubt it." She shrugs, her blue eyes hard as they remain

on the open doorway. "He broke up with me and moved on to Lisa. He doesn't care who I talk to."

"He shouldn't," I agree. "But he does."

Keeley sticks her tongue out at me and I laugh as I bend down to pick up the lid of her detergent, which has rolled beside the washing machine and come to rest against the wall. As I lean in close, I notice that this corner of the wall has ancient, flaking plaster with the carved words "Best friends forever!"

Underneath, there are a bunch of names, and I trace my fingers over them all.

Estelle... Cecelia... Margot...

Noeleen.

"Becks?" Keeley calls, and I stand up so fast, I almost smack my head on a cupboard. "What're you doing?"

I swallow. Compose myself. "Um, I was just grabbing this for you." I wave the detergent lid at her.

She assesses me with pursed lips. "You look like you've seen a ghost."

"Don't be silly, Keeley. Ghosts aren't real," I say with a distracted smile, repeating the words she teased me with last night.

Noeleen. Could it really be her?

She frowns at me as she hops off the dryer. "Something wrong, Becks?"

"No, no. Nothing." I clear my throat, my thoughts moving fast. "Just was thinking I might chat with Ezra about the Indie Music Night. Maybe I can help out with sound or something."

It's not that I don't want to tell Keeley what I just saw, it's more that I have no idea if I've stumbled upon anything at all.

Plus, she's probably keen to get out of this laundry room now that the door is open. It's hardly an ideal time to start up a conversation about my dead grandmother who once lived in this town.

"I still think you should play. But I'm sure he'd love the extra help."

"You haven't heard me sing yet to be making grand statements like that," I say with a smile.

"If you're awful, that'll be all the more entertainment." She grins.

"It'll be good craic," I agree. "With an I-C on the end, for the record, before you start dialing the police."

"Excellent C-R-A-I-C." Keeley laughs.

I glance at the open door and give her a salute. "Guess I'd better be on my way. So little time, so much of this building to explore."

"Sure thing." Keeley returns my grin. I'm about to turn away and head out the door when she calls out, "Hey, Becks?"

I turn back to her, where she's scuffing the toe of one of her black Converse sneakers across the cement floor. "Yeah?"

"I'm glad we're, um, friends now."

"Me too," I tell her, and I mean it.

Suddenly, between meeting Keeley, the Indie Music Night, and discovering what *could* be my Gran's name on the wall, I feel like my summer in Serendipity Springs might be even more serendipitous than I first thought.

Chapter Eleven
Beckett

"YOU'LL NEVER BELIEVE what happened to John McCandless down at the bookies last night," Mam says between sips of her drink. Even over video, her eyes are shining with excitement, and her skin is a nice pink shade of almost-a-tan. She's currently lying on a sun lounger on a beautiful beach in Greece, and I'm glad she's having a good honeymoon.

Even if I have no foggy idea who John McCandless is.

"What happened to who?" I ask her as I move my phone to my other hand and push open the front door of The Serendipity. It's sunny again today, and I slip on my sunglasses before I head down the steps, taking them two at a time.

I'm headed out this morning to do a food shop.

Or, as they say here, *get groceries.*

I've been in Serendipity Springs for a few days now, and so far, I've been living off the supply of basics Mr. Prenchenko kindly left in his fridge for me. But at this point, I'm out of bread, milk, and eggs—and I'm kind of missing having green things in my diet.

Not to mention I'm hoping that the supermarket will have some decent tea.

"Aye, you know John. Tall fella from Clogher, used to hurl with your uncle Packie back in the day."

"Still don't know him, Mam."

"Wise up, Becks. You do know him, surely. Big John McCandless. He came to Conan Fogarty's first communion?"

I pinch the bridge of my nose. "No, Mam. I have never met, nor heard of, this John McCandless you speak of."

"Lawds a mercy." She clicks her tongue—a habit my brother Callan inherited from her—and then launches into a long, secondhand-account story about a man I have only just learned existed and how he won some money last night betting on horses.

Real fascinating stuff.

Nonetheless, I listen patiently, the pitch of Mam's voice soothingly familiar as I head towards the parkade. As I go, I greet a couple of fellow Serendipity residents with a nod—that sweet elderly couple who are always strolling around the building, and a young woman with dark brown hair who gives me a look of intrigue as she nods back, then whispers something to the guy clad in medical scrubs whose hand she's holding.

Mam's just getting to what I believe is the crux of the story—the moment John risked all his winnings on lucky number thirteen, Paddy's Wagon—when the line beeps. She stops mid-sentence. "Ah look, Aoife's on the line. Lovely, I'll add her to this call."

She presses a button, and Aoife's pale, freckled face fills half the screen. I get the feeling that I never will find out if John McCandless's gamble on Paddy's Wagon paid off or not, as my sister starts rapid-firing questions without waiting for an answer. "How's Crete, Mam? Did you hear about that robbery in Sligo last night? Dreadful, just dreadful. Oh, and I bumped into Roisin last night at the hairdresser's, and it turns out she's seeing Frank Doherty now. Remember Frank?

Skinny fella. Had a bit of a lazy eye back in the day before he got those corrective glasses?"

"Nice lad, Frank," Mam says, beaming. "Good for Roisin."

Then, they both stare at me. I realize they're waiting for my reaction.

"Yeah, good for her," I say, and I mean it. I don't think of Roisin much anymore, and I truly wish her well when I do.

I hope Keeley will feel the same in regards to Andrew someday, too. Seeing her face go pale when he came into the laundry room yesterday really irked me, especially when he acted like she was doing something wrong for simply talking to another man.

I know guys like that. Guys who play women for their own gain, who use women to make them feel bigger and better about themselves. And though I don't know her well yet, I already want so much bigger and better for Keeley than that rat of a guy.

I'm judging him without knowing him, and I'm sure my Gran would have a saying about not doing such a thing. But then again, I don't think she would have liked Andrew, either.

And on the subject of Gran, I haven't been able to stop thinking about seeing her name on the laundry room wall yesterday. I don't think Noeleen is a super common name here in America and it seems too convenient. On top of every other convenient coincidence I've encountered lately.

"Mam, are you sure you don't have any more info on Gran's time here?" I ask when there's a brief lull in the Frank Doherty conversation. "Like, she never mentioned where she might have lived or anything?"

"Becks, love, I've told you everything I know." Mam lifts a shoulder. "She went to college there, came home, met your Grandpa, and they got married and had me a few years later. She never, ever spoke about her time there. In fact, I forgot all about it until you found that old student ID of hers."

Ah, yes, that student ID card shocked us all. I came across it in a basket of Gran's things when I was helping Mam clear out her bedroom. I'd had no idea that she'd ever even been abroad, never mind that she'd gone to school in America.

The twenty-year old Gran in the picture looked happy. Truly happy and glowing through the grainy black-and-white exposure.

I wondered why she never told me about going to America. Surely, out of the millions of stories she'd told us over the years, it would have come up.

My gran was a natural storyteller, through and through. What could have happened here to make her never speak of it?

"But Becks, don't you be fretting about Gran, you hear me? Just take it easy over there, enjoy your holiday." Mam's beady eyes suddenly spark with interest. "Speaking of, have you met anyone nice yet? Made any friends?"

The question is reminiscent of the ones she asked me after my first day of "big school" oh-so-many years ago, and it makes me smile. "Yeah, I did."

Keeley Roberts.

I love her name. It just sounds so... American. Like she's one of those Dallas Cowboys Cheerleaders Aoife's always on about.

Although the thought of Keeley with her eyeliner and dark nails and nose ring in a cheerleading outfit makes me want to laugh.

"That reminds me, Becks, Niamh's wondering if you got her that autograph yet?" Aoife asks.

"I've only been here a few days, Aoife."

She scoffs. "Only takes two seconds to sign a piece of paper, though."

"Was Oprah being difficult about giving you her signature?" Mam pipes up indignantly.

85

"No. Mam. I have not seen, nor spoken to, Oprah just yet."

She shakes her head like I'm a half-wit. "What are you waiting for?"

I swear these conversations are like literal roundabouts. With no exits.

Or traffic circles, as I believe they're known on this side of the pond.

"You're right, Mam. I'll just track Oprah down once I'm done with my morning coffee."

Coffee, again. Because I can't seem to find any decent tea in this country.

"There's the can-do attitude I like to see," Mam says with a nod of approval, then covers the speaker on her phone as she turns her head towards Paul, who has just popped up behind her wearing a dashing neon pink and yellow Hawaiian shirt that really sets off his crisp sunburn. A moment later, she's back. "Paul says hi and it's time for us to get ready for our dinner reservations. We're trying *stuffed vine leaves* tonight. And spanako-whatsit. Can't remember what it's called, but it's something with pastry. Very exotic, don't you think?"

I stifle a laugh. Mam thinks adding black pepper to her mashed potatoes is adventurous eating. I don't think the woman even had Chinese food until about a year ago.

"Enjoy that," I tell her.

Aoife tuts. "Hope you don't get food poisoning. Emmett McGee told me his wife got a dreadful upset stomach on her holidays last year."

"Ah, there's a shame. Was she in Greece, too?"

"No, no. She went to Blackpool."

"Blackpool, England? As in, nowhere near Greece in the slightest?" I question.

Aoife gives me a withering look. "Traveler's diarrhea can strike anywhere, anytime, Beckett."

"And on that note, I'll be off," I say firmly, having no wish to further discuss Maureen McGee's bowel movements.

But of course, it's never that easy. And after a lengthy course of goodbyes, about sixteen more remarks about food poisoning, and a quick (not) Google search from Aoife to inform me that if my own stomach starts to play up, I can find Imodium at a place called "CVS," I finally hang up and jump into the truck.

The vehicle rumbles noisily to life, and I exit the parking garage and drive towards Spring Foods, which is apparently the local place to shop for food.

My GPS is on, and my eyes flicker between the suggested route and the road as I drive. I'm paying so much attention to not taking a wrong turn that I almost don't notice the woman with her familiar streak of black hair running down the sidewalk.

It's Keeley. Dressed in sneakers, a tank top, and athletic shorts.

Without hesitation, I swerve to pull the truck over and wind the window down.

"Keeley! What are you doing?"

She halts in her tracks and a look of pure mortification dances over her delicate features, before her eyes flash with something akin to annoyance.

She's covered in sweat, there's a clump of damp hair stuck to her forehead, and her cheeks are glowing bright red beacons... And I find myself simultaneously wanting to laugh and wrap her in a hug. Neither of which are appropriate reactions to greeting your sweaty new friend, I'm sure.

"Wh-what does it"—she pants heavily—"look like I'm doing? I'm running."

"But what are you running away from?" I ask with a

teasing grin, still charmed by those red cheeks and flashing eyes.

"What? No! I'm running for..." She heaves another big breath. "Fitness."

"Aquarobics wasn't cutting it anymore, huh?"

"Shut it, McCarthy!" She glares at me before she leans forward and puts her hands on her thighs, still puffing hard.

"You doing okay over there?" I ask, enjoying myself thoroughly.

"I'm dandy. Just one mile to go."

"You going to make it?"

She looks at the truck longingly for a few beats, before she looks back down at her sneakered feet. "I'm sure I could, but..." She pauses, looks at the sidewalk stretching out ahead of her, and seems to consider something. Then, her jaw sets. "Maybe you could give me a ride."

"Excuse me?" I blink, wondering if too much cardio can deprive someone's brain of vital oxygen or if she really just asked the question I think she did.

In response, she looks at me like I'm very, very slow. "Give me a ride. Like... I would get in the truck. With you. And you would drive me home."

"Oh!" I say with a sputtered laugh. *Wait until Callan and Eoin get wind of this one.* "Wow. Well, let's just say that particular sentence has a *very* different meaning where I come from. We'd call that a 'lift home.' And of course I can give you one of those."

As Keeley grins at me in thanks and comes around to the passenger door, I find I'm delighted by the unexpected turn this morning has taken.

"Thanks, Beckett," she breathes as she sinks into the seat. "Hope I'm not interrupting any plans."

I wave a hand. "Not at all. I was actually just driving around looking for tired runners to collect."

She smirks at me. "My Gramps always taught me not to get in cars with strangers in case I get murdered or whatnot, so I guess it's lucky for me that we're friends now, huh?"

"More like lucky for you, I'm not in a murderous mood today." I gesture towards the pavement, which is currently radiating. "It's too hot for gratuitous violence. I can't believe you were out running in this insane heat."

She pulls at the hair tie holding back her ponytail so her long hair cascades down her shoulders for a moment, before quickly pushing the stray hair off her face and beginning to retie it. "Me neither. I don't know what I was thinking. I guess I hoped a run might help me clear my head."

"Did it?"

A smile. "No."

I smile back as I put the truck in drive again and steer onto the road. "Fasten your seatbelt. I'm still getting used to driving on the wrong side of the road."

Keeley gasps theatrically and grabs the door handle. "Is it too late to change my mind about this?"

"Yes."

"Okay, in that case, you do realize that you're going the wrong way?" She jerks a thumb over her shoulder. "Our building is that way."

"I know." I look over at her and waggle my eyebrows. "I need your help with something quick before I take you home."

"That sounds ominous."

I nod at the GPS pulled up on my phone sitting on the dash. "Just a little trip to Spring Foods."

She grins. "Oh, you can close that. I'll direct you."

"A true local."

"Born and bred."

"Right. You mentioned the other night that your family's been here for generations."

"Yup," she says, then pauses. Frowns. "Well, specifically my dad's family. The Roberts family."

I glance at her hands, which still have chipped black polish and that silver Claddagh ring. "Does that mean your grandpa grew up here? Is he your dad's dad?"

"Yes. Gramps was the mayor's son, and then was also the mayor himself for a time. The Roberts side of the family are part of the furniture in this town." Her smile falters a little. "I just visited him yesterday morning, at his retirement residence. He has dementia now, so he needs full-time care."

"I'm so sorry," I tell her sincerely. While I haven't personally encountered dementia with any of my relatives—Gran was thankfully completely lucid until she passed—I've heard it's an extremely tough condition on both the person afflicted and their loved ones.

A part of me had hoped to ask Keeley if her grandpa could have crossed paths with my gran. It was a stretch, sure—Serendipity Springs is a town of about a hundred thousand people. But the fact that Keeley has that ring from her grandpa seems like an odd coincidence.

Coincidences certainly seem to be a thing around here, though, and this seems hardly the time to dig around for such information. So I let the thought go for now.

"Were you close?" I ask her.

"Yeah. We were pretty close—still *are* pretty close." She frowns. "But things are different now."

"I get it." My hand involuntarily goes to the ring around my neck. "I was close with my grandmother. She passed away last year."

I'm not sure why I'm volunteering this information—it's not something I talk about easily, especially not with people I've recently met. But something about Keeley, about her sharing with me, makes me want to open up, too.

"I'm sorry," Keeley says quietly. She lifts a hand, and I get the sense she wants to place it on mine as a gesture of comfort, but she seems to change her mind and run it through her ponytail instead.

I look over at her and give her a half-smile. "Guess we're a sorry pair."

"A sorry pair of Spring Chickens, you mean."

"I beg your finest pardon?"

Keeley laughs, and the sound echoes happily around the cab of the truck as she digs a key ring out of her shorts pocket. A little white tab on it proclaims: "I'm a Spring Chicken!"

"This explains nothing," I tell her mock-solemnly.

"Springs Foods loyalty card, baby. Stick with me, and I can get you all the best shopping deals in town."

It's my turn to laugh. "How lucky I am to have taken up residence next to you."

"Unfathomably lucky," she declares.

We share a smile, and suddenly, my jokey words feel very true. I'm grateful that Keeley Roberts has become a part of my time here in Serendipity Springs.

Chapter Twelve
Keeley

"Okay, if we're doing this, we're doing it right," I tell Beckett as I hand him a wire grocery basket and take one for myself.

"Lead the way, captain," he affirms as we walk into Spring Foods together, two people on a mission.

Somehow, my morning has transformed from "go for a run to get my head on straight after being kept awake again last night by Andrew and Lisa's footsteps" to "accompany my new friend Becks to the grocery store to help him stock up on *American delicacies*"—his words, not mine. Apparently, while he's here, he wants to try all the delightfully processed foods our great nation has to offer.

Lucky for him, he has a connoisseur assisting him today.

And lucky for me, he pulled up in his truck at exactly the right moment, because I think my head might've exploded before making it home.

I hate running at the best of times. And I must've gone temporarily insane this morning—it's the only explanation for why I was suddenly convinced a run in one-thousand-degree heat would inspire me to work on my article this afternoon.

Although, of course Beckett would see me in yet another state of total disarray.

I'm so inhumanly sweaty right now, I'm sure I left an imprint on the passenger seat of Mr. Prenchenko's truck. Despite the air conditioning Beckett was blasting the entire drive here.

But honestly, I'm not really thinking about my full-body glow at the moment. I'm too busy wondering about Beckett and his grandma. I can't quite believe that I just willingly, openly, shared with him about Gramps and his condition. He, in turn, told me about his own grandmother's passing, and I could tell by the expression on his face that he's pretty torn up about it.

I've been suspecting that Beckett's here in Serendipity Springs for more reasons than just to house sit for Mr. Prenchenko. Maybe he's here to grieve. Get some space. I can totally understand the need for some space from whatever his situation is at home.

After all, isn't that at least part of the reason I'm applying for this job in Boston? To escape being right downstairs from my ex and the woman he left me for?

It was strange to me, the other day in the laundry room, when Beckett told me he thought Andrew was jealous. I doubt he was right. I mean, why would he be jealous? The guy moved on from me quicker than I could practically even have a freaking shower.

Maybe Becks was just saying it to make me feel better. Which was nice of him.

"Okay," I say as I lead Beckett past the fresh produce and straight to the back of the store. "First, we need to hit the freezers."

"I was rather hoping for some apples." He casts a longing eye at a large stack of bright green Granny Smiths.

I shake my head. "We'll hit the aisle with the Minute Maid in a bit."

"Minute Maid?"

"Apple juice," I explain.

"Right," he says. "Because that was clear as day."

I fling open the door to one of the freezers, and a minute later, he's in possession of a basketful of corn dogs, hot pockets, and Eggos.

"Like on *Stranger Things*," he says in wonder, examining the box of blueberry waffles.

"Eleven loved them for good reason, trust me." I throw a couple more boxes of waffles—one cinnamon, one chocolate chip—into his basket for good measure.

Becks eyes his basket warily. "Am I expected to consume all of these, or are we stocking Mr. Prenchenko's freezer for his return?"

"Consume, of course." I tsk. "But in the bizarre scenario that you don't fall in love with them, I'll happily take any extras if Mr. P is also insane and not a waffle guy." I add a box of chocolate chip waffles to my own basket. "Speaking of, how on earth did this house sitting thing come about? How do you even know Mr. Prenchenko?"

I'm prying, I know, but I can't help but be curious. Just as Beckett had questions for me in the laundry room yesterday, I have questions for him, too.

I mean, isn't that what friends do? Get to know each other?

"I don't." He shrugs a shoulder before grabbing a box of chicken spring rolls from the top shelf of the freezer. "As a teacher, I have the summer off, obviously, and a colleague recommended me to house sit for Mr. Prenchenko while he teaches summer courses at the school where we work back home."

This doesn't quite satisfy my curiosity as to why a handsome twenty-six-year-old Irishman would want to spend his summer, alone, three thousand miles from home in a random small town. But this doesn't feel like the time or place to push that, especially if it *does* have something to do with his grandma's passing.

So, I just smile and say, "Well, The Serendipity is a pretty great place to be house sitting—the waitlist for an apartment there is a mile long. I was so lucky to get mine. A few people in the building have lived there for longer than I've been alive, I think."

He studies me for a beat before asking, "Do you happen to know how old the building is?"

"Random," I tell him. "I don't know exactly, but it's probably ancient. It has the same sort of look and style as all the OG buildings in town."

"Hmm," is all he says, but his brow is furrowed, like he's deep in thought. I have to wonder, yet again, if there's more to his being here in Serendipity Springs than just watering Mr. P's plants.

We walk into the tea and coffee aisle, where Beckett squints in concentration at multiple packages of tea before adding about six boxes to his basket. Then, we cross over into the cereal aisle, and Beckett's face lights up with pure delight.

"Lucky Charms!" he exclaims, grabbing a couple of boxes to add to his already overflowing basket.

I stare at him in full confusion. "You don't have Lucky Charms—the most Irish of all the cereals—in Ireland?"

"Nope. I think our government banned them. Too many dyes."

"What a bunch of bores," I tease.

"Despicable," he agrees. "Depriving the entire nation of essential chemicals."

As Beckett and I banter back and forth, I'm surprised to feel a sort of calm contentment falling over me. I was looking

95

for a way to clear my head this morning, and as it turns out, a trip to Spring Foods with my neighbor was apparently the key.

It's a bit strange, but when I'm with Beckett, I feel... relaxed, somehow. Like I don't have to try to escape what I'm feeling.

I lean over and take the box of Oat Bran out of his hand and add a box of Froot Loops and another of Count Chocula to his haul. "Speaking of chemicals, have you been introduced to the wonders of Marshmallow Fluff yet?"

Beckett groans. "You have a secret plan to induce diabetes in me or something?"

"Just trying to get you more enjoyment in your life."

He gestures in front of him with a silly flourish. "In that case, lead the way, Miss Roberts."

Chapter Thirteen
Beckett

"BECKETT!" Ezra looks ridiculously happy to see me. In fact, despite his somewhat menacing appearance at first glance, this guy could be the poster child for that "small town hospitality" Mr. Prenchenko told me about.

A good reminder to never judge a book by its tattooed cover. Fittingly, today, he's wearing a graphic t-shirt with the logo of a 90s punk band on the front.

"Hiya," I greet him with a smile as I head towards the back of the store. Blue Notes is empty again, and instead of standing behind the cashier's desk, Ezra is sitting on it while eating salad from a cardboard container.

"Sorry, I was just on my lunch break," he says, setting down the container. He gestures around the store with a smirk. "Busy morning, as you can see."

"Do you own the place?" I ask, almost hoping for his sake that the answer is *no*.

He senses the poorly veiled concern in my voice and laughs. "I do. But don't worry, we do make *some* money... just not necessarily from retail." He jumps off the counter and beckons me to follow him down a narrow hallway and through a door into a back section of the shop.

He flicks on a light switch, illuminating a back hallway with windows on either side looking into what appear to be spacious, private rooms. "We offer music lessons in these rooms in the afternoons and evenings—usually guitar, piano, and drum lessons. There's also a concert violinist who comes through town every once in a while and gives lessons when he's here." He throws a grin over his shoulder. "So if you, for some reason, decide to stay instead of going home after your vacation, you're always welcome to teach lessons here."

"I'd actually love to give some lessons while I'm here," I offer. "If you need any extra teachers, that is."

"Hey, that'd be great. Thanks, man."

"Not like I have much else going on," I joke, and as he shuts the door on the last lesson room, he gives me a smirk.

"I saved the best for last..."

At the end of the hallway, Ezra gestures with a flourish towards the last and biggest window. I look inside and am shocked to see a recording studio.

An actual, state-of-the-art recording studio, with high-tech equipment and a drool-worthy set-up. A plaque above the door reads "Lucky 13 Studios."

Lucky, indeed.

I'm exceedingly jealous of Ezra's business, which is clearly so much more than just a music store. This guy's got his act together, that's for sure.

Ezra takes in my expression and grins. "Thought you might appreciate it."

"*Appreciate* it?! This is incredible. I'm like a little kid in a sweet shop—er, *candy store,* as you'd say here." In fact, it's all I can do not to press my nose up against the glass as I peer into the sleek facility.

"We get people coming from all over to record here. It's

where the magic happens, to use that cheesy old line. In fact..." Ezra pauses for a moment. "We recently had a certain very-well-known Irish gentleman in here to record a single for his upcoming album. Must've heard about the legend of luck here in Serendipity Springs and thought he'd try his hand."

"We can be a rather superstitious bunch." I laugh, wondering who it might have been but not wanting to ask, and then add without thinking, "I'd give my left arm to record in here."

"You want to book some slots?"

Ezra's question catches me weirdly off-guard. Back before Gran died, I wrote most of an original album, and when I would play at the local pub, I'd alternate between popular covers and trialing my originals on a small—admittedly drunken—audience.

Sometimes, I'd think about what it might be like to record my own music.

But I don't think about that anymore.

In the past year or so, all my creativity has dried up. Shriveled away. The music in me now feels like an itch I can't scratch, buried too deep to access.

I never finished my album.

There was no need.

I've got a real job that I'm grateful for.

"Nah," I tell him with a half-smile. "Thanks, though."

"What about signing up for the Indie Music Night?" he asks without missing a beat.

I laugh. "Keeley talked to you?"

"She did. She said you'd come see me and mention some nonsense about helping with sound, but she was very insistent that I try to persuade you to play instead."

"Of course she did."

"So, will you? Play something, I mean?"

I study the toe of my sneaker for a moment. I meant what

I said to Keeley in the laundry room a few days back—I have thought about performing in the Indie Music Night.

And while I came here today with the intention of telling Ezra I'd help out with sound and behind the scenes stuff, I'll admit a part of me is still thinking about playing.

"Is everyone gonna be playing original music?"

Ezra's eyes spark with delight. "A mix of things. Feel free to do a cover if you want."

It's probably just a sugar high from consuming a lunch of the waffles and chocolate cereal Keeley absolutely insisted I buy. But I feel like this is something I can do.

It's strange. Lately, that deep-seated itch in me to play music almost feels like it's moving closer to the surface again.

It's something I can hardly dare to hope for. But if I play a cover, there's no pressure to channel that creativity again. I can simply just play a familiar song and help Keeley's friend out in the process.

"Maybe something Irish?" Ezra suggests, bringing me back to the present. "People would go nuts for that."

Steve Earle's "The Galway Girl" immediately comes to mind—a song about a man who meets a beautiful woman with black hair and blue eyes, and even though he's not looking for love, he can't help but be totally charmed by her.

The thought makes me smile.

"Sure," I find myself saying.

"Nice!" Ezra says, looking genuinely pleased. "Nori will be so happy to fill the last spot."

He starts talking me through some details, and I nod along, mind whirring with a mix of nerves, trepidation, and excitement, when Ezra casually says, "Keeley will also be helping out, of course."

"Makes sense. She and Nori are good friends."

Ezra smirks knowingly. "You two have been hanging out, huh?"

"A little. Sometimes," I say, because that's easier than telling him that we were locked in the laundry room together for an hour yesterday after I found her in yet another state of partial undress, and that I picked her up from the roadside earlier and basically kidnapped her to be my shopping partner.

A shopping trip that made me the proud owner of an *I'm A Spring Chicken!* reusable tote bag.

Ezra and I wander back to the main floor of the shop, and he picks up his salad container again. "I'm glad she has someone watching out for her in her building. Especially now that she and Andrew have broken up."

I frown at the mention of his name. "What's the deal with that Andrew guy, anyway?"

"They dated for ages, but their relationship always felt... off to me." Ezra's eyes darken. "Like something didn't quite fit."

"Oh?" I ask, trying not to look as keen for details as I feel.

"I think he was just the wrong person for her, and she was trying to make it right for so long that it was habit by the end. After they broke up, she seemed to wake up and consider what she really wants. I feel like he was holding her back in a lot of ways."

I remember what she said about the article she had to write to get her dream job, and I lean forward, curious to know more about Keeley's plans. "Holding her back career-wise?"

"Yeah. Partly. I was happy when she told me she was applying for a job in Boston. It'll be a fresh start for her."

"Oh. I didn't realize the job was in Boston."

For some reason, the thought of her moving away makes me feel... strange. Just for a moment, until I snap back to reality and remember that in a few short weeks, I'll be leaving, too, and we won't be neighbors anymore.

Ezra's blue eyes—so like Keeley's—are steady on me. "You like her, don't you?" he asks bluntly.

I swallow. Consider the question.

I *do* find myself drawn to Keeley in a way that I'm not used to feeling. But I barely know the woman. And when I go back to Ireland, how I feel about her—or don't feel about her—will be an entirely moot point.

"We're just friends," I reply firmly.

"Uh-huh," he counters with a twinkle in his eye, like he very much doesn't believe me.

A twinkle that makes me question if I even believe what I'm saying myself.

Chapter Fourteen
Keeley

"Wow, don't you look nice, dearie. Got a date with that handsome boy?"

I look up to see a smiling, well-meaning Mrs. Hathaway approaching me in the lobby. I've just come downstairs with the intention of holing up in the Spring View library for the rest of the day and working on some elementary outlining for my Evoke article.

"There's a twinkle in your eye that suggests so!" Mr. Hathaway is next to his wife, one hand supportively placed under her elbow and the other wrapped around his cane. He's wearing his trademark bowler hat, like always, while his wife sports what looks like a fresh lilac rinse.

These two are the cutest.

The couple have got to be approaching their nineties, if not there already. They both have deeply lined faces, stooped postures, and move slowly and carefully, like something could break at any moment. But despite this, there's something incredibly, unfathomably youthful about them. Like there's a light glowing from within, reflecting through their eyes and making them appear younger than they are.

The Hathaways are longtime residents of The Serendipity. In fact, they must be the oldest people living here, and they seem to know every tenant by name. You can often spot them in the rooftop garden together, or sitting by the pool together, or reading in the small library room on the building's ground floor... together.

Come to think of it, I've never seen one Hathaway without the other. And I must say, even with my current boycotting feelings towards love, it is pretty darn inspiring to see how in love they still seem to be after a lifetime spent together.

"Oh, no, no. No date. Just..." I look down at my fitted purple shirt with the sweetheart neckline, and my cute light wash jeans with ripped details, then back up at Mrs. Hathaway. "Wednesday," I finish.

What I don't say is that it's been a few days now since my almost-death by running. Each morning since that impromptu and very sweaty grocery store run, I've carefully planned my outfit so there will be absolutely zero risk of running into my new friend Becks again in yet another state of chaotic disarray.

And yes, I might've done my hair and put on mascara and lip gloss, too.

But just because I wanted to feel pretty today, that's all.

I mean, I haven't actually *seen* Beckett since we went to Spring Foods together. I've heard the sounds of him softly playing guitar in the mornings, the musical notes carrying from his apartment. But if I happen to run into him today— or get locked in a confined space with him—while I look presentable, then so be it.

Super weird how that keeps happening. I think the universe genuinely likes to laugh at me.

Surprisingly, Mrs. Hathaway does not seem satisfied by my

response to her question. Instead she smiles like she's sure I'm wrong and I really *do* have a date, after all. She pats my hand, her wrinkled skin cool to the touch. "He's a lucky man."

Her kind words and the small gesture seem intimate in a way that makes me feel strangely emotional. Like she's sealing my worth with her touch.

"Guess you haven't heard that Andrew and I broke up," I say quietly, shifting my backpack on my shoulder.

Mr. Hathaway looks away so quickly, I first worry he's going to tweak his neck. But then, it almost looks like he's... hiding a smile?

When he turns back to me, though, there's no hint of a smile on his face, leaving me wondering if I'm imagining things now. "Oh, yes, we were already aware of that. I think my wife was referring to—"

"That fine specimen of an Irishman who's moved in next door to her?" someone interrupts, and we all turn to see Roberta from the first floor standing next to us. Her eyes are eagerly glowing with the glee of an impending gossip session.

Honestly, this woman knows everything about everyone in this building. It's impressive.

But everyone is clearly misinformed this time.

I shake my head vehemently. "Becks and I just—"

"Got caught in a passionate embrace in the elevator?" Roberta asks with a big smile. "Started doing your laundry together? Went to hang out with your brother already?"

"None of those statements are *quite* accurate," I start, but Mrs. Hathaway is patting my hand again.

"I think it's lovely that new love is already blossoming for you," she says softly.

"Oh, no, we just met—"

"So, what are you waiting for?" Roberta shoots me a theatrical wink. "Lock down that delicious piece of man candy before someone else does. Anyhoo, got to run!" She waggles her fingers at us and continues across the lobby, heels clicking.

I turn back to the Hathaways and hold up my hands as if clearing my name. "Beckett's just a friend and my temporary neighbor, as I'm sure you've heard. He's only here for the summer."

And then, he, like me, will be gone from this place. If all goes according to plan.

"A summer of love," Mr. Hathaway says, clearly not hearing a word I'm saying.

I blanch at the L-word. I am officially allergic to love now. "Nope!"

"True love will show up exactly when and where it's meant to," Mrs. Hathaway adds, not listening to my protests either. "This place has a funny way of working things out the way they're supposed to work out. Or not work out."

She's looking at me rather pointedly, and I wonder—not for the first time—if everyone but me believed Andrew and I were all wrong for each other and would eventually go our separate ways.

Which begs the question: how blind was I?

But Mrs. Hathaway's words have struck another chord—though surely not the one she intended—as the topic of my article-to-be-written suddenly jumps to mind.

I take in the clearly still very-much-in-love couple before me, and I adopt my objective reporter persona.

If I'm going to stick with my ideal article topic—to disprove the legend that this building brings people luck in love—I might as well start with the Hathaways. They're clearly a success story in the love department, but they're also about a million years old. Surely they met and fell in love before they moved in here... which means that their love would have grown somewhere else organically, instead of being the product of a stupid "lucky in love" legend.

"Where did you two meet?" I ask.

Mr. Hathaway smiles. "We met right here in this building."

My fragile hopes are dashed. "You don't say," I reply feebly.

Mr. Hathaway clearly doesn't notice my disappointment, because he continues on excitedly, "We moved into The Serendipity after the apartments opened back in the sixties. We were living next door to each other upstairs when we fell in love."

His wife tuts good-naturedly as she winks at me. "He's conveniently leaving out the part where he didn't even notice me until we got trapped in the elevator together..."

Her words startle me.

"*This* elevator?" I point in the direction of our building's elevator, my thoughts rewinding to the tumble I almost took the day Beckett and I met. How he caught me before the elevator trapped us together.

"That one, indeed," Mr. Hathaway confirms. "And what a lucky twist of fate that was, because from that day forward, I knew Janey here was the one for me. We got married and moved away for a time, but life eventually led us right back here, where we first met, to see out the rest of our days together."

"That's awesome," I say even as my stomach pinches slightly.

Writing about beautiful, lasting love feels disingenuous to me, given my own experiences. I want stories of heartbreak. Betrayal. Being shunned for the supposed best friend, like I recently was.

Now *that* sounds like the type of thing I can authentically dig into.

Not to mention, these kinds of stories are relatable. They pull at your heartstrings. And they'd be popular with readers —especially single twenty-somethings reading a lifestyle magazine like Evoke who've had similar things happen to them.

As adorable as they are, I don't need happily-ever-afters like the Hathaways have.

"Do you know of a lot of people who've fallen in love here?"

Mrs. Hathaway smiles. "Absolutely."

Again, not the answer I was hoping for.

"Hey," I say, needing a change of conversational pace. "You said you moved into The Serendipity right after the apartments opened. What was the building before?"

If I can't get the answers I need for my article from the Hathaways, maybe I can get the answer to the question Becks asked at the grocery store about the age of the building.

"It was a college dorm for Spring Brook." The elderly lady nods decisively. "Back then, of course, it was a women's college, and the campus was in the town center. This place housed some of the students." She smiles fondly. "I imagine they hosted gentlemen callers in the library and held dances in the ballroom."

"Wow, I had no idea," I breathe, feeling like this is information I absolutely *should* have known. A former Spring Brook student myself, I knew the college historically had been all-girls and that the campus had been relocated to its current spot sometime in the 1960s, but shame on me for not realizing that I currently live in one of the old dorms. "That's cool."

"Lots of interesting history 'round these parts," Mr. Hathaway says with a smile. "Now, if you'll excuse us, my wife and I had best be off. We have a date with our bridge club."

"Enjoy!" I bid the Hathaways goodbye and head towards

the front door. And that's when I hear the music coming from the small library room just off the lobby.

Beautiful, unfamiliar music that I somehow know instinctively is *him*. Music that has me ditching my plan to go to the library and instead walking straight towards the sound. Like he's the Pied Piper and I'm completely under his spell.

Chapter Fifteen
Beckett

MY FINGERS MOVE FREELY over the strings, pulling a tune out of me that's brand new, yet somehow achingly familiar. It's soft and gentle, yet taut with an emotion I can't quite name.

It's that old, still familiar sensation of letting music flow from somewhere inside of me, my body channeling it into something tangible that echoes in my ears.

Moments when I feel most myself.

I can hardly believe this is happening. I haven't played like this—*created like this*—since Gran died.

The morning after her wake, I got up and found I'd become numb. Something in me had shut down, and I was on autopilot, both physically and emotionally. And it never really went away.

Instead of mourning in what might be considered the traditional way, I somehow navigated the last year feeling nothing at all. Even when Roisin left, I continued to go about my everyday life without letting myself feel a thing.

It was safe. Still *is* safe.

But right now, something is stirring in me that's been dormant for a long time.

I don't know why it's happening, but I do know that I can *feel* it.

The same way I used to feel it when Gran was around. Like there's magic in the air.

When I woke up this morning, I felt... *inspired* is perhaps the best word for it. Maybe it's because I said yes to the Indie Music Night, but something has suddenly shifted.

Until now, I've been playing on the couch under the window in Mr. Prenchenko's place, but this morning, I put my guitar in its case and wandered around The Serendipity like some kind of vagrant searching for a street corner to busk on.

And that's when I found myself inexplicably drawn to this room.

I thought I'd explored the building thoroughly—over the past few days, I've taken a swim in the pool, had my morning coffee in the courtyard (since I deemed all of the tea I bought at Spring Foods undrinkable, particularly one brand of something called 'Orange Pekoe Black Tea' that should have been a criminal offense), and spent an afternoon reading in the rooftop garden that's bursting with color in full summer bloom. Until this morning, I'd never noticed the room just off the building's lobby.

It's an old library or study of some sort, with dark wood paneling on the walls and aged volumes lining the floor-to-ceiling shelves. The furniture is dated, matching the rest of the room, but it's clean and comfortable. Sunlight streams through the windows, painting shadow patterns all around the comfortable wingback chair I'm sitting in.

I came in here with the intention of rehearsing my cover for the big night, but instead, my own music is flowing once again.

As my fingers move over my guitar, my chest tightens with emotion.

I'm shocked by the physical sensation of it—heavy as it settles over my ribs, but not unpleasant. Just... there.

It's the first time in a long time that I've felt anything.

And then, I hear the creak of a door closing.

I abruptly stop playing, slamming my hand down on the strings.

"Sorry," a small voice whispers. I look up to see Keeley standing just inside the doorway, lit by the streaming sunlight. Her black hair glimmers where the sun kisses it, and her eyes are wide as saucers. "I didn't mean to startle you or interrupt."

I clear my throat, trying to force away the sensation in my chest as I paste on a cheery smile and set my guitar down. "You're fine. I was just messing around."

She blinks. "That wasn't messing around. That was... incredible. What song was it?"

"I don't know," I admit, lifting a shoulder.

Her eyes bug even more. "You're telling me you wrote that?"

This makes me laugh, and I lean forward in my chair. "'Wrote' is a strong word. It's just a little melody that came to me."

Keeley shakes her head. "You have that a lot? 'Little melodies' just 'coming' to you?"

The almost indignant expression on her face makes me want to laugh. "No. Not really, not anymore."

"Oh. Too bad."

I tilt my head at her. "For some reason, I didn't take you for someone who'd be into this kind of acoustic-y stuff."

"What? Just because I wear a lot of black and have a nose ring, you assume I'm a riot grrrl who should be rocking out to Bikini Kill or something?" she asks, placing her hands on her hips.

"I mean, that's definitely something I'd like to witness." I chuckle.

"Careful, McCarthy, you sound like a man who's treading on very thin ice right now."

"That sounds exactly like something a riot grrrl who should be rocking out to Bikini Kill would say," I retort. Then pause. "Whatever on earth a riot grrrl is."

She laughs. "Not important. Because for your information, I'm more of a country music girlie."

"Intriguing. Like Dolly Parton and twangy guitars and songs about beer and heartbreak?"

She points at me. "Now who's stereotyping?"

"Point taken and accepted," I acquiesce. Because I kind of love the fact she's into country music. And Dolly is a literal icon... not that I'd admit that to her right now when I'm having so much fun teasing her.

She's still hovering inside the door, not making any moves to step further into the room, and I find that I don't want her to go. The melody may have died on my fingertips when I realized her presence, but the air is still taut with that magical feeling, like something could happen at any moment. And while I have no idea what that something could be, I realize I want to find out.

"So, questionable musical tastes aside, how's your week been so far?" I grin at her. "I haven't seen you haunting the fire escape at night lately."

She grins back. "Oh, I've been haunting it every night. But I prop my window open to ensure I can get back inside when I'm done."

"Don't you enjoy, you know, sleeping? Or are you more of a nocturnal creature?"

Her face falters for a moment before she says, "Andrew lives right upstairs from me. I can't sleep when I hear multiple footsteps at night because I know Lisa's up there with him."

"I cannot imagine my ex living upstairs from me. That sounds like torture."

"It's…actually more annoying than torture-y. Strangely." She frowns, her expression thoughtful.

"You don't miss him as much as you thought you might?" I ask.

"Yeah." She picks at her fingernail, eyes lowered. "I mean, it's never nice to see—or hear—your ex moving on, but honestly, their footsteps can be *loud*." She shoots me a little smile. "Though, I do think it's more habit at this point to go out on the fire escape than it is necessity to escape the footsteps. I always do my best thinking and article outlining out there."

"Ah, yes, for the job in Boston," I say without thinking.

She looks up sharply. "I don't recall telling you the job was in Boston."

My cheeks heat a little. "Your brother told me," I admit.

"You and Ezra were talking about me." She says this as a statement, not a question, a smile playing at the corners of her mouth.

"We were." I'm unable—or maybe unwilling—to keep the flirtatious note out of my voice. Because despite what might be all my best instincts, I have just realized right this second that ripped jeans and Converse sneakers are my kryptonite. "All about how you meddled to try to get me to play the Indie Music Night."

She grins, totally unashamed. "It worked, though, didn't it? He told me you'll be playing."

"He also said that if I play something Irish, you'll lead the crowd in an Irish dance routine," I add, just for badness.

Her mouth drops open, her expression delightfully stunned, before her shrewd eyes narrow. She points an accusing finger at me. "Liar."

"If I say 'please' can I make it be true?"

She snorts. "Not in a million, billion years am I dancing in public. Or dancing at all. I'm not the dancing type."

I want to tell her that, on the contrary, her eyes are currently dancing, but I refrain. Because boundaries.

"Pity," I say instead, "In my mind, you were line-dancing up a storm in full cowgirl getup."

Which somehow sounds equally as boundary-pushing as what I wanted to say.

She reddens, shifting from foot to foot as she says, "Well, I'd better be going. Have to hit the library to work on my article."

"How's that going?"

She sighs. "I liked your idea of trying to disprove the legend, but so far, I've only encountered happy stories of love in this place, save for my own experience. And if I base the whole thing on my own breakup, it's going to come across as petty. Too personal to be a proper opinion piece. So, I'm a bit stuck... but I'll figure it out."

Keeley steps back and reaches for the door handle. Turns it.

"Oh. You've *got* to be kidding me," she mumbles, turning it harder.

The door doesn't budge.

She spins to look back at me, her face a mask of total disbelief.

Meanwhile, I can barely hide my smile. "It's happening again, isn't it?"

Chapter Sixteen
Keeley

"THERE MUST BE some reasonable explanation for this," I say as I jerk the door handle, rattling it harder than I'm already rattled.

Because here we are again.

And while I know that I somewhat tempted fate earlier by imagining this very scenario, said scenario in my head did *not* include Beckett being bashfully humble about writing the prettiest melody I've ever heard. Not to mention the way he looked at me with flutter-inducing heat in his eyes as he admitted to my face that he'd been talking to my brother about me.

I'm not used to guys like this. Flirtatious and playful, yet unabashedly honest while being so.

Andrew often had me questioning if he truly liked the way I looked or the way I acted. It was subtle, never outright mean or rude or hurtful, but he'd make observations about the way I dressed or the way I did my makeup that had me second guessing myself. Would compliment me when I wore my hair the way he liked it... and give me pointed looks when I pulled it back in a messy bun or braid.

He'd also make comments about how much he liked that Lisa enjoyed going out to bars with friends on weekends. Meanwhile, I preferred to stay at home reading, hang out at the library, or visit Gramps with my brother. He and Lisa would hit the bars together; I'd stay home to do a Korean face mask and order takeout.

How blissfully unaware I was.

With the clarity of hindsight, there was always *something* I couldn't put my finger on in my relationship with Andrew. Something that felt less than fully genuine, like all of his cards weren't quite laid out on the table. Everything was semi-veiled, cloaked in shadows.

But when Beckett looks at me, it's like someone has parted the blinds and the sunlight is streaming in. The way he's looking at me today when I'm perfectly made-up and dressed well is the exact same way he looked at me when I was covered in ketchup, or wrapped in a towel with soaking wet rat's-nest hair.

He looks at me like he likes what he sees.

"Let me help." Beckett smiles oh-so-sexily as he rises from his chair.

I try to ignore the little shimmer of heat in my stomach as he crosses the room, walking with purpose as he approaches me, not stopping until he's right in front of me, his chest inches from my face. He's so close that I feel his body heat, smell that wonderfully intoxicating woodsy, masculine, Irish Spring-tinged scent of his. He's wearing a black t-shirt today that's hugging his chest and shoulders and biceps in the most enticing of ways.

As he leans forward, my heart leaps into my throat and my eyelids flutter...

He reaches right past me, and his hand lands on the door-knob behind me.

All the air leaves my lungs as reality and reason return to

my addled mind. I watch him pull on the door handle as my heart pounds like an anvil in my chest cavity.

Idiot.

"Stuck," he confirms, looking down at me with his hand still on the doorknob, effectively caging me in.

I'm burning with embarrassment, hoping Beckett doesn't notice my body's incredibly visceral reaction to his proximity. He doesn't move, and we stand there for a few loaded moments, his hand outstretched behind my body, our eyes locked on each other, our breathing audible. A tableau depicting being caged, locked, stuck... but in a way I don't hate.

Not at all.

The last thing you need is to be feeling so drawn to your new neighbor, Keeley...

The mental reminder has me stepping backwards. Only there's nowhere to step back *to*, so I end up with my back plastered against the door.

Beckett's smile grows, like he's enjoying this as much as I'm trying not to. "Weird place, this building. Either the doors—and windows, and elevator for that matter—are very old and very broken, or the universe wants us spending time together in enclosed spaces."

"It's definitely the first one!" I practically yell, then cough. Lower my voice to a regular decibel level. "I mean, the apartments have been around for multiple decades now, so of course stuff is going to break. I mean, the landlord had to hire Steve full-time to take care of all the maintenance issues. Have you met Steve? Tall guy, likes a sweater vest..."

I'm babbling on in a way that I'm surprised is somewhat coherent.

The hot, flirty look on Beckett's face morphs into one of surprise. He abruptly lets go of the door handle and steps backwards too, putting much-needed distance between us to allow my brain to function properly and stop short-circuiting. "I thought you said you didn't know how old it was."

"I didn't. But I ran into the Hathaways just now—they've been here forever. They informed me that this building was converted into an apartment block in the mid 1960s."

"Oh?" he says. Casually, in a way that sounds like he's trying very hard to be casual when he actually has zero chill. Which is a little bit adorable. "And what was it used for before that?"

"It was a dorm building for Spring Brook College! I'm shocked I didn't know that, seeing as I went to Spring Brook." I pause for dramatic effect, like I'm announcing a TV show or something. "Back then, it was a women's college, so this building housed female students."

Beckett looks around the room, his eyes suddenly a little wild.

I raise a brow at him. I mean, I was looking for a subject change to get away from my babbling, and it seems to have worked... maybe a little too well, given Beckett's current expression.

"I think my grandma lived here." His voice is so low that I almost think I've misheard him. Until he looks right at me, his face a little pale. "How is this possible?"

"Your grandma?" I repeat, just to make sure. "Like, the one who—"

"Yup," he replies curtly.

My brow crinkles. "Wasn't she Irish?"

"Yes, but she spent some time in Serendipity Springs. I didn't even know about it until after she passed away."

"And you think she lived here, in this apartment building?"

"No." He takes a breath. "I think she lived in the dorms."

Beckett pulls his wallet out of his pocket and shimmies an old, yellowed card out of it. Hands it to me.

The card is an old-fashioned student ID for one Noeleen

119

Quinn, Spring Brook graduating class of 1960. The woman in the picture looks around nineteen or twenty, and even though the picture is wrinkled and weathered and in black-and-white, her resemblance to Becks is undeniable—the sparkling, teasing look in her eyes, the strong cheekbones, the full lips, the confident tilt of her chin.

"She's beautiful," I say.

He smiles fondly. "She was an incredible woman."

I tilt my head. "Spring Brook is a pretty big college, and was so even back then. There were likely a ton of dorms around town just like this one. What makes you think she lived here?"

"I found her name on the wall in the laundry room, carved into the plaster. There were a bunch of names in a row. Estelle was on there, I think. Maybe a Margot?"

"Whoa." I suddenly remember the look on Beckett's face after he picked up the lid of my laundry detergent—the way his face paled, his hazel eyes wide open. I've seen the names written on the wall down there a few times over the years. Never thought much of them. "And she never told you she came here?"

Becks shakes his head. "That's what's really strange about all of this. There must be a reason she never mentioned it to me."

I nod slowly, processing this. I can't imagine Gramps dying and then finding out something completely unexpected about his life. I'd have so many questions... as I'm sure Beckett does. But I'm safe in my knowledge that Gramps grew up here and stayed here his whole life.

Beckett's dark brows are drawn together, his full lips pursed in thought. I can't help but feel for the guy.

"This must feel doubly strange, then," I say gently. "You could be living in the same building where she lived."

He looks at me for a long moment, then quirks a little

smile, giving me a flash of his dimple. "Now, *that* would be very serendipitous."

"I bet there's a way we can find out for sure." For some reason, I feel entirely invested in helping Beckett learn any detail he can about his grandmother's time here in town. Probably because he's my friend. I want him to get whatever answers he needs.

Beckett shakes his head. "I drove out to Spring Brook the other day to see if they could run her Student ID and tell me anything about her time there, but apparently the campus out there was established after my gran attended."

I pause for a moment. "You're right, it's a newer campus, separate from the college it used to be... but you're forgetting something very important."

"Do enlighten me."

"We're currently standing in one of the old campus residences." I gesture towards the bookshelves lining the walls. "I wonder if we can find some answers in this very room."

That wonderful, broad smile is back on his face. "Keeley Roberts, you are a genius."

I flip my hair over my shoulder playfully. "Not just a pretty face."

"Brains and beauty. It's a killer combo." His eyes are warm and liquid as he looks at me with blatant, unabashed admiration. He then abruptly turns on his heel and marches towards the nearest bookshelf... leaving me standing in the wake of his charm with insides that now also feel warm and liquid.

When he reaches the shelf, he looks over his shoulder with a flirty smirk. "Are you coming or what?"

"Sure am," I say as evenly as possible, forcing away the herd of internal butterflies rampaging around my stomach.

Together, we rake the shelves, exploring the old tomes. There are rows of encyclopedias, stacks of Oxford English

121

Dictionaries, and a whole shelf's worth of cartography books boasting maps of the world.

I can imagine the young women of generations past coming in here to peruse the volumes on the shelves, trying to find information for papers they were writing. College during the pre-internet era must have been such a different experience.

I cross the room to another large bookshelf and squint up at a line of thick-spined hardcovers cased in burgundy leather on the top shelf.

"Becks?" I call and he crosses the room in three long strides. "Up there."

He comes to stand behind me, his large body shadowing mine as he reaches up and easily pulls a book from the top shelf. As soon as he cracks it open, a cloud of dust puffs into the air.

His mouth drops open. "It's a yearbook!"

"Really?" My eyes widen even as I fan the dust away from my face. "What year?"

Beckett flicks through a couple of pages. "1956."

Without a moment's hesitation, he slots the yearbook back in place, then counts four spots to the right and eases another one down.

"This one should be 1960," he mutters.

His cheeks are flushed, and his long fingers tip-tap impatiently on the book's cover as he leads us to a small loveseat in a corner of the room. We sink into it, our thighs almost touching, and he opens the book into the small space between us.

Spring Brook College Yearbook, Class of 1960.

We lean forward, my hair falling over my shoulder as we pore through the pages.

Soon, I see a name—and face—I recognize.

"Oh, my goodness, that's Sissy!" I exclaim, staring at the

page featuring my favorite brutally honest Texan librarian. Her hair was just as big back then as it is now, and her smile is toothy and bright and undeniably *her*.

Underneath the photo, a nameplate reads "Cecelia 'Sissy' Brown."

It states her major as English Literature, her place of residence as Serendipity Hall, and there's a quote: "Seize the day, ladies. It's yours."

I chuckle. "She hasn't changed a bit. She's the head librarian at Spring View now," I tell Becks. "'Mayhew' is her married name."

Becks looks at me, his hazel eyes wide. "Cecelia was one of the names on the wall downstairs."

"No way," I breathe. "I never considered that Sissy was really a Cecelia. Do you think she and your grandmother could have been friends?"

"According to the names on the wall downstairs, apparently they were *best* friends."

Becks starts flipping pages faster. In the middle of the book—before we reach the Q's—he pauses over a few photo collages.

"That's the courtyard outside! The Serendipity's courtyard!" I exclaim as I point to a picture in the corner of four girls laughing with their arms wrapped around each other.

Becks's pointer finger lands on the girl on the far right. His voice cracks a little as he says, "And that's my grandmother."

We share a look of triumph before I grab the book and flip ahead, racing past the M, N, O, P names until I turn to a page with a glowing photograph of none other than Noeleen Quinn.

A shiver dances down my spine. "This is crazy."

"I'll say." Beckett's eyes are moving over the page like he's trying to soak up as much information as possible.

I pore over it, too. Her major was Music—fitting, given Becks's musical talents—and her place of residence was also Serendipity Hall.

Her quote, however, makes my breath catch.

"'A light heart lives a long life,'" I read aloud, my voice sounding distant. "My grandpa said that to me once. When he gave me this ring." I hold up my hand.

Becks stares at it for a moment, and then, in a low voice, he says, "Keeley, do you mind if I take a look at that?"

The expression on his face is so intense, I don't bother to question him. Instead, I slip off the piece of jewelry and hand it over.

Beckett holds the ring up to examine it and immediately stills.

A few moments pass where he remains unnaturally silent, spine ramrod straight and expression frozen. I bite my lip as I watch him.

"I assume the writing inside is Irish?" I ask when I can't take the suspense anymore. "I don't know what it means."

My voice seems to snap him out of his reverie. He looks me dead in the eye. "I do."

Chapter Seventeen
Beckett

CALLAN

Becks, let us know what you find out today.

AOIFE

Aye, call us after. I still can't believe Gran
had this whole scandalous past none of us
knew about.

BECKS

We don't know anything yet for sure. I just
found a ring like hers, it could mean
anything. She could have given them to all
of her friends here.

AOIFE

Nah, that's not it. There's a scandalous story
here, I'm sure of it. Gran was a dark horse,
and she had to have some sordid secrets up
her sleeve.

MAM

Your Gran was not in any way sordid or
scandalous. She was an upstanding
member of the community.

NIAMH

She for sure had a wild side. Remember Ronan McGinty's wedding?

EOIN

😄 Was that the night she drank too much Baileys and got Father Houlihan on the dance floor to do a jig with her?

AOIFE

Oh, I remember that… Father Houlihan threw his back out, didn't he?

CALLAN

Fair play to him, though—the old man's got moves. And Gran was totally oblivious coz she was trying to get everyone up to do Rock the Boat.

MAM

Hush, now! Your grandmother will be turning over in her grave with all this chat!

EOIN

Ach you gotta admit though, Mam, that was a fierce good night.

MAM

So it was. But Beckett, do let us know what this Sissy character says.

BECKS

Will do, Mam.

CALLAN

Also, hurry up and send more truck pictures, will ya! Or a Hummer, that'd be class.

BECKS

You got it.

I HAVE to laugh as I close out of the McCarthy Clan group chat and bring up my maps app to check that I'm still on the right route towards Oldford Park, where I'm meeting Keeley.

After she and I discovered yesterday that our Claddagh rings bear matching Gaelic inscriptions—and that my Gran had that same quote in English in her yearbook—we were both a little stunned.

And also unsure what, exactly, to do with this information.

The story that Gran used to tell me about a boy she loved and lost because fate had other plans for them jumped to my mind.

Could she have been telling me a story about my new next door neighbor's grandfather?

The thought seems almost too crazy to be true.

I texted my family about the rings and the yearbook, but of course, that just led to twenty-four hours of pure speculation about Gran's "sordid and scandalous" past.

Keeley is pretty sure her grandfather wouldn't be able to help—he struggles to remember people. I also don't want to potentially upset the guy by confusing him with questions he might not be able to answer.

Especially since, at this point—as I just mentioned in the family text conversation—it still could all be a big coincidence.

Unlikely, but possible. And I don't want to be rash.

So, Keeley and I settled on stopping by the library—which is on the edge of Oldford Park—to see Sissy.

My grandmother's apparent past best friend.

I wanted to go yesterday right after we found the yearbook, but Sissy takes Wednesdays off, and according to Keeley, nobody comes between Sissy and the hair salon.

My stomach rumbles—a reminder that it's midday and I haven't eaten yet. I spot a quaint-looking sandwich shop up ahead, and on a whim, I duck inside with the intent to grab some lunch for us. Keeley's been at the library working all morning—I think she said something about horoscopes, which surely can't be right—and I bet she's hungry, too.

"Hey, there." The teenage boy behind the counter greets me with a smile. "What can I get started for you?"

"Hi. I'll have, um..." I pause as I peer at the menu, unsure what Keeley would like. "What's a lobster roll?"

The kid blinks at me through his glasses. "Dude, you've never had a lobster roll?"

"I don't think so."

The kid shakes his head, like this is the most disappointing thing he's heard all day. "You're seriously missing out. It's lobster meat mixed with mayo and seasoning, served on a soft bun, and you *really* need to try one, my man."

His description makes me smile as I remember my conversation in the elevator with Keeley the day I moved here. "Sounds delicious. But do you happen to have anything with Miracle Whip?"

Chapter Eighteen
Beckett

"ARE you trying to replicate Jesus's miracle of feeding the five thousand?" Keeley asks.

We're sitting on a bench in Oldford Park, right by a pond full of ducks that are staring at me intently. Forget my earlier notion that birds don't stare at people; these ducks are mega zoned in on us and look ready to strike at any moment.

"Are you sure that it's safe to sit here?" I shift on the bench uncomfortably as I gaze at the army of ducks lining the edge of the pond, beady eyes trained on us. "And 'thank you' is usually the appropriate response when someone brings you lunch."

"Stop being such a wuss," she says with a grin, then picks up the huge brown paper bag of food I bought from Relish. "And indeed, thank you very much for the fifty pounds of lunch."

"Hope you're hungry."

I left the sandwich shop ten minutes ago armed with a lobster roll, something called a "grinder"—which the boy made with Miracle Whip instead of mayo—and two back-up subs: a Philly cheesesteak, which sounded delightfully American to me, and a vegetarian sub on gluten-free bread, just in case Keeley has any allergies.

I might have also picked up an assortment of drinks and crisps.

"Starving," she says as she dives into the bag and selects the grinder sub. I can't help but grin as she takes a massive bite and then closes her eyes dreamily as she chews.

She looks great again today—her hair's in a messy ponytail held back with a leopard-print hair thingie, and she's wearing a baggy short black dress with those Converse sneakers again.

I've never paid too much attention to women's fashion, but I love the way Keeley dresses. It's like her clothes tell you something about her, show off a part of who she is.

I select the lobster roll for myself and dig in.

The guy working at Relish was right. I've been missing out.

This lobster roll is everything I've ever wanted in a sandwich. And if it weren't for the sadistic ducks staring me down, this would be the perfect picnic.

One of the brown ones takes a waddly step out of the pond, black eyes still intent on me, and I try not to flinch. I had no idea that ducks make me uncomfortable until right this second—America is teaching me so much about myself.

"Should we move?" I ask.

Keeley bites down on her lip like she's trying to contain her laughter. "I'd hate to see you come face-to-face with a coyote or a bobcat if you're this shaken up by a few cute little ducks."

"The duck that just got out of the pond has the face of a serial killer, so I have no idea where you're getting the 'cute' descriptor from." I turn to look at her. "And I was expecting more of a 'yes or no' sort of answer to my question."

"No."

"No, what?"

"No, we should not move."

"Okay, well, for the record, if Ted Bundy over there pecks your eyes out, you'll only have yourself to blame."

"Oooh, okay, scenario for you: would you rather fight one hundred duck-sized horses, or one horse-sized duck?" Keeley responds cheerfully.

"The horses, obviously. How is that even a question?"

She giggles. "I think I'd take the horse-sized duck."

"You frighten me, Keeley Roberts," I say. *In a good way*, I find myself adding.

She grins at me, and as our eyes meet, my heart jumps in my chest.

The sensation is almost shocking, and I forget all about the killer ducks as our eye contact holds for longer than it should. I let myself sink into the dark blue of her irises, just for a moment.

"You've... got something..." I reach out to brush away a little spot of sauce at the corner of her mouth.

The pad of my thumb drags along the edge of her lip, and she shivers. The sensation buzzes right through me in a way that feels electric.

Alive.

Her eyes widen, and I pull my thumb away quickly. She looks back down at her sandwich and busies herself pulling a pickle off it.

She doesn't like pickles. Noted.

"Gramps and I used to come here every Saturday to feed the ducks, and we'd ask each other 'would you rather' questions like that one," she says nonchalantly. Like those sparks between us didn't just happen and we're simply hanging out, casual as can be.

"He sounds great," I say.

"He is." She screws up her face for a moment before looking at me, eyes full of question marks. "Do you think it's

possible that my gramps and your gran had some kind of...
thing when she lived here? Romantically, I mean?" She frowns.
"Or is that just the journalist in me asking questions about
love that she doesn't really want to know the answers to
again?"

I cock a brow at her. "Article's going well, huh?"

"Swimmingly," she replies sarcastically.

I chuckle. "I mean, it *is* possible they dated when my gran
was at Spring Brook." I shrug, her story of ill-fated love still at
the forefront of my mind. "Gran married my grandpa when
she was twenty-seven and had my mam a couple of years later.
So it's very possible she had a relationship years before."

Keeley nods, then picks up the last bite of her sandwich.
"Ready to go find out?"

"Ready as I'll ever be."

Chapter Nineteen
Keeley

I FIND myself impatiently tapping my foot as Beckett and I wait for Sissy, who is currently giving a mortified-looking middle-aged woman a full run-down of the bodice-ripper romance novel she's trying to subtly check out.

"Oh, my days, I couldn't put this one down. Duke Rufus is the swooniest rogue I've ever read. Those pantaloons of his had me all hot and bothered," Sissy says with excitement.

The woman trying to borrow the book goes crimson from head to toe. Next to me, a muscle in Beckett's jaw tics as he clearly struggles to keep a straight face.

"Wait until you get to the chapter where the duke smuggles Lady Penelope onto a cargo ship. The captain weds them at sea, and then the duke has his wicked way with her in the galley!" Sissy's voice projects around the entire reception area.

I bite down on my bottom lip, and Beckett ducks his head, a lock of that bronze-tinted hair falling over his forehead as he (badly) disguises his laugh as a cough.

I forget my jitters for a moment as my fingers itch with the urge to reach up and push that piece of hair back into position. Sweep it back and feel it under my fingers—the way his thumb traced over the sensitive skin on my lip a few minutes ago.

All I wanted to do in that moment was lean into his touch, hold onto that feeling for as long as possible. But I had to remind myself that he wasn't touching me to be sensual and was instead *cleaning Miracle Whip off my face* like I often have to do with Everett. Which was embarrassing enough to begin with, never mind the way I reacted to his touch.

I tried to play it as cool as possible. Although, I have to wonder if my current state of nervous impatience has more to do with the lingering memory of Becks's touch than it does with finding answers from Sissy.

At that moment, Sissy pauses her verbal book review long enough for the romance-reading woman to swipe her book with impressively quick reflexes. She chucks it in her bag and practically flees the scene.

"Now, I wonder why Renee was in such a rush," Sissy mutters to herself as she pats her fresh blowout with nails that are metallic silver with rhinestone tips.

Claudia at the salon has clearly upped her nail game this week.

The elderly librarian looks around in bewilderment, and that's when she finally spots Becks and me standing near the counter.

"Keeley, darlin," she greets me warmly, but her eyes are already roaming all over Beckett with undisguised interest. "Pray tell me, *who* is this devastatingly handsome young man accompanying you?"

"Handsome young man? Where?" I ask, making a big show of looking around in confusion.

Becks catches the smug grin on my face and grins right back at me. A sly grin that says *challenge accepted.*

He goes on to flash that charming, dimpled smile at Sissy and extends a hand to her. "Pleasure to meet you, Sissy," he says, and her heavily-made-up eyes fly wide open in surprise. "I'm Beckett McCarthy."

"An Irishman," she says, her startled tone matching her expression. "Honey, that accent of yours brings back some wonderful memories." The librarian shakes her head as if in wonder. "Been a long time since I heard an accent like that."

Becks and I share a look, and I'm pleased when he cuts straight to the point. No B.S.

"I'm Noeleen Quinn's grandson," he tells Sissy with a pleasant smile.

Her eyes widen even further. "Well, I never!" she breathes, pressing one wrinkled hand to her heart. "Of course, you are. I see it now—you look so much like her."

Exactly what I thought when I saw Noeleen's picture.

"I believe you two were friends?" Becks asks.

Sissy claps her hands, bangles jangling on her wrists. "Friends? Please, we were *soul sisters*, your grandmother and me. Born worlds apart but cut from the exact same cloth."

My heart starts to thump excitedly. Beckett smiles wide but his eyes are soft as they focus on Sissy, clearly hanging onto her every word.

"How is she?" Sissy goes on. "I always wondered what became of her. Haven't heard from her for, gosh, sixty-odd years now."

Beckett's smile falters. "Um, she died. Last year."

Sissy looks stricken as she reaches for Beckett's hand. "I'm sorry to hear that, honey. Your grandmother was one of the good ones."

"She was my favorite person," Becks says, and Sissy smiles sadly.

"Mine too, at one point." She winks. "Don't tell my husband that, though."

"Wouldn't dream of it," Beckett promises solemnly.

"We were thick as thieves, lived in the same dorm during college. We did everything together."

"Did Noeleen know my Gramps, too?" I pipe up, unable to keep my question quiet any longer.

Sissy nods. "She did."

Becks touches the ring on his neck, and I can tell the motion is totally reflexive, unconscious. "Were they... together?"

I lean forward eagerly.

Sissy pauses, her shrewd eyes noting Becks's gesture. "They were, for a short time. In our last year of college." Her eyes get a little misty, like she's plucking memories from deep inside her mind. "Wow, it's been a long, long while since I've thought about that. Noeleen was so in love with Douglas, and he was head-over-heels for her. In fact..."

She frowns at us both, then nods at my right hand. "They got each other matching rings back then from an Irish guy in Boston who owned a jewelers' store there. If I'm not mistaken, the very same rings you're both wearing today."

I twirl Gramps's ring around my finger, processing all of this information.

I figured Douglas and Noeleen were once an item ever since we found out yesterday that the inscriptions on our rings match. But hearing Sissy confirm it as fact—alongside the fact they were very much in love, and the matching rings were, indeed, theirs during their relationship—makes my head spin. "Whoa."

"Ah, the double dates we had! She and Douglas, me and Roger. We were the talk of the town back then. Noeleen was so magnetic, drawing people in without even trying."

Sounds just like her grandson. I shoot a surreptitious look at Beckett.

"I was so upset when she went back to Ireland," Sissy continues. "I missed her every day for a long time. We wrote for a few years—last I heard from her was a good few years after she left. She'd married and just had a baby. Bridget, I think her name was."

"My mam," Beckett says with a smile.

Sissy looks at Becks fondly. "I was happy Noeleen had finally found love in her life again and had started a family. But we eventually lost touch. It was harder to stay in contact back then, as you can imagine. Snail mail was our main form of communication."

Becks shoves his hands in his pockets, looking genuinely sorry. "Do you know why she left Serendipity Springs?"

Sissy shoots a little look in my direction, then looks back at Beckett. Shifts on her chair. "She had a life back in Ireland..."

She hesitates, looks like she wants to say more but is debating what to say.

"And?" I ask, unable to help myself.

"Well, right before graduation, she and Douglas broke up, right out of the blue." Sissy frowns. "It was totally unexpected —the two seemed so happy together. To this day, I'm not sure why they broke up, exactly. She never told me."

"Would Estelle, or maybe Margot, know what happened?" Becks ventures, and Sissy gives him a smile.

"You've really done your research, young man. But unfortunately, Noeleen told us nothing, never even a hint of a whiff of what might have happened between them. And then, one day, she told me she was going home to Ireland."

I'm instantly empathetic, seeing a mental picture of a young Noeleen heartbroken and wanting to escape having to see her ex all the time. Did she, like me, climb out onto the fire escape after her breakup, unable to sleep as she gazed up at the stars and wondered what on earth to do next with her life?

"Next thing I knew, she was packing up her things and

getting on a plane," Sissy goes on with a sniff. "She never came back. A while after that, your grandfather met and wed your grandmother, Keeley. And the romance between Noeleen and Douglas was never mentioned again."

"Did my Gramps break Noeleen's heart?" My question comes out way more loud and demanding than I mean it to, and I lower my voice before adding, "Sorry."

Sissy apparently doesn't even notice that I've practically yelled in her library—something that she's usually unbelievably precious about.

"Yes, I think he did." She swallows. "And when she left, I believe she broke his, too."

Chapter Twenty
Keeley

I CAN'T SLEEP AGAIN.

But this time, it has nothing to do with the footsteps upstairs, which are loud as ever. I can't bring myself to care about Andrew and Lisa in the slightest right now.

I also can't blame my AC for my insomnia—it's miraculously working, even though I still haven't gotten Craig to come look at it. Or, as Steve the building manager haughtily informed me, "There was nothing wrong to begin with."

Which is false, but he wasn't accepting that for a moment.

No... tonight, I'm tossing and turning in my (blessedly cool) bed as I think about Gramps and Noeleen.

On the way home from the library earlier, Becks told me his Gran often talked about a boy she once loved—a love story that, in the end, wasn't written in the stars. He thought it was a fairy tale when he was growing up, a story she made up to entertain him and his siblings.

Now, he thinks that boy in the story might have been my Gramps.

I think he might be right.

I wish we could have gone to visit him right after we left

the library. It would be so helpful to have a firsthand account of what actually happened between him and Noeleen.

But I'm not sure what I'd say, exactly. Not sure how much he'd even be able to tell me.

The last thing I want to do is upset him or confuse him further.

I'm surprised Sissy didn't know why they broke up when she and Noeleen were so close. And, apparently, Estelle and Margot won't be much help either—Estelle passed away a few years ago, and Margot now lives in Australia.

So for now, Beckett and I are going to gather up all the crumbs we can find and see what we can piece together.

Because now that we know that Noeleen and Gramps were once in love, all I want to know is more. Why did they break up? Why did she *leave*?

I shift in bed a few more times, maneuvering my pillows around.

But I eventually give up, climb out of bed, and head for the living room.

Ever since the Korean-face-masked-banshee-incident I've been playing my late-night fire escape trips super safe.

For one, I keep my button-down pjs on.

For two, when I open my window, I grab two books from my desk—one, a notebook I slide under my arm to work in while I'm outside, and the second a thick novel to carefully position on the ledge so the window can't close and lock me out here again.

Never let it be said that I don't learn from my mistakes.

Once I'm on the fire escape, I take a seat and loll my head back against the cool brick wall behind me. It's cloudy tonight, and the stars in the sky aren't visible. You can't even see the moon.

The distant flicker of streetlights below don't cast enough light for me to work—on fuller moon nights, I've been jotting down ideas for my article in my notebook—so instead, I wrap my arms around my legs and draw them to my chest, taking a moment to enjoy the dark quiet of the night.

And when I say "moment," I literally mean it because...

"Evening."

Beckett's lilting voice cuts through the night, and for some reason, I'm not surprised in the least when I turn to see him—or rather, see his shadowy outline—standing next to me on the escape, his living room window open behind him.

I nod my head toward it. "If I were you, I'd prop that open. Things seem to have a bad habit of locking themselves around here."

In the darkness, I see his white teeth flash as he smiles.

"Ah, I don't know about that," he says easily as he folds his body to a seated position. He's wearing a soft sweatshirt that grazes my arm as he sits down right next to me. "I know of worse habits than that."

"Like?"

"Smoking. Biting your nails. Chewing with your mouth open." Another flash of teeth. "Drinking so much coffee to get through prolonged jet lag that you end up becoming as nocturnal as your neighbor."

"That's a real bad one," I say solemnly. "How much coffee does one need to achieve that?"

He faces me, leaning the side of his head against the wall. We're only inches away from each other like this, face to face, and I can make out his features in the darkness. "Honestly? I think it has less to do with the coffee and more to do with what we learned today that's keeping me awake. How about you? Andrew's footsteps bothering you again?"

"The man has the tread of an elephant, I swear."

"Did you guys date for long?"

"A few years. He was my first real relationship."

"Those can be tough to get over." Beckett's eyes move to

141

mine, and his lips pull into a small smile. "But if you want my two cents, he's an eejit for letting you go."

His words are sweet, but they don't quite hit the truth.

"No, I actually don't think he is," I say slowly, the creeping realization that's been niggling at me lately finally coming into words. "I'm beginning to think we never were right for each other."

Picking at the chipped polish on my nails, I pause. Realize how true these words are.

I had a lot of love for Andrew, at one point, and we got along just fine, for the most part. But I feel like we were stuck in a routine together. I was letting my circumstances dictate what my heart wanted, instead of vice versa, like Gramps once told me to do.

Some hindsight makes me see that clearly now.

In a way, I can understand why Andrew moved on to someone like Lisa. The two of them are friends in a way that me and Andrew never were. She makes him happy like I never did.

I think that, by the end, I was hanging on by a thread—the thought of being left motivating me to try for a relationship that was maybe already in the dust.

"Honestly," I say, "a part of me wondered if the two of them might make a good match. But maybe I chose to ignore that doubt, and in the end, it came back to bite me. The breakup caught me so off guard that my first reaction was to be more annoyed with myself for not seeing it coming than annoyed at Andrew for actually breaking up with me. Isn't that messed up?"

Beckett thinks about this for a moment, then shakes his head. "No. I don't think so. I think it's possible to feel a lot of complicated things at once, but to focus on one of them as a way of coping with a situation." He looks down at the ground. "Or focus on none of them at all."

"That makes sense." I nod. "I guess I haven't been able to admit to myself that the sting of sudden rejection may have hurt more than losing the relationship itself. My parents had a really messy divorce when I was a kid, and my dad left my mom for someone else. I was totally blindsided, didn't see it coming at all. I thought they were happy."

At the time, it felt like my dad thought my mom wasn't good enough for him, and I was angry with him for hurting her.

But after that, when my mom in turn left me and Ezra, I was angry with both of my parents—Mom for leaving, Dad for driving her away.

But more than all of that, seven-year-old Keeley was angry with *herself* that she hadn't been enough to make her own mother stay.

I swallow thickly, pushing away my ugliest, most painful, memories.

"I guess I felt some of those emotions again when Andrew blindsided me," I conclude. Because that much of the truth I can speak—Andrew leaving me for Lisa scratched at an old wound that's buried deep in me but smarted the second it was prodded again.

"I understand that feeling," Becks says quietly.

"Have you ever been in love?"

He's silent for a long beat, and I'm about to apologize for overstepping when he lets out a sigh.

"I thought I was in love, once," he says quietly. "But what Sissy was talking about earlier? How Noeleen and Douglas loved each other so fiercely that it broke their hearts when they went their separate ways? Well, I've never been in love like that."

"Me neither," I say softly.

"I was with my ex for a few years, but when we split up last year, I almost felt relieved because then she could find

143

someone who was better for her," Beckett confesses, his eyes fluttering closed for a second. "Someone cut out to be a good partner."

"What makes you think you weren't a good partner?" I ask, surprised.

"A lot of things," is the response I get, and when I glance at him, there's a distant look in his eyes as he stares through the darkness.

I want to reach for his hand. Thread my fingers through his. Instead, I place my hands in my lap and entwine my own fingers. Change the subject so I don't push him farther than he wants to go in this conversation. "It's weird our grandparents were once in love, isn't it? Like, what if they'd stayed together? Gotten married and had kids?"

Beckett snorts a laugh. "I guess we wouldn't exist to even be having this conversation in the first place. Kind of crazy, when you think about it, that one breakup can rewrite generations of people."

"Trippy," I say, considering this. "And on top of that, what are the chances that her grandson and his granddaughter would end up being next door neighbors?"

"Slim, at best." He moves a little, like he's shifting to get comfortable. His movement is casual, nonchalant, but when he stills again, the small space between us has been eliminated. My shoulder is resting against his arm, and our thighs are pressed together as we sit here in the darkness, side by side. "But here we are."

"Here we are," I echo.

There's electricity everywhere we're connected. An exciting, zippy kind of spark that makes me want to lean in and see what happens next. Which would be crazy... but the pull between us currently feels *that* strong.

"Maybe the universe wanted us to meet," I find myself saying, my voice a little throaty.

It's strange to think of something outside of ourselves operating on a bigger scale than what we're used to in our everyday lives. I'm not sure I like the idea of the universe having a hand in our decisions, of fate determining the course of our lives... but then again, maybe there's some comfort in that.

"If not the universe, then it has to be this crazy building that keeps locking us in confined spaces together," he jokes. At least, I think he's joking.

I crane my neck to look over at my windowsill, half expecting the book to be gone and the window to be firmly shut.

But it's propped open, just like I left it.

"We're not locked together now." I turn to face him again, and just looking at him makes my heart beat double-time. I've never felt chemistry like this, a draw to someone that feels like it could overtake all logic.

All reason.

We're only inches apart, and his hazel-green eyes appear black in the darkness as they hold mine captive. "We're not," he says, his voice low in a way that makes a shiver wrap itself around my spine.

He's close, oh so close, his warm thigh still pressing into mine, his minty breath skimming my cheeks in the cover of darkness.

Is he leaning closer? Am I? All I know is that my eyelashes are fluttering closed, and I'm surrounded by his clean, woodsy smell, reminiscent of babbling brooks and fields of four-leafed clovers and golden sunsets over heather-clad moors and—

Far below, on the street, a car alarm sounds, snapping me out of my reverie.

His head jerks back in surprise, and the second I lose his closeness, my cheeks burn hot. My breath comes shakily, and

I'm mortified by the stunning realization that I think I might've just tried to kiss him.

Did I imagine him leaning in? Am I so behind on sleep that I'm losing my marbles?

"So, what are you going to do for the rest of the summer?" I blurt the first question that comes to mind, trying to force my voice to sound somewhat normal.

"Aside from hanging out with you on fire escapes and playing at Indie Music Nights, you mean?" he says teasingly, but I'm gratified to hear the hitch in his breathing. Like he's affected, too.

I try to match his jokey tone, play it as cool as he is. "Speaking of Indie Music Night, I'm not sure where to put my giant leprechaun and shamrock decorations for your performance..."

"You'd better be kidding, Roberts." He pokes me right under my ribs, perfectly hitting that sensitive spot that makes me giggle and squirm.

"Kidding!" I hold up my hands, and his fingertips graze over my side again as he pulls his hand back.

"Good." His eyes dance in the fractured moonlight. "And as for what I'm doing, I've signed up to give some guitar lessons at Ezra's shop... and then I also intend to find out exactly why our grandparents broke up, because now I'm hooked on this story like it's a serial soap opera or something."

"Our very own cross-continental family drama to unpack." I smile, happy he is on the same trail of thought as me. "I was wondering if I could go see Gramps to ask him about Noeleen... I'm not too sure how to approach the subject with him."

"We wouldn't want to upset him," Beckett agrees, and I'm grateful for his sensitivity.

I get the sense that this is important for Beckett, that

being here and connecting with a part of his grandmother's life he didn't know about until recently means a lot to him.

Now that I know him a little better, I also get the feeling that his looking into her time here in Serendipity Springs is potentially a form of delayed grieving for him, and that if and when he gets the answers he's looking for, he'll be able to come more to terms with the loss.

"Agreed," I say. "But it really would be nice to know what happened. If anything, it's a lot more interesting to learn about my grandfather's long-lost love than to write an article about my own failed love life—which I'm beginning to think I'm going to have to do, because apparently this building is full of happily-ever-after love stories."

The Hathaways are super in love, Cash and Nori met here, and heck, even Andrew seems to have found the right person for him...

"Gosh, even our grandparents fell in love when one of them was living in this building."

Becks tilts his head at me. "Wait, what if you wrote your piece about Noeleen and Douglas? You could write about how she lived here in the building, but their love didn't last, so the legend is flawed, at best. You could even tie it to us, if you like. How Douglas's granddaughter now lives in the building too, and it also brought her no luck in love... and Noeleen's grandson is the biggest single sad sack to ever walk the planet."

"Is that a direct quote I can use?" I ask, laughing. But my heart is picking up speed.

"I think the alliteration has a real ring to it."

"But seriously, Becks, all joking aside, are you sure you're okay with me using your—and your grandmother's—story for something like this?"

Because while I was feeling entirely opposed to writing about love before, I don't really feel that way anymore. Throughout the course of this conversation, I realized that

I've made my peace with my ex, and I'm no longer writing this article to escape my situation, but rather for the sole purpose of furthering my career. Of shaping my life the way I want it to look—living and working in Boston, while still remaining close with my family here and visiting them often.

He shrugs. "Sure. She loved being the center of attention, this would totally have given her a kick, knowing you're researching and writing her story for publication."

"I'll have to talk to Gramps first," I say, still mulling it over. "I'm not sure how much he will comprehend, but I'd feel like I was going behind his back by not asking him about it."

Beckett smiles. "Maybe he'll surprise you and have more answers than you think."

"And even if we don't get answers on why it ended, it still makes for a great story." It's whimsical, like Freya wanted, and though it might not be a fun, sexy story of stars aligning, instead one of star-crossed lovers that tugs on the heart-strings, I think she'll love the unique angle and how it's personal to me. This feels like a much more genuine story for me to tell.

And it's also a great reason to spend more time with Beckett.

Who, as it turns out, I like spending time with.

A lot more than I'd care to admit.

Chapter Twenty-One
Beckett

WHEN I WAS A TEEN, my morning routine was to wake my younger siblings and make sure that they brushed their teeth and put on clean(ish) school uniforms. Mam was long gone to work by the time we woke up, and I liked to let Gran—who was getting up there in age by that point—sleep a little longer.

So, I made it my job to make sure the five of us got to school in one piece. Aoife was old enough to help, and she'd braid Niamh's hair while I made tea and toast for everyone and checked to make sure the younger ones had put their homework in their school bags.

While my siblings ate their breakfast, I'd assemble five brown-bagged lunches, and we'd set off—Aoife to the girls' grammar school on the hill, where she had a scholarship, Eoin and Niamh to the local primary school a short walk away, and Callan and I to the comprehensive school we'd have to take two buses to get to after dropping the wee ones off.

The morning routine, I didn't mind so much. I liked helping Mam and Gran and looking after my siblings. My family were—still are—the world to me, and I'd do anything for them.

But the actual going to school part, I *did* mind. Very much.

And so, it's kind of funny that, in adulthood, my morning routine has come full circle with me making myself a lunch and heading off to school every day. This time, as a teacher.

It's a routine I'm falling into, once again, in Serendipity Springs: leaving my apartment with a bagged lunch of a breakfast roll—*sandwich*—and an apple and heading straight to Blue Notes to spend my morning teaching guitar lessons.

Today is my first day, and I'm already enjoying every second.

"Good, just like that," I tell Sammie, whose face is pinched up in concentration as she attempts to hold a G chord with her little fingers. "You're doing amazing."

As if on cue, her finger slides out of place, and when she strums her guitar, the sound is flat. Off-key.

"No, I'm not." She looks up at me, all big brown eyes and wobbly lower lip. "I suck, Beckett."

It's nearing the end of her forty-five-minute lesson, and I'm assuming that both her mind and her fingers are tired. So what's happening right now is understandable.

But I know better than to say that to a six-year-old. Logical explanations are not the way to make Sammie feel better about herself and her abilities—she needs to *feel* it to believe it.

"Hey." I set down my own guitar, which I was using to show her finger placement, and hop out of my chair. Walk over and crouch in front of her. "Sammie, can I ask you a question?"

She nods cautiously, lip still wobbling, like she's unsure she wants to say *yes* in case she gets the answer wrong.

"Okay." Her expression is so reminiscent of how I used to feel in school that my stomach twists in empathy for her.

I wasn't good in school. I found it hard to concentrate and spent a lot of time staring out of windows, zoning out and humming tunes to myself in a way that was—needless to say—not conducive to drumming up popularity. Or making teachers like me.

They figured my behavior was due to laziness. An unwillingness to try.

If I had a penny for how many times I was told to "apply myself"... well, I'd have a good few more euros, at this point.

Or "bucks," as they say here.

Back then, the only place I could escape to was the music room. Music was the one thing that made me feel like I didn't "suck," as Sammie just said. And when I enrolled in teaching college, it was with the intention of paying this feeling forward.

So, the fact that I've ended up teaching in a private school for the academically gifted—a school that would have never let me through its doors as a student—is an irony that's not lost on me.

It's one of the main reasons I took up giving volunteer guitar lessons on the side.

This type of teaching is important to me exactly because of moments like this one. Where I can use music to make a difference to how a kid feels about themself.

"Can you name me three people you love?" I ask Sammie gently.

Her face brightens. "Yes! My mommy, my daddy, and my brother Zachary."

"Brothers are great. I have two brothers, and I love them very much."

Sammie smiles in solidarity. "My brother is the best. He's four."

"I bet you're a great big sister to him." I lift my eyes to meet hers. "Do you ever teach Zachary things?"

"Yup." Her little chest puffs with pride. "I taught him how to color in the lines! And I help him on his scooter because he can't balance yet, so I show him how."

"And is he getting better at balancing on his scooter now, thanks to your help?"

"Mm-hmm." Sammie grins, her cheeks flushing.

I pause. Drop my voice so it's as gentle as possible. "And when he falls off, do you help him back up and encourage him to try again?"

"Yes, because practice makes perfect, my mommy always says."

"Your mommy sounds really clever. And hey, what do you think Zachary would say to you if he heard you saying you suck?"

She pouts out that lower lip—no longer wobbling—for a moment, before screwing her nose up. "He'd say I shouldn't say mean things about myself."

"And would he encourage you to try again until you get it?"

She sniffs. Looks down at her pink flip-flopped feet. "Yeah."

"So is that what we should do now, with the G chord?"

"Yeah," she says again, but this time, she looks up. And when I see the determined set of her chin, the conviction in that one syllable word, I know I've won her over.

In the remaining five minutes of the lesson, she completely nails the chord.

"Great job today, Sammie," I tell her as we finish off with a huge high-five. The grin on her face tells me she believes it, too.

"And my mommy was even here to see me do it!" She points towards the window of the lesson room, and I turn around to give her mom a wave where she's watching through the glass.

I'm momentarily distracted, though, because Keeley's standing next to her.

And though I'm expecting her, the sight of her—dressed in an oversized Dolly Parton t-shirt and cutoff jean shorts, a leopard print scrunchie holding back her long black hair— makes my heart jump in my chest.

Like, palpably.

"Oooh, she's *pretty*," Sammie says from beside me.

"She is," I agree wholeheartedly, before snapping myself out of it and walking the little girl towards the door.

"Is she your girlfriend?" Sammie asks.

I smile, looking at Keeley through the glass. She smiles back at me, and I notice she's holding two paper cups. "No, not my girlfriend."

We're at the door now, but before Sammie opens it, she levels serious dark brown eyes on me. "Why? Does she think you suck? Because you don't."

This makes me snort.

"Thanks for that, Sammie," I say with a chuckle, patting her head.

"Anytime," she says, then throws open the door. "Mom! Beckett learned me a G chord today!"

"*Taught* you a G chord," her mom corrects, looking down at her daughter indulgently.

I spend a couple of minutes chatting with Sammie's mom and reviewing the lesson. As they're leaving, Sammie shoots me a huge, gap-toothed smile over her shoulder and yells, "Bye, Beckett! See you next week!"

"Looking forward to it," I call back.

Then, Sammie turns her focus on Keeley. "Bye, Beckett's friend!"

She grins at the kiddo. "Bye, sweetie."

"Beckett thinks you're pretty, by the way!"

Keeley's mouth falls open.

"Sammie!" the girl's mother chides, barely hiding her smile.

"She's not wrong," I say with a shrug and enjoy the way Keeley's cheeks flame red.

She waits until the mother-daughter duo exit the hallway before she turns to me. "Um, hi."

"Hi, yourself." I'm ridiculously happy to see her even though we just saw each other this morning, when she knocked on my door to confirm we're still on for this afternoon before going off to work at the library.

Today's the day we're going to talk to her grandpa at his retirement community. And while I'm not sure what to expect, not sure how much Douglas will be able to tell us about my gran, I'm glad Keeley wanted me to come with her.

Not only because I'm beyond curious to know his side of the story and learn more about my Gran and her past, but also because Keeley wants to introduce me to someone so important to her.

I get the feeling that she doesn't allow people into her inner circle very often. It's an honor I don't take lightly.

"You didn't tell me you were excellent with kids," Keeley says in an almost accusing tone that makes me laugh.

"It didn't really come up in conversation," I reply with a grin.

"Well, I *was* bringing you coffee to recharge after back-to-back-to-back forty-five-minute sessions with six-year-olds." She holds out a steaming paper cup towards me. "But you look more energized and recharged than I've seen you yet."

"Oh, I could definitely use that caffeine, so thank you," I say as I accept the cup from her. I've turned into quite the coffee drinker since coming here. "But I do like kids, and I

154

like teaching kids. Especially kids who love music and want to learn it."

"I can tell." She shakes her head. "I love my nephew, but after spending forty-five minutes with him, I often feel like I've aged forty-five years."

"Ah, but the good news is, you don't look a day over forty," I tease.

"Rude!" She glowers at me playfully as she reaches out to whack my arm, but my reflexes are quicker, and I intercept her weak hit easily, wrapping her outstretched hand in mine.

The sensation of her small, warm hand against mine sends an immediate tingly feeling down my arm, and we both still, our hands mid-air, entwined.

After a moment, I drop my grip, and Keeley shoves her hand in her pocket. Looks down at her Converse.

Meanwhile, I rub the back of my neck, trying to play it like I didn't just feel a million sparks travel through me.

Sparks just like I felt a couple nights ago, when we sat out on the fire escape.

For a long, loaded moment, I had the almost insatiable urge to kiss her. That heavy, almost intoxicating feeling of desire hit me out of the blue. I haven't felt sparks like that—raw want like that—in a *very* long time. Maybe ever, if I'm being honest.

And it felt like she wanted me to kiss her, too...

But then, that car alarm went off, and she jumped back like a scalded cat. I couldn't see her expression in the dark, leaving me to wonder if I'd very much misread the moment.

"Should we go?" I ask, all casual-like.

"Sure," she says quickly. Almost too quickly.

Like she feels the same sparks I do when we touch.

Chapter Twenty-Two
Beckett

TWENTY MINUTES LATER, we're walking into a beautiful facility with country-club vibes, and any sense of calm or happiness or excitement I might have felt back at Blue Notes has been replaced with sheer nerves.

I'm about to meet someone who is a complete stranger to me but who was once important to my Gran. Someone I've heard countless stories about over the years without really knowing if they were true.

The person at the center of all the tales Gran told of a boy she loved and lost. And the likely owner of the Claddagh ring I wear around my neck.

Keeley greets the receptionist by name, and she waves us inside with a smile. We walk down a brightly lit corridor decorated with floral and landscape paintings and into a sort of living area, where groups of people are scattered about, playing cards, sipping coffee, and chatting.

In one corner, a man with a lined face and kind blue eyes brightens as we approach.

"Hi, Gramps!" Keeley gives him a hug. "I've brought a

friend to visit you today, if that's okay. He's really looking forward to meeting you."

The older man cranes his head towards me. "Oh, how nice."

"This is Beckett McCarthy," Keeley says, and I extend my hand.

"It's a pleasure to meet you," I say, smiling warmly. "Keeley's told me so much about you."

Douglas's hand stiffens in mine, and his eyes widen. "You're Irish?"

I pause for a moment, eyes darting to Keeley.

As we discussed prior to coming here, the plan was to chat with Gramps for a while, gauge how he's doing today, and then, she would take the lead on asking any questions about Noeleen.

We didn't consider the fact that my accent might throw him off.

"I am," I say, keeping my tone gentle. "Visiting Serendipity Springs for the summer."

Luckily, Douglas just nods. "Summer's a great time to see the town. So much life and greenery." He drops my hand and looks at Keeley. "Wouldn't you say so, Rose?"

Keeley winces—just barely—before she swallows. "Rose was your sister, Gramps. I'm Keeley, your granddaughter."

And though her voice is steady, kind, and patient, her blue eyes flare with emotion. I can immediately tell how much she loves him—and how hard this is for her. It feels all the more poignant that she's allowed me to share this moment with her.

Gramps blinks. "Oh, of course. My granddaughter."

Keeley pastes on a smile and sits next to him, taking his hand. She starts gently reminding him of a time when she was eight years old and he took her to Boston to see the penguins at the aquarium.

157

Douglas nods along and laughs occasionally, though his eyes are slightly glazed, like he loves hearing the story but can't quite place himself within it.

I don't sit. Instead, I hang back and give them the moment together. Study Keeley as she talks animatedly, sharing this precious memory. She swallows more thickly than she usually does, her smile a bit more forced than it usually is, and I find myself feeling a little emotional, too, as I take in the scene.

Keeley has only been a part of my life for a couple of weeks, but I already know that she's made up of many layers. Layers I can't get enough of peeling back and seeing. She's strong and feisty and funny yet vulnerable and sweet and caring all at once. The best person I've met in a long time.

My Gran would have loved her.

The thought pops into my mind out of nowhere, but the second I think it, I realize how true it is. Gran always took to multifaceted people, people who had a combination of rough and soft edges. Who cared deeply about those they love.

That's Keeley.

It's becoming more and more apparent to me that this sudden resurgence of feeling, of tapping into my emotions again after having them lie dormant for so long, has as much —if not more—to do with *her* than it does to being here in Serendipity Springs.

It's like seeing daylight after so long in darkness.

Keeley has been a key part of every meaningful moment I've had in this town so far, and I am really happy to be here with her in this one, seeing another side of her that makes me like her even more.

"Becks?" her soft voice cuts through my thoughts, and I startle.

"Yes?"

"Want to sit with us?" Keeley pats the chair to her right, across from her grandfather. "Gramps would like to play Gin Rummy."

"I love that game," I say with a smile. "My Gran taught me how to play."

Keeley's blue eyes dart to mine as I sit beside her, and she flips her long black ponytail over one shoulder as she turns to her Gramps. "How did you learn to play, Gramps?"

Douglas squints for a moment and then looks right at me. "A lady from Ireland taught me."

Under the table, Keeley's knee begins to bounce almost frantically. Before I can think too much about my actions, I place my hand on her knee to still her anxiety.

"Noeleen?" Keeley asks gently.

And then, something incredible happens.

Douglas's lined face breaks into a beaming smile and his eyes clear. "Yes, Noeleen Quinn. She was a wonderful woman."

Keeley finishes dealing the cards and picks up her hand, as does Gramps. She very casually asks, "How did you know her, Gramps?"

His eyes get a little misty. "I had two great loves in my life. Your grandmother was my second. Noeleen was my first."

"What happened with Noeleen?" Keeley asks, and I can tell she's purposefully trying to keep her tone light.

Douglas's forehead wrinkles in confusion. "I... I... I'm not sure."

Keeley shoots me a sideways glance, and I realize that at this point, she's digging for my sake. She wants to get me an answer as to why they broke up that might help explain why Gran left so suddenly. Why she never mentioned this place.

But it's an answer I don't need right now. I just want to be here to support Keeley.

I give her knee a little squeeze under the table, then use my other hand to gesture to the deck of cards on the table. "Why don't we play a round of Gin Rummy?"

Chapter Twenty-Three
Keeley

THE NIGHT after Becks and I visit Gramps, I can't sleep again.

Although this time, I'm not even trying to sleep.

In fact, I'm almost *too* enthusiastic to leave my bed and make my way to the fire escape—by way of a detour to my bathroom to brush my hair and apply lip balm.

As I slide open my window, I'm surprised how much my heart is racing. How much I'm hoping he's out here.

I step out onto the metal platform... and find Beckett already sitting down, looking in my direction. Like he was waiting for me.

Butterflies swirl in my stomach as little Sammie's words from earlier ring in my ears again:

"Beckett thinks you're pretty, by the way!"

Then Beckett telling me, *"She's not wrong."*

I mean, way to make a girl blush.

"Evening," Becks says now in his lilt, and I get a little flash of his dimples when he gives me a quick smile.

"We meet again," I joke as I sit next to him. A couple of

inches away, so he can't feel my heartbeat, which is currently vibrating through my body.

"It's almost a routine at this point," Becks replies. "Insomniacs Anonymous's nightly meeting."

I smile, because I know all too well that I could've fallen asleep tonight if I really wanted to. The footsteps upstairs no longer bother me; when I came out here a moment ago, I was simply driven by hopes that Becks would appear.

And he did.

I *also* know that he's been in town long enough that there's no way he can blame jet lag for his insomnia.

Which means that we're both out here tonight because we want to be. It's a realization that makes me want to lean closer. Inch towards him until I feel his arm pressed against mine again.

"Thanks again for coming to see Gramps with me earlier," I say instead. "He loved meeting you."

"I loved meeting him, too. Although the old man sure kicked my arse at Gin Rummy."

"That he did," I say proudly.

Becks was wonderful with Gramps, which just made me warm to him even more. In fact, *hot* is a better descriptor than *warm* when it comes to how I feel towards Beckett. Because at this point it's clear that he's not just good looking; he's also a good guy.

A *great* guy, in fact. The type of guy any girl in this town would feel lucky to call theirs... if he were sticking around, of course.

I was touched how well he read the situation while we were at Silver Springs earlier. How he could tell that Gramps was getting confused, and so he gently redirected the conversation towards calmer waters—even though I know how badly he must have wanted to ask about his gran.

Later in the visit, I managed to gently bring up Noeleen

once more. Not wanting to risk upsetting my Gramps again after such a nice time spent together, I didn't ask about what might have happened between them, but I did tell him that I was writing an article about their courtship.

Gramps, to my relief, seemed delighted. Said it "brought back fond memories"—though he couldn't recall exactly what those memories were.

Either way, it definitely puts my mind at ease about what I'm penning for Evoke.

"So how was the rest of your day?" I ask, lolling my head back against the brick wall. It's cloudy tonight, no stars. "Anything crazy happen?"

"It was very uneventful. I practiced for the Indie Music Night for a while, and then I made that box of that macaroni and cheese you put in my shopping basket at Spring Foods." Beckett grimaces. "I don't know why they call it Kraft Dinner, because there was absolutely nothing edible inside that box."

"What?" I demand. "It's got pasta, cheese, milk, butter... all of the essential food groups."

"Calling that orange powdery stuff 'cheese' is a massive stretch." His eyes crinkle at the corners. "I'm amazed you're still alive, eating like that."

"What's your favorite dish back in Ireland, then?" I ask. "Cabbage with extra cabbage on top, served with a side of carrots?"

Becks laughs, and the sound is sweet as honey. "Add some beef and potatoes and you pretty much have an Irish stew."

"Sounds... delicious," I say, sounding as entirely unconvinced as I feel.

"Hey, don't knock it til you try it, Roberts," Beckett teases. As he says this, he leans over and pokes my side, his finger easily finding that sensitive spot under my ribs which sends shivers coursing through me.

163

But instead of jerking away, my instinct has clearly left the building because I find myself leaning into his touch. Savoring those shivers he's conjured in me.

I'm gratified to hear a catch in his breath, like he's affected by our contact, too. He lets his fingers linger for just a beat longer on my hip, before he pulls his hand away almost wistfully.

He gives me a bashful smile in the darkness. "Maybe one day I'll make you Irish stew so you can find out what you're missing."

"Don't threaten me with a good time," I shoot back with a matching smile, and in response, he pokes my ribs again.

This time, I laugh and squirm away, giggling as he tickles me.

"That can be your next article for Evoke," he says with a twinkle in his eye. "After you get the job there, your next pitch can be about a girl who was proved very, very wrong about her presumptions of Irish cuisine."

"Sounds like something that will really speak to the site's target audience." I laugh self-deprecatingly. "They'll have me fired within a week and I'll have to slink home with my tail between my legs."

I'm still kidding around, so I'm surprised when Beckett's expression grows serious.

"I lied," he says, hazel eyes honed in on me.

"What are you talking about?"

"A few minutes ago, when I said nothing else eventful happened today aside from the disastrous dinner I ate. I lied."

"Oh?"

"I actually spent the remainder of the afternoon reading everything I could on the Serendipity Springs website—well, everything with the byline *Keeley Roberts*."

My cheeks heat. "Oh my gosh, you did not."

"You're super talented, Keeley. You bring even the most

mundane of topics to life in a way that made me want to keep reading. Despite me not giving a single toss about what happened at the last town council meeting here, you had me entirely hooked."

His compliment is delivered in a tone that's straightforward, totally sincere. He's not trying to butter me up, he's telling me what he really thinks. And for some reason, I find myself willing to accept the type of praise that normally makes me feel uncomfortable.

"Thank you, Beckett," I say. "That means a lot to me."

And it really does, coming from him.

"I'm just telling the truth." His eyes are still focused on me, and I'm held captive by his stare. My whole body feels alive, crackling with energy, and I know the chemistry between us is getting harder for me to deny.

I've never felt sparks like this before, ones that set your skin alight and make your insides fizz and bubble like champagne...

Champagne that I've tried to cork tightly within me, but currently feels like it could pop open at any moment, if I gave it half a chance.

Chapter Twenty-Four
Keeley

"You're here!" The door to Serendipi-Tea flies open, and a flushed Nori stands in the doorway, beaming. Her eyes move from me to Beckett next to me, and her smile grows. "You're *both* here."

"Why are you so out of breath?" I ask my friend with a teasing wrinkle of my nose. "Did we interrupt you and Cash having a hot and heavy make out session or something?"

Nori laughs. "No, no, we were just setting up the chairs. If we'd been making out, I would have never answered the door."

"Fair," Beckett says with a grin. Nori grins right back at him.

"It's nice to finally meet you, Beckett. I've heard so much about you." She gives me a wink, and I feel my cheeks going fire-engine red.

"She's heard only normal things," I jump in. "About you being my neighbor and... stuff."

"Yeah, yeah." Becks gives me a teasing little nudge, then extends a hand to Nori. "Nice to officially meet you, too, Nori. I've also heard a lot about you... and your tea and coffee shop. Everyone always raves about it. I'm excited to finally check it out."

Nori beams with pride as she shakes his hand. "That's so nice of you to say, Beckett."

"Please, call me Becks."

"You are such a charmer," I mutter under my breath as Nori ushers us inside.

He's walking just a step behind me, and he dips his head so his lips are close to my ear. "Are you charmed, Keeley?"

A shiver rolls through me. "Absolutely not."

His responding laugh lights me up from the inside.

"Nori, it looks great in here." I swiftly pirouette to a less shiver-inducing subject as I set my tote bag on the counter and look around the space.

Almost a week has passed since Becks and I went to visit Gramps. Since then, I've been hard at work on said article, writing about how Noeleen and Douglas were brought together when she lived in The Serendipity, but ultimately, their love wasn't written in the stars.

I have a lot of the piece written—and it's an effort I'm really proud of—but I'm having a hard time knowing where to go next with it.

It's hard to write towards any kind of conclusion when I don't know what the *moral* of the story is.

All I know is that Noeleen and Douglas loved each other, for a time.

And then that love hurt them.

I suppose my lingering question is that I have no idea if loving and losing someone is better than not loving at all.

But tonight, I'm taking a little break from writing, because it is the first official Indie Music Night. The cozy coffee shop looks even cozier than normal. The lights are dimmed atmospherically, and the sofas and loveseats have been pushed closer to make room for extra chairs that have been set out. Nori's best friend and old roommate, Hayden, has apparently taken over Nori's task and is setting out more chairs alongside her husband, Jasper.

In the front window, Nori's boyfriend, Cash, is lying on the floor, maneuvering some wiring around a makeshift stage. Meanwhile, Ezra's standing on the stage, setting up a microphone.

"Thanks, my friend." Nori smiles almost nervously. "I'm really hoping it'll be a success."

"Everyone is going to lose their minds," I say confidently. "It'll be a packed house tonight, and you'll get a ton of new customers putting your shop on their radar."

"I hope so." Nori turns to Beckett. "And I must thank you, Becks, for stepping up to fill the closing slot. I've had a few customers come in over the past couple of days who've been super excited to experience some authentic Irish music."

He gives her a crooked grin. And even though Nori is my friend and fully in love with Cash, a strange flicker shimmies through me. It's not that I don't want him to smile at Nori... more that I want that smile directed at me. Always.

And I'm not exactly sure what to do with that information.

Nori grins at me knowingly before tugging Becks by the elbow to meet Hayden and Jasper.

I watch Hayden's eyes move over him appreciatively, which I can totally understand. Becks looks even more gorgeous than usual this evening in a soft blue denim button-down shirt with the sleeves rolled up to expose his muscular, tanned forearms. After she's done checking him out, she turns to give me a subtle (not) double thumbs-up.

In response, I roll my eyes at her, and she grins before going back to setting up chairs.

Becks moves on to chat with Cash and Ezra, earning a warm bro-shake thingy from my brother and a huge backslap from Cash. To absolutely no one's surprise, he's already charmed by Becks, too.

Funny how Beckett's been in this town all of five minutes, and he's already drawn so many people into his orbit.

Nori helps Hayden and Jasper with the chairs, and I'm tasked with lighting a bunch of tealights and placing them strategically on tables. But first, I duck behind the coffee bar and unpack the contents of my tote into one of the fridges.

I'm armed with tealights and approaching one of the back tables when Hayden sidles up behind me.

"He's *hot*," she says in a teasing, singsong voice as she eyes the stage area, where the boys are working on rigging up sound equipment.

"Mm," I say, noncommittally.

"Are you guys, like, a thing?"

"Just friends," I reply primly.

"Really?" She smirks. "Because I heard through the grapevine that you guys have been spending a *lot* of time together."

"Bahaha," I spit out, but my laugh sounds forced, even to my ears. "That's just gossipy Roberta from the first floor stirring the pot."

What I don't say is that over the past week, there have been multiple days when I've found myself walking towards Blue Notes after a morning at the library to pay Becks a visit between his lessons, and every night I've climbed out onto the fire escape, hoping for another "Insomniacs Anonymous" gathering for two.

And every night, my hopes have come to fruition. Some nights we've stayed out there for hours, talking about anything and everything under the darkness of the sky.

Despite what I just said, we *have* been spending a lot of time together.

169

Of our own volition, mind you, and not because we were somehow locked somewhere together.

"I don't know, Keels." Nori is suddenly at our side. "He keeps looking at you."

"He does?" I blurt as my gaze flies across the room.

Beckett is, indeed, looking at me. Those hazel-green eyes of his crinkle at the corners as he smiles.

Hayden's cackle is borderline evil. "Just friends, huh?"

I duck my head and shake it with a laugh.

"I... kinda like him, okay?" I admit under my breath, chipping a little piece of candle wax off the edge of a holder. Make that like him *a lot*. So much for my thinking I could avoid the smug pretty boy I met in the elevator a few weeks ago.

"I knew it!" Hayden pumps a fist, while Nori lets out a whoop, which she quickly disguises as a weird cough-splutter.

"Y'all are subtle as bricks," I drawl in a Sissy-esque accent. "And it doesn't mean anything. He's nice and funny and good-looking, but he's also here temporarily. And I might be moving to Boston soon, too."

Nori's mouth falls open. "Really?"

"Really." I fill the girls in on the job opportunity at Evoke, and how excited I would be to get it.

For some reason, I leave out the article topic I'm working on in order to actually *get* the job, as well as the fact that Becks and I discovered that we're connected. Have a shared history we could never have expected.

And the fact that, right now, it seems like it's a whole lot more than just the historical thread drawing us together.

"So, what about a summer romance?" Hayden asks the same question the Hathaways asked me a while back. "See out the rest of your August with that fine, fine man over there?"

For some reason, this time, it doesn't seem nearly so improbable.

I'm clearly attracted to Beckett. Probably too attracted to

him. And I clearly think way too often about the sparks between us. To the point where I might need to put up a "Danger, High Voltage!" sign in my head.

"I don't know," I tell Nori and Hayden hesitantly, taking a mental step back from the metaphorical electric fence in my mind.

I'm not in the market for romance. Right? I'm focusing on my career, working towards my future. And like I mentioned, Beckett's only here temporarily. In a couple of short weeks, I might never see him again.

"Don't know what?" Nori tilts her head.

I shrug. "If I'm a summer romance sort of person."

Or any kind of a romance person.

"Maybe you could be," Hayden says thoughtfully. "Maybe that wasn't you in the past, but you could try something new this summer."

Nori nods. "He's a good man. I think he'd be good for you."

I steal another glance at Becks, and of course, my silly heart picks up pace.

A change in pace that has me considering things...

Maybe I could open myself up to something new, explore this positively magnetic chemistry between us. A chemistry that's tangible; that's becoming harder and harder to brush off.

With Beckett leaving at the end of the month, and me already knowing this, there's no way I can be blindsided again. He can't hurt me by leaving if I already know there's an expiration date on anything we could possibly have together. If I'm aware upfront that this is temporary, then I can make sure it doesn't hurt me.

I can protect my heart because I know what's coming— and at the end of August, we can go our separate ways, entirely unscathed.

"Maybe a summer romance could be good for me. And maybe one could be good for him..." I find myself saying.

Apparently, I'm just leaping the fence now, no inhibitions. And I'm kind of liking the thrill of it.

"Yeah, girl!" Hayden cheers.

"Oh, by the way," Nori says, biting her lip. "Sorry to change the subject so abruptly, but I should give you a heads up. I ran into Andrew and Lisa in the hallway this morning, and they said they're coming tonight. Together."

I nod as I digest this information. Wait to feel... something.

Nothing comes. So I shrug. "It's good that they're coming. The more we pack this place, the better, right?"

"You don't mind?"

"Nah," I say, and it's the truth.

I don't care about Andrew anymore. Not like that. To the point where I'm glad he's happy.

"Good for you," Hayden says, but I'm barely listening as I sneak another glimpse at Beckett. He's standing onstage in front of the microphone now, pushing a lock of hair that's fallen over his forehead out of his eyes as he helps Ezra with the sound check.

I've seen what an incredible teacher he is. Heard what incredible music he can create.

And now, I get to see him bring his passion to life on the stage right in front of me.

I can hardly wait.

Chapter Twenty-Five
Beckett

THIS PLACE IS BURSTING at the seams.

Like, to the point where I'm thinking about fire code.

Or maybe it's that I'm thinking about later tonight and hopefully seeing Keeley on the fire escape.

Our nightly meeting there really has become a routine for me—one I *really* like.

I lean back in my chair and let my eyes travel over the crowd. I recognize a handful of people, including the teen boy from Relish, Sissy from the library, and Steve the building manager.

There have been a few excellent performances, and the musician who's currently onstage—a teenage girl playing a Taylor Swift cover—is really giving the audience something to sing along loudly to.

Two more performances, and then I'm up, closing out the night.

I'm glad that with or without my performance, this Indie Music Night is already a hit. I'm happy for Keeley's friends, who are super welcoming and friendly. Nori's boyfriend Cash, who used to be a pro baseball player, invited me to watch a game with him soon.

The dude was enthusiastic. Like, almost *too* enthusiastic.

I figured he was just like that with everyone, until Andrew walked through the door (late, I might add) and Cash gave him what can only be described as a death-glare. He's clearly also not a fan of Keeley's ex, which made me warm to him even more.

Andrew's now sitting at a table, holding hands with his new girlfriend. She's a nice-looking girl, I guess, if you're judging objectively.

But she can't hold a candle to Keeley. My eyes sweep back to her for what must be the thousandth time this evening. She looks incredible tonight in her tight black tank top with a plaid flannel shirt worn open over top. Her hair is pulled into a messy bun, and she's wearing the ripped jeans and Converse that I apparently cannot resist.

There's a pause between songs, and applause rings out.

As I clap, I stand and walk towards the coffee bar, where Keeley's chatting quietly with Nori. There's a jug of water on the bar, and I move in that direction—as if I'm thirsty—but I obviously fool no one, because Nori gives me a knowing little smirk before darting across the room to sit on Cash's lap.

"Hi," Keeley says softly.

"Hi," I reply, equally quiet. "You doing okay?"

She looks at me quizzically, pretty blue eyes narrowed. "Yeah, why wouldn't I be?"

"Because Andrew's here with Lisa." I nod in their direction.

"Don't care. I'm here to watch you, not them."

She pairs her words with her pretty smile. And man, if I don't feel it straight in my chest.

"Are *you* doing okay?" She throws my question back at me.

"I'm grand, yeah." I eye the stage, then venture towards the truth. "Nervous, I guess. I haven't done this in a long time."

"Well, I'm no performer, but when I was nervous to present in school, my Gramps always told me to pretend everyone was in their underwear to help ease the nerves."

Oh, boy.

Her belly button ring and freckled stomach immediately jump to the forefront of my mind.

As if I wasn't already a jumble of nerves.

"Don't say that," I groan.

Her eyes fly to mine, and as our gazes clash, the flash of heat that moves between us is palpable. Her cheeks are flushed, eyes bright.

There's no misreading the moment this time.

She feels these sparks, too.

The revelation excites me way more than it should.

"I didn't mean for you to picture *me*." Her voice cracks over the words.

"Too late," I tease, but my own voice comes out weird, like a cat being strangled. Which I'm sure is incredibly sexy.

She whacks my arm playfully, but her eyes are still wide, her cheeks still flushed. She looks around somewhat frantically, as if grasping for a change in subject. "Oh, great. Ezra's looking over here."

I follow her gaze across the room, and indeed, Ezra and a petite Asian woman are watching us. Ezra's face is positively smirky, the woman's curious.

"Is that Ezra's wife?" I ask.

Keeley nods. "That's Mae. They have a little boy, Everett."

"Cute name."

"He's a cute kid." She grins. "By the way, I told Ez about our gramps and your gran."

"Was he surprised?"

"Shocked as we were." She shrugs. "I think he's fully invested in the soap opera now, too."

"As he should be." I nod my approval.

"Hey." She gives me an almost-shy look from under her eyelashes. "I'm going to a barbecue at Ez and Mae's place tomorrow night. Ezra says he has an old box of Gramps's stuff for me that could maybe give us some clues about Noeleen. It could be nothing, but either way, it'll be a fun night. Mae's a great cook. Do you... want to come with me?"

I shoot her a flirty smile. "Are you asking me on a date, Keeley Roberts?"

I'm only kidding around, but the second the words are out of my mouth, I realize how much I don't want them to be a joke.

Since that first night we sat together on the fire escape, thoughts of Keeley—of more than a friendship with Keeley—have pretty much consumed me. I've been out of the dating game for a long time now, but Keeley makes me want to explore and lean into my feelings.

And I know I'm going home soon enough, but in the time we have left together, I find that I want to show her she deserves more in her dating life than what her ex gave her.

She sighs and flicks her eyes heavenward. "Of course, because all good dates involve your brother."

"Fair." I look down at her, my pulse picking up as I decide to take a risk. "But what if I took you out afterwards for dessert—or a drink, if you prefer? Then, could it be a date?"

My words have her flustered, and she stuffs her hands in her pockets. Takes them back out. Pockets them again. It's adorable.

She scrunches up her eyes for a moment—almost like she's mustering up courage or something—and then says, "Uh... not no?"

"Would you *want* it to be a date?"

Her cheeks glow red, and she looks down at her sneakers. "Maybe... also not no."

"Good." I can't help the huge smile that creeps across my face. I'm on cloud nine. "In that case, I'll drive, and you can be my human GPS again. I'll pick you up tomorrow night at six?"

"Okay. Sure."

Somehow, my smile gets even wider. "It's a date."

"You're trouble, McCarthy."

"You like it, Roberts."

We're so engaged in our flirty conversation that I don't notice the applause until Ezra takes the stage. "Thank you, Whitney! And now, I'd like you to put your hands together for our final performance of the night—a very special guest from all the way across the pond. Please welcome... Beckett McCarthy!"

Applause rings out. Sissy cheers. Cash puts two fingers in his mouth and whistles.

"I'm up," I say to Keeley.

Quick as a flash, she pulls me into a hug.

For such a little woman, she's *strong.*

Our bodies press together, and her hands are cool on my back. My nose buries in her hair so I'm breathing in the scent of raspberries and vanilla as I squeeze her tight.

It's the first time we've hugged. I hope it's not the last. So much so that I keep my arms wound around her for what I'm sure is way too long.

"You should probably get up there," she finally says

"I should."

She pulls back, and I almost wish I could swallow my words. Cancel my performance, shut this Indie Music Night down, and stay here with her in my arms all night.

But my regret is short-lived, because before I can walk

away, she stands on her tiptoes. Her lips brush against my cheek before she whispers, "Good luck, Becks."

It's the fuel I need, and as I take the stage, all the nerves leave my body as I sling my guitar over my neck and realize I'm ready. I'm exactly where I should be at this moment.

Exactly where I *want* to be.

Chapter Twenty-Six
Keeley

I'M MELTING.

Like, literally. We need a clean-up on aisle three because I'm an actual puddle.

Beckett's guitar playing is beyond anything I've heard live. And he has a voice like butter. Sultry, smooth, melted butter that I want to order a vat of so I can drown in it.

It's not just that, either. He has this... *presence* onstage. It's just him, his guitar and the mic stand, but it's almost overwhelming. His confidence, his pure and unadulterated charisma, forces you to stop what you're doing and watch. Forces your breath to catch.

Holy moly was the man downplaying his talents with that bashful act of his.

He should be performing for the masses. Selling millions of records worldwide, flying in private jets, headlining Coachella, and booking out Madison Square Garden.

But instead, he's here, in Serendipity Springs.

In cozy, warm, familiar Serendipi-Tea, singing for our townspeople.

Singing for me.

Because from the moment he took the stage, he hasn't taken his eyes off me. And I haven't been able to take my eyes off him as his beautiful, low voice sings an Irish song I vaguely recognize. A song that's all about a girl with black hair and blue eyes.

Not that I'm reading into that part too much... okay, fine, I'm totally reading into it. And also wanting to jump up and down like a little kid with excitement because I have a freaking *date* with this unbelievably hot, talented man tomorrow night.

He sings the last line, strums the last chord, and there's a moment of still, still silence. Like, you could hear a pin drop.

And then, everyone's on their feet.

The applause is raucous. Thunderous.

People whistle and shout, "Encore!"

Nori looks like she could burst with happiness—her first Indie Music Night is a literal roaring success. Ezra looks beyond impressed, his eyes popping wide. Even Andrew's taking part in the standing ovation, on his feet and clapping loudly.

And all the while, Beckett stands on the stage with his head slightly dipped and the tips of his cheekbones pinkening. The picture of humility.

"What a beautiful serenade." Next to me, Sissy wipes away a tear as she turns to look at me. "That one's a keeper, Keeley."

I just nod dumbly. I wouldn't dare trying to speak through the huge lump lodged in my throat, anyway.

Who knew music stirred up so much emotion in me?

My eyes meet Beckett's once again, and he gives me a special little smile, sending my heart slamming against my ribcage.

Maybe it isn't just the music, then...

I swallow the pesky lump, put on my biggest smile, and cup my hands around my mouth so I can cheer as loudly as possible.

After Becks closes the show, Serendipi-Tea doesn't clear out for another couple of hours.

To Nori's delight, people stick around, mingling, chatting, and sampling some of the teas and pastries on the menu.

And, of course, they want to talk to Beckett.

The man is a hot commodity, being dragged from conversation to conversation. I try not to let my hackles rise too much when a beautiful young blond woman places her hand on Beckett's arm as she laughs at something he said.

I'm thoroughly placated when he looks down at her hand on his bicep, then gently releases his arm from her clutches with a murmured excuse and moves on to talk to a woman I recognize as Sammie's mother.

Every time I think of his conversation with the little girl last week, my heart squeezes. I couldn't hear everything through the window, but I heard enough to know how incredibly gentle Becks was with her. How he handled her emotions carefully and made sure not to disparage or discount her feelings as he led her to a place where she could see herself more positively.

It was nothing short of, well, swoon-inducing. Between that sweet moment with Sammie and his gentle joking with my grandfather, I have to wonder why on earth he thinks he would be a bad partner.

I've never seen a man so in tune with how others feel. Which I would think is a great quality in a potential partner.

"Want us to help clean up?" I ask Nori as I drain the last of my decaf mocha latte and set the cup on the counter.

"Us?" she squeaks. "You guys are an *us* now?"

My face takes on the color of a burnt lobster. "I just assumed that Beckett will want to help, too."

"If you're here, I'd say that's a safe bet," she says with a cheeky wink, then heads for the front door as the final stragglers step outside.

She turns the key in the lock, then puts her back against the door with a happy sigh. "Phew!"

It's now just me, Becks, Nori, and Cash. Ezra disassembled the sound equipment earlier before he and Mae went to relieve their babysitter. And Hayden and her husband went home a while ago because he has an early start in the morning.

So, here we are. With a massive array of strewn cups, glasses, and empty cake plates.

"You got a broom so I can get cracking on this mess?" Becks asks, gesturing to the crumbs and napkins on the floor.

"He cleans, too?!" Nori stage-whispers—loud enough so he can hear, of course.

Beckett takes it in his stride, laughing as he rakes a hand through his already-tousled hair. "What can I say? My mam taught me well."

I dart behind the coffee bar. "I've got something for us before we tackle the cleaning," I say excitedly. I open the fridge to retrieve the six-pack of Guinness I brought in my tote bag. I hold it up high and look at Beckett. "So we can toast like true Irish people tonight."

"Yes!" Cash whoops. "Nice one."

"That's so thoughtful of you, Keeley," Becks says, and the smile that lights up his face makes my knees go a little weak.

"I've never tried Guinness," I admit.

182

"Me neither," adds Nori.

Becks shrugs. "Well, I've never had it from a can. But as they say, there's a first time for everything."

We each crack open a can and hold it up.

"Sláinte," Becks declares.

"Come again?"

"Cheers, in Gaelic."

"Sláinte!" we all cry in unison, slamming our cans together.

I take a sip and immediately regret it.

Guinness is disgusting. Like, super gross.

I try not to gag as I set down the can, wiping the foam from my mouth.

Yuck.

I see Nori wince in my peripheral vision and get the feeling that she's not a fan either. But the boys sure seem to like it. As we continue to clean up, Cash and Becks sip on their cans. At some point, someone pairs their phone with the cafe's Bluetooth, and upbeat pop music blares through the speakers as we laugh and joke together, recapping the highlights of the night.

Andrew and I never hung out with other couples like this —not that Becks and I are a couple, of course.

But Beckett has this breezy way about him that just seems to put everyone—me included—at ease.

I mean, Cash and Nori are both already treating Becks like he's their lifelong friend.

It's a nice feeling.

Beckett comes up beside me as I put away the last clean latte glass, and he slings a casual arm around me. "This was a good night," he proclaims, and when I turn to look at him, I notice how loose his body language is, how bright and shiny his eyes are.

"Beckett McCarthy, are you a little drunk right now?"

His grin is equal parts sheepish and adorable. "I warned you I was an awful lightweight, didn't I?"

This makes me laugh. "You did, I will admit."

"Hey, Keeley?" His Irish lilt is even stronger than usual. "I want to say thank you."

"What for?" I ask, turning fully to face him. I glance around to see if Cash and Nori are around, but they must be putting the last of the chairs into the back room because we're currently very much alone.

He takes a step forward, his feet coming between my legs, his body hovering just an inch or two from mine as he effectively cages me in by the counter. His hand comes up to tuck a stray lock of hair behind my ear, and his callused fingertips brush over the sensitive skin there as his eyes lock on mine. "For encouraging me to play tonight. For calming my nerves before I went up there. For buying Guinness and pretending to like it when you clearly hate it."

"Busted," I whisper, biting my lip as I hold his gaze.

"You had to have at least one flaw," he says, his grin crooked, his hair mussed, his eyes sparkly.

"Believe me, I have many."

"I don't know about that," he says, his voice low.

His fingertips graze the nape of my neck—

"Annnnd that should do it! We're all cleaned up and good to go."

Cash's voice fills the room as he and Nori reappear, looking a little mussed themselves, which makes me smirk. Beckett jerks backwards a little too fast, almost losing his footing as he stumbles slightly, then rights himself.

"Whoops."

I smile. "C'mon, McTipsy. Let's get you home."

It's a beautiful, balmy night, and the four of us decide to walk the two miles to The Serendipity under the stars.

Cash throws an arm around Nori, pulling her close. And

as we set off, fingers brush against my hand—almost tentatively, like they're asking a question.

A question there's only one answer to.

My heart picks up as our fingers thread together, intertwining seamlessly.

It's the perfect end to a perfect night.

Chapter Twenty-Seven
Beckett

"Just a second!"

Keeley's voice carries through the closed door of her apartment and into the hallway, and I step backwards, putting a foot of space between me and the door. You know, so I don't look *too* overly keen.

Not that that particular ship hasn't already sailed.

To be fair, I am five minutes early. I'm dressed in the smartest outfit I could find in my suitcase, and I'm holding a bottle of wine.

Oh, and a potted plant.

I was leaning towards getting a cheerful bunch of yellow and orange flowers, but the cashier at the store reckoned a houseplant was a better gesture to say, "Thank you for having me for dinner."

He was very persuasive, apparently, because here I am. Plant and all.

The door flies open, and Keeley's standing there, grinning a tad sheepishly. She's wearing an oversized t-shirt, holding an eyeliner pencil, and her hair is gathered sloppily in a claw clip.

And she honestly looks incredible, just like that.

"Sorry, this will likely take longer than one literal second." She gestures down at herself. "But come on in..."

She trails off as her eyes sweep over me, taking in my lightweight black bomber jacket, ironed t-shirt, and dark jeans. And, finally, the plant.

"For Mae," I explain, holding out the wine bottle in my other hand. "In case she doesn't like wine."

An indecipherable expression flits over Keeley's features, and for a moment, I wonder if I've made some kind of error.

But then, she smiles. It's a big, broad, sunshine-y smile that transforms her pretty face. It's a specific smile I haven't seen her wear before. One I can only think she doesn't offer over nothing.

"You're so thoughtful," she says almost shyly, blushing a little as she steps aside, gesturing for me to come inside.

As I walk into her apartment, she holds up a finger and darts into what I assume is her bedroom, leaving me alone to take in her space.

It's the first time I've been in here, and I set down my wine and plant on the counter so I can soak it all in. Fairy lights are strung haphazardly across the ceiling over a small white couch covered in throw pillows. A messy desk with mugs full of colored pencils and a board covered in colorful post-it notes sits below the window, the laptop on it open to the Evoke website. There's a furry blue rug and a Banksy print on the wall and stacks upon stacks of books on the coffee and side tables.

The room is filled with an eclectic, splashy mix of oddities that somehow all come together to feel exactly like *her*.

It makes me wonder how long she's lived here and if she's going to miss it when she goes.

And I say *when*—not *if*—because I've read some (all) of

187

her content on the Serendipity Springs town website. She's a brilliant writer, and I have complete faith she will score this new job.

As if on cue, there's the thud of footsteps upstairs, and I remember why she wanted to escape in the first place.

Will she be sad to leave this apartment? Or will she welcome the change?

Crossing the room, I take a tentative seat on the couch, sliding over a stuffed capybara who's wearing a backpack in the shape of a goose. I set the stuffed animal in my lap and retrieve my phone from my jeans pocket.

One new email from Rory Cassidy, the principal of the school where I work.

It's an email blast to all teaching staff. I can only assume it's filled with housekeeping items for the upcoming school year.

I ignore it, for now. Even though today brought in colder weather, it's still summer. I'm not officially on the clock again for another two weeks.

I'm catching up on Mam's recap of her recent introduction to scuba diving in Greece (which apparently went very poorly because Paul got chased by a rather aggressive little octopus and is now scarred for life) in the family group chat when the bedroom door opens and Keeley comes out. "Sorry about that. Ready now!"

She's dressed in a short black skirt that wraps around at the front, and a scoop neck t-shirt that's the same color as her eyes. On her feet are the ever-present black Converse.

Her hair is long and loose and shiny, her cheeks flushed and pink.

"You look..." Still a bit dumbstruck, I fumble for an appropriate word. "Wow."

Nice one, Beckett. Real smooth.

For some reason, she smiles at my idiocy. "Well, you came in here looking so fancy, I had to match your energy."

"My jacket was getting lonely, hanging out in my suitcase by itself," I say with a chuckle. "Today's the first day that it's cool enough to actually wear the thing."

For the first time since getting to Serendipity Springs, I woke up this morning to overcast skies full of gray, swollen-bellied clouds. A chilly breeze has filled the air all day.

"Nothing worse than a lonely jacket," she confirms solemnly, reaching for a deep blue sweatshirt that's draped over the back of the couch. She shrugs it on, then spots the stuffed animal in my lap. "Or a lonely capybara, so thank you for getting acquainted with him while I was getting dressed."

"The pleasure is all mine," I say as I set the little fella down on the couch and stand up. "He's cute."

"His name's Bert. Gramps won him for me at the fair a few years ago."

"There's a fair you haven't told me about?" I demand playfully.

"Every August." Keeley's eyes sparkle. "End of summer kind of thing. Rides and cotton candy and funnel cake and games that are rigged so you can't win unless you get super lucky."

"Well. Now I know where I'll be at the end of the summer."

"Oh, yes, we should totally go!" she says, and I love her use of *we*. "You can't leave the USA without trying a deep-fried Oreo, now, can you?"

"I'd never be able to forgive myself," I say gravely, and I'm rewarded with a laugh.

"It's a date," she says. "And speaking of dates, we should get going."

I pick up my plant and my wine. "I thought the first

portion of the evening wasn't a date given the fact that your family members will be present."

"It wasn't meant to be." A wicked little smile dances over her face. "But then, I saw you in that jacket, carrying that plant, and I changed my mind."

Chapter Twenty-Eight
Beckett

EZRA AND MAE live in a renovated Victorian a few neighborhoods over from The Serendipity. It's got high, sloped ceilings, dormer windows and a wood burning fireplace, the mantel of which now hosts my gifted plant.

I love the place on sight.

I also love Everett the second I lay eyes on him. It's the first time I've met Ezra and Mae's three-year-old, and his energy is infectious, his cheeky smile adorable. Even after sixty-five rounds playing on his plastic Fisher Price bongo drums with him while crouched uncomfortably on the hardwood floor.

Keeley is out back with Ezra, assisting him with plating the meat, which we're going to eat inside now due to the cooler weather. I offered to help, of course, but she said she'd do it so I could continue playing with Everett, who apparently digs me as much as I dig him.

Which feels nice, not gonna lie.

"I can grab you a chair, Beckett," Mae offers for approximately the fifty-seventh time, but I decline with a smile. I don't know much about little kids—I mainly teach tweens and teens—but I know it's important to connect with them on their level.

"Do you have any nieces or nephews?" she asks, smiling fondly at her son. "You're so good with Ev."

"Not yet," I say, tapping on the bongo in a rhythm that makes Everett giggle with glee. "But I will shortly—my sister is pregnant with her first."

"I didn't know you were about to be an uncle," Keeley says as she walks through the sliding glass doors from the yard, holding a platter stacked high with chicken thighs glazed with Korean barbecue sauce.

"Yeah, my sister Aoife is due in October." I grin. "Last time I talked to her, she said she felt like a cross between an elephant and a house, and she was hoping for an early arrival."

Mae chuckles. "I remember the feeling all too well."

Ezra comes in with a stack of ribs and announces that it's time to eat. It feels good to be able to stand and stretch my legs, finally.

"I wanna sit next to you and Kiwi," Everett declares, smiling up at me. *Kiwi* might be the cutest nickname I've ever heard.

"Deal, little man."

We all gather around the dining table—me across from Keeley, and Everett perched between us on one end of the table in a booster seat, like he's the king observing his subjects.

"Thanks again for having me," I say as Ezra passes me a bowl of glass noodle salad. "I've been subsisting on a diet of sugar-coated cereal, thanks to Keeley's grocery shopping tactics." I give her a little smirk. "Nice to be reacquainted with some vegetables."

"Vegetables are overrated," Keeley declares, then seems to register what she's currently shoveling onto her plate. "Except for your bibimbap, of course, Mae."

"Saved yourself in the nick of time there, Keels," Mae retorts with a wink.

As I fork a mouthful of deliciously hot, flavorful food into my mouth, Keeley, Mae, and Ezra banter back and forth. I love the way they communicate—kind of like my own family, only much, much less chaotic. Oh, and people actually seem to listen when someone else speaks.

Must be refreshing.

I'm enjoying myself thoroughly, and I take a backseat in talking in order to just listen to their conversation... until talk turns to the Indie Music Night.

"You were so good," Mae says, and I thank her, dipping my head. It's weird—I never know how to take compliments of this nature. Like accepting them will make me look ego-centric or prideful or self-indulgent.

"Did you know he writes his own music, too?" Keeley pipes up suddenly.

I wave a hand. "Ah, barely."

"No, seriously, I heard him playing a tune he wrote. It was incredible."

Ezra's eyes spark with interest. "Really?"

"Just something I'm dabbling with," I admit. A few days ago, I might have shrunk away from a question like that, but after performing last night—after asking Keeley out and walking home holding her hand—I've been feeling musically inspired.

So much so that I spent most of today working out the kinks in the new melody that's been moving through my mind. Even adding some lyrics.

"Would you be interested in recording it, Becks?" Ezra asks.

"I'm sure you're fully booked with lots of actual song-writers with real songs to record," I say. I know it's self-deprecating, but honestly, as much fun as recording might be, what would I even do with a recorded song?

"Yeah, we actually had a cancellation for next week that we'll never fill again in time, so the spot's yours if you want it. On the house."

"I—"

"No pressure," Ezra says. "But it could be a blast."

"It could be." Keeley's voice is soft and accompanied by the sensation of her foot gently pressing against mine under the table. I meet her eyes, and she swallows. "And I'd love to be able to listen to it again after you leave. It was so beautiful."

How on earth can I possibly argue with that? I think as I gaze into her hopeful eyes.

And honestly, I don't really have a good reason to say no— save for potential embarrassment that the finished song will turn out rubbish and Keeley and Ezra will hate it.

But something in me, something deep and intangible, already knows that's not the case.

"Sure," I find myself saying and then feel an accompanying shiver of excitement. Although I'm not sure how much of that has to do with the idea of recording, and how much has to do with the fact that Keeley is now playing full-blown footsie with me under the table.

Almost experimentally, I press my foot back against hers. Not going to lie, I have never thought of feet as sexy. Not my thing. At all.

But I might be reconsidering that. Because I like everything about Keeley Roberts. Including her feet, apparently.

And for the rest of dinner, as wonderful as Ezra and Mae are, the only thing on my mind is being alone with her later.

I've planned a few things that aren't maybe the most traditionally romantic or popular first date ideas, but they're things I think she will like. That will show her I'm paying attention. Doing everything I can to *see* her clearly.

After we're done eating, I'm happy to be tasked with scrubbing pots. I like that they don't make me sit down but instead let me help. Like they've accepted me as one of their own...

Not that that's what's happening here, of course.

My first date with Keeley does not officially start until later this evening, so I really shouldn't be thinking about being accepted into the family when we haven't even gone out together yet.

After everything's cleaned up, Mae gives us both huge hugs goodnight before she whisks Everett upstairs for bath time. We're about to say our goodbyes to Ezra when he holds up a finger.

"Let me grab you that box of Gramps's things." With that, he retrieves a box from the basement—one of those thick legal-looking cardboard boxes, a thin layer of dust on top.

"He gave me this box a while ago, before he moved to Silver Springs. It's mostly records, but there's a couple of old photo albums in there, too." Ezra shrugs as he passes it to me. "Maybe your Gran is in some of the pics or something. Might be worth a look."

Keeley smiles at her brother. "Cool. Thanks, Ez."

"Yeah, thanks, man," I say as well.

I'm grateful for Ezra's thoughtfulness, and while it's a long shot that we'll find anything useful in a box of old records, it's obviously worth looking through. But honestly, I'm in no rush to look at the moment...

Because right now, I get to take Keeley Roberts on a date.

Chapter Twenty-Nine
Keeley

BECKS HAS DONE HIS HOMEWORK.

As we climb into his truck, he tells me that he doesn't need my human GPS skills tonight. Instead, he puts on a country playlist and drives straight towards the outskirts of town.

There's only one possible place we could be getting ice cream, and it happens to have my favorite ice cream in the world.

As he pulls off at an exit in the middle of nowhere, I gape at him. "How did you know about this?"

"Ezra might've given me a couple of tips." Beckett parks the truck, then rubs the back of his neck. "I wanted to give you a good first date, and I only had dessert to work with." He turns and gives me that lopsided, dimpled grin of his I love so much, and adds, "I wanted to make sure you were suitably impressed."

I'm not sure what's got me in my feels more—the fact that he took the time to learn my favorite dessert in preparation for tonight, or the fact that he said *first* date.

As in, there are going to be more dates following this one.

"Consider me impressed," I tell him as we climb out of his truck. It's still dark and gray and overcast, and I'm glad I grabbed my sweatshirt.

When people talk about the best ice cream in Serendipity Springs, most mention Calaway Creamery—an awesome spot downtown that offers hundreds of delicious flavors and comfy booths to sit in. It's popular with tourists and locals alike, and it's a favorite for people cozying up on dates, sharing a sundae. It's actually where I went on my (admittedly awkward) first date with Andrew. We shared a double scoop sundae—I chose mint chip, he chose coffee, and it turned out those flavors totally clashed. Didn't work or blend together at all.

It's where I assumed we'd go tonight.

But Beckett, once again, has surprised me. In a good way.

Because while I love Calaway Creamery's ice cream, my favorite dessert in the world is found in this little spot on the side of the highway.

Dippity Doo Dah is an old-style ice cream truck that serves creamy soft ice cream dipped in the best chocolate coating on the planet. It's one of Serendipity Springs's best kept secrets, in my opinion. The owners are snowbirds who spend their winters in Florida, so their ice cream is only available in the summer months. Which, of course, makes it even better, because every year, you have to enjoy it while it lasts.

Gramps used to bring Ezra and me here all the time when we were growing up.

Beckett smiles as he looks around. The truck's cute striped awning is lit up with hanging lanterns, and small clusters of people sit at the few picnic tables surrounding the truck.

"When we started driving out here, I got nervous for a minute," he admits. "Thought Ezra might've been having me on and we were actually on a wild goose chase."

"He likes you too much to sabotage our date," I reply with

197

a laugh as we get in line. "But believe me, the drive out here is totally worth it. What are you going to order?"

"Two of whatever you want," he says, and I have to say, I love that he wants to try my favorite thing on the menu. At every turn, it's like he's searching to know more about me—from the little things to the big ones.

When we get to the front of the line, I order two large caramel vanilla swirl cones dipped in chocolate. The elderly man smiles at me. "Excellent choice."

We take our cones, and I'm about to walk towards a free table when Becks smoothly intertwines his hand in mine and pulls me in the other direction. I look at him questioningly, and he looks back at me with a heat in his eyes that makes my heart pound.

"I don't want to sit with all those people," he says in a low voice that I feel in my very core. "I've been waiting to get you alone all night."

And that's how we end up sitting on the tailgate of his truck in the parking area, overlooking a mostly deserted highway as we eat our ice creams... and somehow, it's the most romantic date I've ever been on.

Because it's exactly what I would have picked. And he somehow knew it.

"I give this a ten out of ten," Beckett says after swallowing a bite of ice cream. He's sitting close to me. So close that I can feel his body heat, which is somehow even more comforting than the cozy sweatshirt I'm wearing. "You have great taste, Roberts."

"I know," I say with a smile as I lick a droplet of ice cream from my finger. I'm hyper aware of the way his eyes follow my movement, how they linger on my mouth.

And I like it. A lot.

"Glad we didn't stay strangers," he says, and the sleeve of

his jacket scrapes tantalizingly along my skin as he casually moves his arm.

He's so casual, so composed. And I'm... well, I'm melting faster than the ice cream cone in my hand.

A veritable puddle of a person.

"Me too," I say into the night, my eyes on some headlights moving down the highway because I hardly dare look at him. Everything about Becks captivates me. Draws me in. Makes me want more. He fits in with my friends, my family, even my apartment building, with an ease that makes it feel like he's a piece of the puzzle that's been there forever, but is finally in its correct place. Finally where it was always meant to be.

And while all of that feels so right, it also feels... scary. Like I made the decision to do this because I was sure I could protect myself from getting hurt at the end of it, but somehow, I'm already falling for him too fast, too hard, and in a way I can't prevent. In a way that I won't be able to escape.

In a way that I don't *want* to escape.

Sure, this is a budding summer romance, but even though I know this is all it can and will be, it already doesn't feel like *just* a summer romance. It feels like something bigger. Something that's going to leave its mark on me when it inevitably ends, however that mark may look.

And instead of fleeing the idea of potentially being hurt again, I'm leaning right in.

I scoot impossibly closer to him. Lay my head on his shoulder like it's something I've done a million times before. Soft suede-like material against my cheek. Woodsy, fresh scent in my nose. My stomach is full of a million butterflies, all vibrating in anticipation of.... something.

"I'm always going to remember this summer," Becks says suddenly, like he's reading my mind.

"Agreed," I reply. "This will always be the summer I got

locked in the elevator, trapped on the fire escape, stuck in the laundry room..."

I feel his smile in his voice. "The summer you experienced all of the above with your charming, handsome new neighbor."

I chuckle. "The summer my incredibly modest new neighbor hit a whole new level of humble."

"The summer I met Keeley Roberts."

I wait for him to elaborate. To add something I did or said that was funny or embarrassing.

But he says nothing further.

I twist my head to look at him, and he shrugs, his eyes burning into mine as he says, "That's it, that's what I'm going to remember. You."

"Beckett..." I breathe.

That electric feeling is only growing. Crackling with energy. With possibility, like anything could happen.

My breath becomes shallow as his hand tightens on my knee, and his pupils dilate as I tilt my chin up towards him.

What I want is surely written all over my face as he leans closer...

"Aghhhhh!" I shriek as what feels like an entire bucket of water washes over my head.

The heavens have opened, the sky has exploded, and screams echo around the parking area as people flee to their vehicles to escape the downpour. Within seconds, I'm a sopping wet mess holding a sopping wet ice cream cone, and my brain has short-circuited—the rain has clearly fried my already overheating circuit board.

Because I'm sitting here, frozen, until the sound of Beckett's laughter snaps through me like a rubber band. Deliciously deep, almost dirty, laughter.

In one swift, impressively accurate motion, he pitches the

remains of his ice cream cone into a nearby trash can, then removes his jacket and holds it up over my head.

In a world of boys, he's the gentleman of all gentlemen.

He hops down from the tailgate and tosses my soaking cone into the trash too, before helping me down. Together, still laughing, we run around to the driver's side of the truck, and he steers me in front of him so I can climb in first.

I tumble into the cab of the truck, soaking and giggling. He's hot on my heels, and I scoot across the bench seat to make room for him.

We're both breathing heavily, and the cab fogs up within seconds. Becks throws his soaking jacket into the back seat, and I peel off my sweatshirt, which is plastered to my skin. My scoop-neck tee underneath hasn't fared much better, and Beckett's t-shirt is sticking to him, almost completely see-through.

"We haven't had rain like this all summer!" I say, running my fingers through my wet tangles.

Becks leans his head against the headrest, still laughing. Droplets of water cascade down his handsome face. "Clearly, I brought the Irish weather tonight." He turns the key in the ignition. "Let me get some heat going."

"Does it rain on most of your dates, then?" I ask. It's not very graceful, nor subtle, and I'm sure he'll clue in pretty quickly here that I'm digging, but I don't care.

"What dates?" he asks with a wry smile. "I haven't gone on a date in forever."

"Yeah, right." He told me that first night on the fire escape that he split with his long-term girlfriend last year, and despite his apparent opinion that he's not good boyfriend material, I am certain that a newly single Becks would have been an extremely hot commodity in his hometown.

Anywhere, actually.

"I'm being serious." Beckett pushes his hair back off his

face and then holds his hands to the vents, where warm air is blasting. "This is the first date I've been on in forever. In fact, it's the first first date I've been on in like a decade."

"*Why?!*" The word blurts out of my mouth before I can stop it, and I hastily follow up with, "Sorry, that was nosy. You don't need to answer that. Obviously."

I'm blabbering again.

But he just shakes his head with a smile. "Because I didn't feel like dating. For a long while there, I didn't really feel much of anything."

"What do you mean?"

"After Gran died, I shut down for a while, was essentially just going through the motions of life. I handled my grief badly, I think."

His eyes flit to my face. I get the feeling he doesn't talk like this easily, doesn't share this with everyone, and I find myself feeling sheer privilege.

He runs a hand through his hair. "I dealt with it all by looking after everyone else, while not really letting myself feel or lean into my emotions... that is, until I met you."

"Me?" My voice is high-pitched and squeaky, like a mouse.

"You," he confirms. His voice, in comparison, is deep and even and loaded with conviction. So much so that the single one-syllable word brings goosebumps to the surface of my skin, all over my arms and legs.

Because under Becks's sunny, carefree surface, he's a complex person who feels deeply. Who loves deeply and puts the people around him before himself. I think, in the process, he's neglected himself, emotionally—a fact that hurts my heart.

Yet somehow, I've been able to play a role in changing that for him. And that means the world to me.

He looks at me for a long, loaded moment, and before I can reply—before I can even attempt to express what I'm feeling—his eyes move away and focus on my goosebumps. "I'd better get you home, you're freezing," he says quietly.

The physical reaction happening within my body right now isn't from the cold, but he's already throwing the truck in reverse.

The highway is slow-going, with cars lined up and moving slowly. The rain is relentless, with pelting sheets of water hopping off both the vehicle and the road ahead, but Beckett's relaxed. He leans forward intermittently to wipe the fog from the inside of the windshield while claiming that he's "used to driving in these conditions."

I don't mind the slow drive, either. I want to savor every possible moment of this date. This night.

"I'm sorry our date got cut short," he says when we finally pull into the parking garage next to The Serendipity. He looks more than a little disappointed as he adds, "I don't think tonight is going to be a good night for a fire escape chat, either."

"I was just thinking the same thing," I say—I'd been hoping we could meet up out there later, but this rain is relentless. "Thank you for taking me for ice cream. I had a great time, despite the weather." My hand hovers by my seatbelt, but I don't unbuckle it yet. Instead I bite my lip, then say, "And thank you for telling me that stuff earlier. About your grief. I'm glad you're letting yourself feel again. I... really care about you, Becks."

He turns his hazel green eyes on me. But unlike earlier—when his gaze was hot and electric and loaded with desire before we got near-drowned in the rain—his eyes are sparkling with a totally different emotion. Something I feel tangibly in my chest.

"From the second you crashed into my life in the elevator, Keeley Roberts, I started feeling things that I hadn't felt in a long, long time. Maybe ever. And for that, I will always be thankful to you."

We look at each other for a moment, and a spark of hope jumps in me as his breathing shallows. But then, his eyes move over my soaked hair and clothes almost regretfully before he says, "I want to get you inside and warm. Are you ready to make a run for it?"

I can't deny the disappointment that wells in my chest, but I know it's unfair—I can't fault the guy for being a gentleman, for putting my needs first. Like he does with all the people he cares about.

"Let's do it," I agree. Although I think my need to kiss him is burning much stronger and brighter than my desire to get warm and dry.

We leave his jacket, my sweatshirt, and the box of Gramps's stuff Ezra gave us in the backseat, and we make a break for it. As we run through the pouring rain together, his hand reaches for mine.

We're both soaked to the skin as we run, hand in hand.

Me squealing, him laughing.

We bolt up the front steps to the building and stop at the front door. It's locked, and he looks back at me and grins as he fumbles in his pockets for his keys.

He finally puts his key in the lock. Turns it.

"Come on. Come on, come on," he mutters as he wiggles the key back and forth.

The door doesn't budge.

"Hang on, I'll get mine." I wipe a hand over my face, then root through my shoulder bag and produce my set.

The rain pounds on my back and Beckett comes to stand behind me in an attempt to shield me with his body, but there's no shielding anything from this crazy rain.

I slot my key in.

Turn it.

It doesn't budge.

"I can't believe this is happening!" I exclaim as I wrench the key again with no luck. I'm breathless and frazzled and soaking wet, my heart beating too fast at the sensation of Beckett's warmth so close to me.

He wraps his fingers around my forearm, his very touch sending a bolt of heat coursing through me as he spins me around to face him.

Water is coursing in rivulets down his face, his t-shirt looks like it's been glued on, and his hair is a soaked mess, but his eyes are blazing pure fire. A fire that lights me up from the inside on sight.

"I can," he says.

And then, his lips are on mine.

Chapter Thirty
Keeley

AT FIRST, Beckett's kiss is feather-soft. The sweet yet torturous feeling of gentle hands with callused, rough fingertips cup my chin as warm lips skim almost experimentally over mine.

It's a shocking sensation that steals my breath, and I let out a shaky gasp.

He responds by moving his hands to the nape of my neck and his fingers thread into my hair as he deepens the kiss. Water is coursing over both of us, streaming over our faces and plastering our clothes to our bodies, but I'm burning hot, almost feverish, as I melt into the kiss.

Beckett tastes cool and sweet, like the caramel swirl ice cream, and nothing has ever been more perfect. I twist my hands in his shirt, dragging him closer. I can't get close enough. My legs are shaking, and my skin feels like it's been sparked with a million volts of electricity, and I can feel his heart pounding against my fist as the kiss goes from soft and sweet to absolutely scorching in a matter of seconds.

He tilts my head and moves his mouth over mine, kissing

me wildly, with total unbridled passion. Totally unrestrained emotion. Like he's pouring everything he's feeling into this earth-shattering, axis-tilting kiss.

I marvel at the exquisite feeling of his thumbs moving gently over the hypersensitive skin on my neck as his fingertips tighten in my hair. The way a delicious shiver coils around my spine as his teeth scrape over my bottom lip. The sensation of his breath coming in short gasps that match mine as we lose ourselves in each other.

"Keeley," he groans, pulling back for a moment to look at me with heavy-lidded eyes. The sound of my name in his mouth makes me feel like I'm unraveling, coming undone.

Both of us are letting our guards down and exposing raw, vulnerable sides of ourselves in a way that would usually feel terrifying, but right now, it feels terrifyingly *right*. With every movement we make, every sound that spills from my mouth as he uses his lips, his tongue, his teeth on me, every reverent touch of my skin, Beckett is communicating a message to me...

We're safe here, with each other, like this. To let ourselves feel and experience every last bit of this kiss.

"I didn't think I'd get to do this tonight," Beckett murmurs into my skin as he buries his head in my neck. His breathing is labored, his voice low. Achey. He trails his lips along the column of my neck. My pulse leaps. "After the rain came, I thought the moment was over, that I'd have to lie awake in bed tonight imagining this. Imagining you, in my arms." He kisses away a raindrop on my collarbone. My head spins.

"I think the building had other ideas for how we should end our night," I say shakily, my voice raw.

"I like the way the building thinks," he says roughly, his eyes glittering, his beautiful mouth curling into a smile.

"Can't believe I'm admitting this, but maybe there is some truth to this whole magical matchmaking building thing," I say, and as soon as the words are out of my mouth, his lips find mine again. I can't help but moan as his hands slide down the sides of my body and curl around my hips, holding me like I'm *his* in a way that makes me never want him to let go.

I don't know how much time passes as we cling to each other in the pouring rain, him kissing me absolutely senseless. But by the time we break apart, no amount of freezing rain could be capable of cooling me off.

I'm on fire for this man in a way I've never felt before.

But he's still so in tune with everything I might want or need to be comfortable, because the first thing he does is rest his forehead against mine, both of us trying—and failing—to catch our breath before he mumbles, "I really should get you inside before you catch your death out here."

"Catch my death?" I ask, nuzzling my forehead against his. Not wanting to ever break apart.

"Just something my Gran used to say about catching colds from being out in the rain too long."

"Colds are from germs, not weather," I tell him.

"That's what I always said." He chuckles, and I feel his laugh vibrate through me. "Why do I feel like I've known you all my life, Keeley Roberts?"

His words make my heart swell.

Because right here, right now? This was clearly meant to be.

A moment destined to happen.

One that's undeniably ours.

"Because we were meant to meet each other this summer," I reply with confidence. "Be here together for this time."

As if to compound my point, I glance at the front door of the building, where my key is still lodged in the lock.

I reach out, turn the key again, and right away the door springs open.

"Well, would you look at that," Beckett says. He's still holding me.

"Would you look at that," I echo as I clutch him tighter.

Chapter Thirty-One
Beckett

"*WE WERE MEANT to meet each other this summer.*"

Keeley's words stay with me through the night and into the next day.

Her words, and the kiss to end all kisses. The kiss that put all other kisses to shame, that shook me to my very core.

My entire world has been turned upside down, and I am not sure I'll ever be able to flip it back.

Not that I'll ever want to.

Kissing Keeley in the pouring rain last night broke a dam in me. A dam that's contained everything in my life and has not let me feel for a long time now.

The rain may have derailed all of my original plans for a romantic first date—believe it not, ice cream while sitting on a truck tailgate wasn't all I had planned for the night. After all, I'm a man who was raised by two amazing women —Mam and Gran—who taught me way better than that. But what transpired was better than anything I could have planned.

I wasn't expecting or planning to kiss her. My goal for the night was simply to make her feel safe and desirable and cared for. I only intended to do something thoughtful and meaningful for her.

Our apartment building, on the other hand, clearly has a mind of its own and provided us the perfect setting for a perfect first kiss. It was the most passionate, romantic moment of my life. One that will be seared into my brain forever.

So much so that this morning, when I wake up to find that the rainstorm has passed and the sun is once again shining and bathing the world in gold, I find myself wishing for rain as I walk to Blue Notes.

Which is absurd. I mean, I live in Ireland. Rain is our only constant, and we love to complain about it. I never, ever thought I'd see the day when I would find myself longing for it.

"Are you lost?"

The voice startles me, and I look up from where I'm standing in the middle of the street outside Blue Notes like a halfwit to see Andrew, of all people, standing in front of me. He's holding a brown paper bag with grease stains at the corners, and he's frowning.

"Oh. No." I keep my gaze steady and cool as I look at him. Not lost, just lost in thought.

"You sure?" Andrew presses, his brown eyes suspicious.

I want to tell him to go take a hike, but instead I say, "I'm grand, thank you."

My words are polite, but my tone is anything but. I can't help it. Seeing Andrew brings up this protective, almost primal instinct in me. I know he's old news for Keeley now, but the fact is, he hurt her. Therefore, I kind of want to deck him in the face.

I've never punched someone before. Or even wanted to.

I'm a musician, for goodness sakes. My hands are exceedingly important.

211

But these are the kinds of feelings Keeley's stirring up in me. Emotions I didn't even know I had—ones that run so deep, so thick, so strong, that they make me want to do things that are totally out of character. And potentially unhinged.

Andrew must read at least some of this on my face, because he takes a step back, his eyes darting back and forth before landing uncertainly on me. "I know you don't like me. And I get it, bro—"

"Not your bro."

Andrew scrubs a hand over his face. "I was a jerk, okay? There, I said it. Happy now?"

My cool tone becomes cold. "No."

He sighs. Swallows. "Look. That day, when I saw you guys in the elevator, my behavior was not okay. I see that now, and I'm sorry."

His apology catches me off guard. Every time I've met him, he's acted so condescending towards Keeley, I'd taken him for someone who thinks he's never wrong.

But I don't want to speak for Keeley or her feelings by accepting his apology, so I just give him a brusque nod.

"I know you and Keeley are tight," Andrew goes on, dragging the edge of his sneaker back and forth along the sidewalk. "And that seemed to happen so fast. I think... I was jealous."

"You were with Lisa," I say pointedly.

He holds up his hands. "And I had no right to be jealous. I was—*am*—with Lisa. It took me a while to understand why I was feeling that way. I actually talked with Lisa about it at length before coming to the conclusion that the jealousy I felt was misplaced. A gut reaction to watching the woman I dated for years look so happy and content and relaxed with someone she'd just met. More so than she ever acted with me in the five years we were together."

I can... kind of understand that. The fact that he's apologizing actually makes me think he's grown somewhat with Lisa. I feel some of my iciness towards Andrew begin to thaw.

"I think, deep down, Keeley and I both knew for a long time that we weren't right for each other. And it took me a while to accept that." He shrugs. "I'm happy with Lisa. She fits with me in a way Keeley never did. And when I see Keeley with you, it's clear I didn't fit with her either, no matter how hard I tried. Whereas you seem to fit with her so effortlessly." He clears his throat. "And I get why you feel the way you do about me. But for what it's worth, I want you to know that I'm happy for her. For you both."

"Thank you, Andrew," I say. "I appreciate you saying that —although I do think you're saying it to the wrong person."

Because what else is there to say? It's the truth.

I know this feeling all too well. It's what I had with Roisin —a relationship that was wrong, but that was hard to let go of in the moment, and with hindsight, it ending was clearly the right thing. Allowed her to find the right person in Frank Doherty, apparently.

Now, I have found the person who is oh-so-right for me in so many ways. And if what Andrew's saying is true, I'm right for her in those ways, too.

We were meant to meet this summer...

Keeley's words mingle in my mind with Gran's favorite saying—*what's for you won't pass you.*

I have no idea what the future holds, but if anything is crystal clear to me in the present, it's that what's for me is spending time with Keeley for whatever time we have left. Not letting it pass without making the most of it.

"I know." Andrew nods at me. "And next time I run into Keeley, I'll tell her all of this too. Apologize to her."

I nod back. "Good."

"I'm... glad she has you."

"I'm glad I have her," I reply. Because it's true—for whatever time I have with her, I'm exceedingly grateful. "See you around, Andrew."

As I walk into Blue Notes, I take my phone out of my pocket.

> **BECKS**
>
> Are you free tonight?

The response is almost immediate.

> **KEELEY**
>
> Yes.
>
> **KEELEY**
>
> Why do you ask?

> **BECKS**
>
> Because I'd like to ask you on a second date.

> **KEELEY**
>
> I'd like to accept.

I smile.

> **BECKS**
>
> Without even knowing what we're doing?

The next message that comes through makes my smile even wider.

> **KEELEY**
>
> Not worried. If our last date was anything to go by, this one will be great craic.
>
> **KEELEY**
>
> Did I use that word right?

My response is simply the truth.

You were perfect.

Chapter Thirty-Two
Keeley

I GOT SET up on a blind date once in my freshman year of college.

It didn't go well. He was a preppy, clean-cut type—which I have no problem with, in theory—but he seemed to have a bit of a problem with the way *I* looked.

In my defense, I was nineteen. A broke student who only knew other broke students. Every date I'd been on up to that point had been sharing popcorn at a movie or getting cheese-burger spring rolls at The Cheesecake Factory and forgoing a main course or dessert in case the guy wanted to go Dutch—because I had to make sure my checking account would survive my half of the check.

So, on the day of my date—which was organized by my roommate at the time, who was lovely but the definition of a total girlie girl, AKA nothing like me—I put on my makeup and dressed the way I usually did for dates. I turned up in black leggings, Converse, and a forest green sweater

My *nice* sweater. The one without the pasta sauce stain on the sleeve.

Unfortunately, after I shook hands with my date—who

was wearing a blue button-down shirt, khakis, and Sperry topsiders—I came to find out that he'd booked us a table at Aria.

A nice restaurant not usually frequented by broke students.

I ordered a starter-sized salad and made precisely one hour and seventeen minutes of stilted conversation with the guy before thanking him for a lovely evening (which wasn't entirely accurate, but manners don't cost a thing) and getting my butt out of there as fast as possible. I never saw him again.

Now, as I look in the mirror and finish my mascara, I smile at the memory of that awkward date. Tonight is the first time since then that I'm going on a date with no idea of our destination.

But I do know *who* I'm going with. And because of that, I also know that it won't matter how I dress. What I look like.

I'm confident that, no matter what, Becks just wants to spend time with me. He has no regard for what I look like or how I'm dressed. So, I'm wearing clothes I *feel* confident in: the cute purple tee and ripped jeans I was wearing the day we got locked in the library room together. When he saw me that day, his eyes flared in a way that made my insides turn to Jell-O.

I hope to inspire the same reaction in him tonight.

When I'm done getting ready, I go to the living room to wait.

Becks was a little elusive with details, simply telling me that he'd "come get me after it gets dark." The sun's just set, so I figure that should be soon. In the meantime, I curl up on the couch with Bert the capybara.

Then, I spy the box sitting on my coffee table—the one Ezra gave me last night. Becks rescued it from the back of his truck earlier and dropped it off at my apartment with my blue

217

sweater I discarded in the vehicle, which was fluffy and dry and folded neatly and smelled like fabric softener.

Because of course Beckett washed my sweatshirt for me—he's *Beckett*. The man's always thinking of other people.

I can't hear any footsteps in the hallway, and there are no new text notifications on my phone, so with a shrug, I reach for the box and pry the lid off.

Like Ez mentioned, there are a ton of records, which makes sense as Gramps and Ezra always bonded over music. I flick through them, scanning the names of old bands I've never heard of, before finding a little metal box tucked at the bottom of a stack of sheet music.

I fish it out, dust it off.

And when I crack it open, I smile.

The first thing I see is a wedding photo of my Gramps and Grandma—him, dashing in his tuxedo with his dark hair slicked back, and her, glowing in a delicate lace veil and copious amounts of creamy satin.

And I mean *copious*. Her dress looks like it's been inflated with a bicycle pump.

But her smile is pure radiance. Glowing from the inside. And Gramps is looking at her like she's a unicorn—rare and mystical and beautiful.

The sight of it pinches under my ribcage, nipping at my heart.

My Grandma died when I was little and I barely remember her, let alone remember how she and Gramps were together. But this picture tells me a thousand words—*thousands* of words.

They were happy.

I flip the picture over. "1966" is written on the back. A few years after Noeleen and Gramps would've parted ways.

My heart beats a little quicker as I continue through the small stack of photos. They're all snapshots of my grandparents' early marriage—Grandma wearing a tea-length powder blue dress as she poses by a Ford Mustang, hands clad in short white gloves cradling her swollen belly. Gramps holding a diaper-clad baby. A dark-haired, blue-eyed toddler—my dad—sitting between them on a floral loveseat.

While my Gramps always has a photo of his and my Grandma's wedding day on his bedside table, I've never seen any of these pictures before.

I'm so engrossed that the knock on my living room window almost makes me jump out of my skin.

I look up, wide-eyed, to see the outline of Beckett's long body crouched on the fire escape.

He beckons for me to come to the window, and I jump up. Open it.

"Hey, did you get locked ou—*whoa*."

My question dies on my tongue as I look out on the fire escape.

Or, what *used* to be the fire escape. Because it now looks like something out of a 90s rom-com movie. You know, the ones set in New York apartments you have no idea how the characters can afford, that seem to set the stage for ultimate *romance in the city* vibes.

"Beckett, what on earth?" I ask.

In response, he smiles. Extends a hand to me.

I take it, and he helps me step out of my window. And when I'm standing in front of him, his eyes sweep down my outfit, and they flare just like I hoped they would.

Meanwhile, I look around in awe. Fairy lights are strung along the railings, bathing the small space where we usually sit in a golden glow. Paper lanterns surround a cozy blanket on the ground. Soft country music plays from a speaker. There's a bottle of sparkling wine and a spread of...

I laugh when my eyes land on the food.

"Wait, are those Eggos?" I ask, elated. Because when I

asked Becks how he liked the ones we bought at Spring Foods, he said something to the effect of "they're good... for toastable cardboard." But he knows *I* love them.

"They are," he confirms. "I know how much you're into breakfast for dinner, little weirdo that you are."

He's standing next to me, wearing that gorgeous bomber jacket again, and though he's smiling and teasing like he usually does, he's also rubbing the back of his neck as if he's a little embarrassed. The embarrassment—the sheer effort of all of this—is so incredible that it makes half of me want to pounce on him and kiss him senseless, half want to burst into tears.

I do neither of these things. Instead, I turn to him.

"It's perfect," I say. And I mean it. Every single last detail is so thoughtful.

"This is how I wanted to finish our date last night," he admits. "But the rain derailed my plans."

"I liked the derailment," I say softly.

His eyes meet mine, lit by the glow of the fairy lights. The heavy-lidded, heated expression he gives me tells me he's thinking about what happened between us last night, too. How magically amazing that kiss was. "Same."

The song playing on the speakers comes to an end, and I blink, breaking the moment. I'm nervous, I realize. Have a stomach full of butterflies over a boy who makes me feel like I'm beautiful.

"Shall we eat?" he asks, gesturing towards the spread of food. There's more than just Eggos, I realize. He's got bacon and sausage and eggs and a whole platter of fruit. When he sees me eyeing the strawberries, he laughs. "I had to bring something with vitamins in it to help us avert scurvy."

"Sexy," I tease, loving how he pronounces the word "vitamin" with an "it" sound in the middle instead of a long vowel like Americans do.

His eyes sparkle. "Yes, I do find the atmosphere on dates tends to be a little sexier when debilitating diseases caused by extreme nutritional deficiencies are not involved."

"That's weird," I reply. "Can I expect any further dates this summer to be nutrient-dense too?"

He places a hand on his chest. "I solemnly swear to get as many vitamins and minerals into your diet as possible until the day I board my plane."

We grin at each other, and some of my nerves settle as we take a seat on the blanket.

"What were you doing when I came to get you?" Becks asks as he pops the top on the sparkling wine and pours me a glass. He gives me that dimpled grin as he passes me the glass and adds, "I feel like I gave you a banshee-level scaring. Which I'm not going to say *wasn't* karma..."

I laugh and bump his shoulder with mine as I reach for a cinnamon Eggo. "I was actually looking through the box of Gramps's stuff that Ezra gave us."

Becks turns to look at me. In the glow of the fairy lights, his eyes are more green than hazel tonight. "Find anything?"

I swallow my bite of waffle before replying, "Nothing with Noeleen. But I did find wedding photos of Gramps and Grandma, as well as some family pictures. I'd never seen them before." I take a sip of wine and hold the liquid in my mouth for a moment, letting the cold bubbles fizz on my tongue. "They looked so happy," I tell him.

His eyes soften. "I'm glad. Your gramps seems like a good man."

Just like you are, Beckett McCarthy.

"Was Noeleen happy?" I ask hesitantly, my teeth pressing into my bottom lip. "Did she find love and happiness in her life, too?"

Beckett rests his forearms on his knees, which are drawn up in front of him. "She never stopped believing in love," he says. "Even though her marriage with my grandfather didn't work out, she loved my mom and her grandchildren something fierce. She had a lot of love surrounding her." He screws up his eyes a little. "I don't think she died having any regrets, if that's what you mean. I think she and Douglas were happy for a time together, and then both went on to live their own separate, very full lives."

"Worth the broken heart to have had that time together," I whisper, mostly to myself. Then, I hold up my glass to him in a toast. "And speaking of time together—to tonight."

"To *you*, Keeley Roberts," he counters, and his dimpled smile is everything. "My favorite neighbor of all time."

"To an incredible summer with Beckett McCarthy," I agree as we clink glasses. "Who comes a very close second to Mr. Prenchenko as a next-door neighbor."

The look Becks gives me is positively sizzling as he reaches out and runs an index finger slowly, sensually across my lips. "I would've thought that, after last night, I'd be at the top of the neighbor leaderboard. But I guess I still have some work to do."

"Ah, Mr. Prenchenko's a pretty decent kisser, too," I tease, and enjoy how appalled Beckett looks—in a really cute, jealous way—before he realizes I'm joking.

"Menace." His voice is somehow soft and rough at once, his thumb still scraping over my lip. "I didn't think I'd have to compete with a senior citizen with multiple wild boar paintings on his walls for your affections, but maybe my ego got the better of me."

The tone of his voice, his teasing lilt mixed with something overtly sensual and weighted with desire, sends my stomach into freefall.

"Last night was the best kiss of my life," I admit.

"I think we can top it," Beckett says as he takes my wine

glass out of my hand with purpose, a man on a mission as he sets it aside.

Knowing what's about to happen puts my entire body into metaphorical freefall.

Just like that date all those years ago, I'm out of my comfort zone, but this time, it's not the atmosphere or the person I'm with that's pushing me there. It's the fact that this is probably the most romantic moment of my life, and I'm here for it.

These sparks, this crazy crackling energy between us, is palpable as ever. But on a deeper level, that invisible string— the irresistible pull that's been bringing us together over and over these past few weeks—feels stronger than ever.

We're connected. And somehow, that makes the risk of letting myself experience romantic feelings for Becks feel like a lifeline.

No, a bungee cord. Because no matter how uncomfortable it is to be outside of my comfort zone—leaning into love when it's burned me before—this time, there's something to catch me when I fall.

The promise of the forever memory of what's happening here and now.

At that moment, a love song by a country artist I'm a huge fan of starts playing. An acoustic guitar, pretty words, and a gravelly voice that's fantastic but that doesn't hold a candle to Beckett's.

I can hardly believe that I'm sitting here, surrounded by fairy lights in the darkness, a man straight out of my dreams about to kiss me right as my favorite love song comes on.

"I love this song," I whisper.

Beckett shoots me a crooked smile. Extends his hand to mine.

"Would you like to dance with me?" he asks, grinning at me like he's waiting for me to shoot the suggestion down.

Which is my first inclination, but instead, I find myself doing something I never, ever do. Or even consider doing. But the moment is too perfect to let this go.

"I'd love that," I tell him, placing my hand in his outstretched palm.

I can tell by his expression that I've surprised him, but he recovers quickly, his lips tipping up at the corners. "I thought you didn't dance."

"Tonight, I do."

He doesn't waste a moment. Within seconds, he's on his feet and helping me to mine before he tugs me close to him.

My cheek rests against his chest, and his heartbeat pounds in my ears as his arms wrap around me. We sway to the music together in the darkness, something that feels almost more intimate than him kissing me senseless.

It's this kind of intimacy I want. No, I *welcome*.

After Andrew and I broke up, I didn't want to give love any time. I wanted to take control of every situation that involved my heart and avoid anything that looked in any way like love.

But the universe clearly had other plans, basically propelling me into Beckett's arms. It makes me realize that, sometimes, we don't get to make decisions about who we meet, or when or if or how we fall for someone. Or how long we might have with that person.

Sometimes, we've just got to be thankful for what we've got, in the moment we've got it. And trust that, no matter how the chips fall, the eventual outcome will be okay.

I look up at Beckett with wonder, and the look he gives me is nothing short of scalding. A searing heat that etches along my skin and sinks into my bones as he slowly, tenderly, touches my face, dragging the back of his knuckles along my jaw and making me erupt in shivers.

I'm endlessly glad that he's here with me right now. And

no matter what the future holds, we will always have this moment.

Just like Noeleen and Douglas had theirs.

And as Beckett leans down to kiss me—another head-spinning, heart-pounding, almost out-of-body-experience kiss —I realize with startling clarity that I know exactly how to end my article.

Chapter Thirty-Three
Beckett

THEY SAY baseball is the great American pastime.

And I get it. Because honestly, it feels like an eternity has passed since Cash and I took our seats in Fenway Park to watch today's Sunday matinee Red Sox game.

At first, I leaned into the excitement of it all. On my way into the stadium, I bought a baseball cap with a large red B on the front—for Boston, not Beckett—and a keyring boasting a pair of socks. Once we got inside, there were hordes of screaming fans and huge foam fingers and foot-long hot dogs—all of which I photographed and relayed to the McCarthy Clan group chat, to Callan's delight ("Lethal!").

But honestly, after three and a half hours sitting in a plastic bucket chair in the splitting sunshine, the initial high has worn off. My arms are as red as the B on my new hat, and my backside is so numb that I don't think I'm going to be able to stand up when this is finally over.

Cash, on the other hand, is having the time of his life. He's sitting forward keenly, elbows propped on his knees and his eyes shrewd under his ball cap. A ball cap which does not bear a B, like mine, because apparently, the Red Sox are a big rival of the pro team he used to play for.

As Cash watches, he's relaying all kinds of statistics that may as well be recited in Mandarin for all I'm comprehending.

Apparently, it's the ninth (or possibly ninetieth) inning, and there's a lot on the line for the person who's about to try to hit the ball with his bat.

He hits it, the stadium erupts in cheers, and I stumble a little numbly to my feet to join in with all the clapping.

Down on the field, the red-shirted players cheer and slap each other on the back in an apparent show of congratulations. I can only assume that they're all so excited because the game is over.

Finally.

As he claps, Cash leans towards me. "So, what did you think? You enjoy it?"

I give him the biggest smile my lying self can muster. "Yes."

"You're a terrible liar, Becks."

"I enjoyed the first... hour or two?" I amend, my expression remorseful.

He laughs. "That's fair. It's a long game in the first place, never mind if you don't know the rules."

"To be honest, it's not *all* the game's fault."

Tonight is my spot at Lucky 13 Studios. I'll be recording my song—*Keeley's song*—for Ezra and Keeley, herself.

I'm both nervous and excited about it all. I haven't performed any of my original music live in any capacity since Gran's passing—thought I never again would. But here we are... plus I'm still riding the high of our incredible date on the fire escape the other night—and every night we've spent kissing and cuddling on the fire escape since—and I am insanely glad she wants to be by my side when I do this.

227

I can only hope she likes the song I wrote for her. I finished it this week, and I really poured my heart into it. Which was a cathartic experience I'm immensely grateful for.

Cash nudges my arm. "Excited to get home to Keeley?"

"Yup," I respond, unabashed. "But I'm glad I came with you, for the experience. Thanks again."

"Anytime, man." We start making our way towards the exit. "So, what sports do you have in Ireland if baseball isn't a thing?"

"Gaelic football, rugby, and hurling, mainly."

"Hurling?" Cash cocks his head.

"It involves big sticks. Hard balls flying in the air." I grin. "Helmets are necessary if you still want to be in possession of all of your teeth by the end of the game."

This makes my new friend chuckle as he slaps me on the back jovially. "Ah, forget baseball, in that case—we have to take you to see a *hockey* game. I'll get us tickets for the Bruins. I think that'll be way more up your alley. "

"Sounds great," I tell him. My only ice hockey knowledge is from watching *Mighty Ducks* as a child, but it's enough to make me want to go to a game.

"Perfect. Their season starts in late October, but we could go to a preseason game in September."

I screw my nose up. "Unfortunately, I'll be gone by then."

Cash looks as genuinely disappointed as I feel. "I keep forgetting that you're leaving after the summer."

Wish I could say the same.

It's feeling all too real that I'm leaving soon, especially as, earlier today, I got an email from the school where I work with some information about policy changes for the upcoming term. Boring stuff I don't even want to think about.

Work has seemed so far away this summer, and I'm happy to keep it that way until I'm back in Ireland and actually have to face it.

Which is a little ostrich-y, I'll admit. But they're known to be nice birds, right?

Bit dim. But nice.

"Sure am... but I'm not ready to leave yet," I find myself saying.

The admission surprises me—I'm usually so good at keeping how I feel bottled up. I guess I'm still getting used to the dam Keeley's cracked open in me, just spilling things when I least expect.

It's funny—when I arrived in Serendipity Springs, my only focus was on finding out more about my Gran's time here. I saw it as a way to feel closer to her, and I think I convinced myself I'd somehow feel differently about her passing if I knew more about her story—about exactly what brought her here and why she left.

But as time has gone on and Keeley and I have put some of Noeleen and Douglas's love story together, I realize I no longer *need* those answers. While it would have been nice to know what happened to break them apart—and why she left Serendipity Springs and never once talked about it—I'm no longer disappointed that we never found out.

Because what I *have* found this summer is about so much more than just Gran.

I've learned about myself. Learned about why I've been the way I've been for the last couple of years. Numb. Aimless. Throwing myself into a job that doesn't inspire me, closing my creative channels that provoked all of my emotions. I thought that if I didn't feel anything, I could be a pillar of strength for my family to lean on, but in that process, I ended up shutting myself off from moving forward in my life. Shutting myself off from my own happiness.

Now, I've opened myself up to my feelings—to happiness—again. And it's Keeley I have to thank for it.

Because I also realize that there's something else I've opened myself up to: love.

"Serendipity Springs has a habit of doing that to people," Cash says, raising his shoulder in a shrug like he's totally unsurprised to hear that I'm not ready to go.

"What do you mean?"

"When I first moved to town, I thought I would be there temporarily."

"And then you met Nori?" I guess.

"Yes. Nori made me want to change my goals, my plans. And in the process of changing those, *I* changed. My life became something different than it had been before, or how I envisioned it being." Cash looks at me again with that shrewd gaze of his. "And I became a better man for it."

"I'm happy for you guys," I tell him.

"You know, Nori says that, lately, Keeley is happier than she's ever seen her."

"Really?" I ask, unable to hide my stupid smile.

Cash nods. "She and Andrew weren't a great match."

I think back to my surprising conversation with Keeley's ex last week—how he owned his past faults and seemed to credit Lisa with helping him work through it. Like being with the right person, the right match for him, made him a better person. Just like Cash said being with Nori made him change for the better.

"Yeah, I think she's better off without him," I agree.

"Or, just throwing something crazy out there." His expression turns playful. "Maybe she's better off with *you*, you doofus."

His words feel like wind in my sails, inflating parts of me that felt flat and lifeless for way too long.

For so long after Roisin left me, I told myself that it was because I was a bad partner. That I wasn't cut out to be with someone.

And while some of that is absolutely true—I wasn't there for her emotionally when I should have been—that doesn't mean *I* can't change. That I can't be good with, or for, someone else.

The reason I thought I made a terrible boyfriend was because I was closed off emotionally, but Keeley cracks open all of my deepest, darkest emotions without even trying. By just being *her*.

She makes me believe in better.

Believe I can be better.

Maybe it wasn't so much that I was unfit for love, but that real love simply hadn't found me yet. And what I feel for Keeley is undeniably real love.

It's a startling realization that should have been simple.

What's for you won't pass you.

Maybe the flipside is: what's not for you will just... pass.

Fate will have its way with you either way.

"Earth to Becks!" Cash waves a tan hand in front of my face, smirking. "Lost you for a moment."

I blink. "Sorry, did you say something?"

His smirk gets impossibly smirkier. "I asked what time you're meeting Keeley tonight, but you were too busy daydreaming about her to hear me."

This makes me laugh. "Busted," I admit readily. "And... seven."

He grins as we walk out of Fenway Park. "Well, then, let's hustle to get you home to your woman. And me to mine, of course."

As we walk onto the street, I look up to see no less than three magpies sitting together atop a lamppost.

Three for a girl.

And there's one girl I *really* want to see right now.

A girl who's changed my life in so many ways.

231

I turn away from the magpies with a smile and give Cash my salute. "Lead the way."

Chapter Thirty-Four
Beckett

"Okay. You all set, Becks?" Ezra is in the control room, looking at me through the glass as he leans forward to press a button to talk to me. Behind him, on the back wall, there's a spray painted "Lucky 13" logo, and beside him stands Keeley. Her hair is long and loose, thrown over one shoulder, and her eyes gleam with anticipation as she watches me.

I'm currently sitting in the live room, perched on a high-backed stool. A large condenser mic is set up in front of me, and my guitar—which I've just finished tuning—is in my lap.

The sound check is done, and it's go time.

"Ready," I tell Ezra, but my eyes are on Keeley.

Though she heard the initial tune I strung together in The Serendipity's library a while back, she hasn't heard the song since.

Every moment that I haven't spent with Keeley or teaching lessons this past week, I've been holed up in Mr. Prenchenko's apartment, working on this track. First perfecting the melody, then putting words to it.

Words that echo everything going on inside me.

"Okay, and we're recording in three, two, one..." Ezra flashes me a thumbs-up.

I nod, then strum my guitar with the opening chords of the song. As I begin to sing, nerves claw at my throat and I find myself a little terrified to play in front of her... yet, somehow, also so ready.

Because this is the final piece of the album I wrote before Gran died.

This is what was desperately missing for so long.

And so, I close my eyes and try to forget who's watching, forget where I am, as I sing my song and let myself be raw and vulnerable and in the moment.

No more refusing to feel, because falling for Keeley requires—no, *demands*—to be felt in full. Sometimes the feeling is so strong, so overwhelming, that it seems like it could swallow me whole and drown me at any moment... but I'm not reaching for any life preserver. Not scrambling to get to the surface like I usually would.

Instead, I'm diving in headfirst. Fearless.

And it's all for her. All *because* of her.

When life led me to you, the stars aligned,
A twist of fate that redefined,
In a single moment, my world was changed,
Love found me where I least expected,
I'm rearranged...

When my voice cracks over the last word of the song, it's like I'm coming out of a trance, coming up for air.

I blink my eyes open in something akin to shock.

I'm peaceful for a moment. Calm.

But when I look through the glass, my stomach drops.

Ezra's standing there, looking at me with a slightly shell-shocked expression. But I pay that no attention because my focus homes in on Keeley's departing figure.

She's leaving.

Was it too much? Did I say too much, somehow violate the unspoken terms of whatever this is that's undeniably blooming—growing—between us?

I swallow thickly. Set my guitar on the guitar stand next to me. Have I chased Keeley away? Let my feelings pour out of me so freely that I scared her into escaping?

The door to the live room flies open, and a streak of black moves across the room so fast, it's a blur.

And then, Keeley Roberts—quite literally—launches herself into my lap, wrapping herself around me like a little spider monkey.

I barely have time to register the abject relief that washes over me—nor Ezra's eyeroll before he steps out of the control room—as I pull her into my arms, holding her as tightly as she's holding me. I breathe in the sweet scent of her skin, her hair, and relish her presence. Her closeness.

She didn't leave when I showed my cards, exposed myself.

In fact, she came closer.

"Beckett," Keeley says, her voice wobbly and choked as her hands fist in the back of my t-shirt. She looks up at me, her big blue eyes rimmed with tears. "That was—"

She doesn't get a chance to finish whatever she was going to say because I'm already kissing her, tangling one hand in her hair as I pull her as close as I can.

The kiss is not eloquent or careful or measured or controlled. It's an unraveling of all these things, an explosion of sensation that sears through my body. My lips meet hers in a fervent, frenzied rush of sweetness and heat, the salty taste of her tears mingling with the mint on her breath, her finger-tips digging into my skin like she's clinging to me for dear life as I take the kiss deeper.

If my song told Keeley how I feel about her, then this is how I *show* her.

I hold nothing back, kissing her lips, her face, her neck,

losing myself in every single sensation that is *her*, committing to memory how she tastes, feels, smells. I nip at her bottom lip and then swallow the whimper that escapes her mouth as my lips close over hers again.

It's like I've unlocked some inner caveman-like instinct inside myself. A primal, almost feral, possessiveness of her that meshes with an unparalleled cherishing of her.

You're beautiful, I tell her with my hands as they tighten around her hips.

You're more special to me than I could ever tell you, I say with the hot kiss I press against her pulse point, my own pulse picking up as I feel hers jump beneath the touch of my lips.

You're everything I want, everything I never knew I needed, she moans as she threads her hands into my hair and almost desperately brings her lips back to mine.

When we finally pull apart, we're both panting. I feel her heartbeat coursing through her like a drum, pounding in tandem with mine.

I press my forehead against hers, hands cupping her face as I struggle to catch my breath. "Sorry I cut you off mid-sentence."

"That was incredibly rude, McCarthy," she says on a breathy gasp, lips curling into a sassy smile I want to kiss right off her.

"It was," I say solemnly, before I smirk. "But I'd do it again in a heartbeat."

"I'm surprisingly okay with that," she murmurs.

"Out of interest, what were you going to say?"

She laughs, rocking her forehead against mine. "If you couldn't already tell, I was a fan of your song."

"I'm a fan of you," I reply. I've turned into a walking romantic cliché, but I don't care in the least as I kiss her again, more slowly this time. More deliberately.

Unhurried and languid and oh-so-sweet.

I don't know how long we're tangled there, her in my lap, my hands tracing over the ridges of her spine as I savor every second with her. But when Ezra's voice booms through the room—*"Hey, stop defiling my recording studio, you heathens!"*—and we break apart laughing, I realize no amount of time will be enough with Keeley.

I couldn't get enough of her if I tried.

Chapter Thirty-Five
Keeley

OKAY, so I *might* have just thrown myself at Beckett.

Like, literally.

It's becoming quite the habit for me, apparently—first, when I tripped into the elevator the day we met, and now, because being on the other side of the glass when his song ended felt like way, way too far away.

I *needed* to be close to him. And so, the second he sang that last note, I practically catapulted out of the control room, raced down the hallway to the door to access the live room, all while Ezra's knowing laughter chased me.

Right now, I'm still sitting on top of Becks. But as my brother walks into the live room and I shift in an attempt to slide off his lap, he grins at me cheekily, his dimple popping as his hands tighten on my waist, holding me in place like he doesn't ever want to let go.

"Stay," he says softly, under his breath and only for me to hear, and chills erupt over my skin.

"Okay." Ezra stands in front of us with his hands on his hips. He's trying to look disgruntled, I can tell, but his lips are twitching like he's fighting a smile. "I'm just going to breeze right past that make-out session I just had the displeasure of witnessing."

I smirk at him. "You came back too soon, didn't give us enough time to wrap it up."

Becks chuckles, and the vibration of the sound moves through my body.

My big brother, however, rolls his eyes at me. "As I was saying, I'm going to breeze right past all of that, because dude!" His gaze moves to Becks, eyes shining with something akin to awe. "I've had a lot of artists come through here, had the honor of watching some of the greats perform right where you're sitting. And, hand on heart, I have never, ever seen a performance like that. Or seen anyone get everything perfect on the first take."

Becks ducks his head a little, but I don't miss the flush rising on his cheekbones. "Ah, thanks for that."

He takes one of his hands off my waist and rubs the back of his neck, a seemingly subconscious habit he does when he's bashful or being complimented.

I think it's endearing that Beckett—who was completely and utterly unabashed that my brother saw us locked in an intensely passionate embrace just a minute ago—is now embarrassed that my brother was impressed by his performance.

His *musical* performance, that is. Get your head out of the gutter. Sheesh.

Ezra's still staring at Becks. "Would you be interested in coming in tomorrow night after-hours to record some more? We could do a whole demo, if you're up for it. Something you can bring back to Ireland if you were thinking about pursuing this professionally." He grins. "Which you absolutely should be, in my humble opinion."

"I don't know about that," Beckett says with a laugh. "But

239

as for recording a demo..." He shoots me a look, then smiles. It's a peaceful, calm smile. "I'd love to."

In that moment, I get the feeling that he's recalling the dinner we had at Ezra and Mae's when I made my request for him to record *that* song so I could have it with me after he's gone. And now, he's going to make sure I have a whole demo's worth of songs.

I squeal and wrap my arms around his neck, wriggling like an overexcited puppy.

"Can I come tomorrow?" I ask Ezra.

He wags a finger at me jokingly. "Only if you promise to stay in the control room."

"Fi-ine," I whine, drawing out the syllable.

But I cross my fingers behind my back.

Beckett snorts with laughter.

We pack up and head outside, then say good night to Ezra before making our way to Beckett's truck.

"I'm so proud of you," I tell him as we climb inside. "You were amazing. And I know nothing about music or recording studios, but let me tell you, I've never seen Ezra so impressed."

"You inspired me," he replies easily, turning the key in the ignition. "You're pushing yourself to do something hard, stepping outside of your comfort zone, and tackling an article topic that brings up some uncomfortable feelings for you."

"Speaking of that, I think I've figured out how to end the piece." After our date we spent dancing together on the fire escape without a care in the world, it was like I knew exactly how to tie all of the remaining aspects of the story together without needing any more answers. "I was working on it all day today while you were watching boresball, and I'd love your take."

This makes him laugh.

"Man, it was like watching paint dry," he agrees. "Cash

240

didn't seem to mind that I was so bored though. He actually assured me I'd like hockey better."

"Pity the season doesn't start until the fall," I say with a sad smile. It's strange to think of him not being here by the time baseball season ends and hockey rolls around. "Same with basketball. I'd love to take you to a game—our team in Boston is called the Celtics."

"Why on earth would a Boston-based team call themselves Celtics?" He looks baffled.

"They have a mascot named Lucky the Leprechaun and everything."

"Between Lucky Charms and now this, I truly believe you Americans have more leprechaun-themed things than we do on the entire island of Ireland."

I grin. "And I haven't even told you about the college football team in Indiana who call themselves 'The Fighting Irish.'"

"Well now I really wish I could stick around for the fall sports season to witness some of this," he exclaims, and even though we're joking around, I get a little dash of wishful thinking. How nice that would be.

"Me too," I say softly. "That would have been fun."

"It would," he agrees, somewhat wistfully. Then he blinks and his expression clears. "So, what did you come up with for your article, then?"

"I realized that it made sense to focus on the fact that fate brought Noeleen and Douglas together for a time, and they clearly relished that time. And maybe the legends surrounding the building are true, but that fate works in a multitude of ways—its intervention might not be just for everlasting love, but for something that meets us where we need it, in that moment."

There's a moment of silence when I'm done talking, one that makes me realize that everything we've just been talking about—the upcoming fall sports schedule he won't get to witness—feels very relevant.

"I love that," he replies after a beat, and the look on his face makes me smile. "How you turned something that most people would've viewed through a sad lens into something positive. Inspirational."

"Is it okay with you that we didn't find out what happened? Why Noeleen left? Because even with the article being done, we can keep searching."

Becks shakes his head. "It's totally okay with me to leave things as they are. I like the idea of not focusing on things ending, but on the process of growth and change instead."

"I think I'm going to submit it tonight." I look up at him with big eyes. "Scary. But I think I'm ready. Do you want to read it?"

"Of course I want to read it! But I want to read it on the internet, with your name and picture next to it, when you get the job and they publish it."

His belief in me getting this article published—getting the job—is everything.

"I'm really happy right now."

"You look happy as a tiny little clam," he agrees solemnly.

This makes me cackle.

But he's not wrong.

I had such a jaded opinion of love going into this article after Andrew. I wanted to reject everything about the lore and legends surrounding The Serendipity because I couldn't make sense of love, so therefore, I couldn't make sense of leaning into the legends.

Yet, somewhere on this journey, I fell head-over-heels into a summer love I didn't believe would—*could*—happen to me.

And it's clear that the building where we live was drawing us together so we could experience this feeling together.

It's magical. Special. Beautiful. Burning bright.

If only for a time.

And that's how I concluded my Evoke article—that an investigation into an old town legend about a building in which I happen to currently reside has made me a believer in love and magic.

Because love can enter your life in different ways, at different times. And maybe the answer isn't how love begins or ends, but the journey on which it takes you. How it shapes you and molds you and makes you grow. Changes you, for the better.

And after spending this summer with Beckett, I will always have that piece of magic with me, no matter what the future holds.

Chapter Thirty-Six
Keeley

"MMMPF," I mutter as I roll my head against a warm, firm surface that smells like clean laundry and Irish Spring.

"Morning, sleepyhead," Becks replies, and my eyes flutter open to see that I must have dozed off plastered to his chest. Leaving behind a drool line, apparently.

With this mortifying realization, I shoot up to a seated position on the couch, wiping my mouth with the back of my hand. "How long was I asleep?"

It can't have been too long. It's still light outside, and the end credits of *Leap Year*—he had never seen it, and I obviously needed to right that terrible wrong—are rolling on the TV.

I'm not usually a napper, but I guess all the late nights on the fire escape are catching up with me. The rest of August has flown by, with Beckett recording more music and squeezing in some last lessons around spending as much time together as we can.

We've been pretty much inseparable—going for dinners and walks and watching movies and feeding the cranky ducks at Oldford Park before we retreat to the fire escape every night and sit under the stars together.

But every single day, I fight letting myself feel sad about a new reminder that our time is coming to a close. A few days back, he took the truck to get detailed as a thank you to Mr. P for letting him use it. Yesterday, I walked into his apartment to find that he'd moved Mr. P's couch back to its original position. This morning, I spotted an open suitcase on his bedroom floor, closet doors open like he's beginning to pack up his life here.

Like I always knew he would.

Now, Beckett shifts in his seat, stretching his chest and the arm that was around me. It hits me that he must have been sitting stock still while I used him as a pillow, bearing through being uncomfortable so as to not wake me.

The realization of this is... well, nothing short of butter-fly-inducing.

Seriously, I think I might be obsessed with this guy. I'm not sure what they put in the water in Ireland, but let me tell you, that country produced a man who should be the proto-type for all men in the world. MIT should be studying Beckett McCarthy for potential cloning purposes.

But then, he has to go and spoil all my thoughts of cloning him by grinning at me wickedly. "You were snoring soundly for, oh, about an hour."

"Snoring?!" I demand, a blush rising to my cheeks.

He smirks. "Yeah, you should get that checked out. Real guttural stuff, like a bulldozer at work. Or a jackhammer. The walls were practically shaking, and then you started talking in your sleep..."

"Did not!" I squeak, my face crimson.

"Did too." His eyes dance as he stretches both arms above his head, causing his (drool-stained) t-shirt to ride up at the bottom and give me a tantalizing glimpse of taut, muscled stomach. "You were saying something about how Beckett McCarthy is the sexiest man you've ever known. Which I'd actually love for you to elaborate on, now that you've rejoined us for the afternoon—"

I smack him with a couch pillow.

In response, he tackles me, swatting the pillow out of the way before easily pinning my wrists with one hand as his other hand tickles the sensitive spot under my ribs. I squeal and try to squirm away from him, cackling with laughter as we playfight and tease... and one thing leads to another, of course, and we end up tangled in each other's arms, him kissing me in a way that burns me from within.

We kiss until our lips are swollen, and the adoring look Beckett gives me as he presses a kiss to my forehead positively melts my heart.

"I'd better go," he says grudgingly. "I need to shower and change before we leave."

I nod. This evening, we're going to the fair—which is now open for business, marking the official end of summer. But first, we're having dinner with Cash and Nori at a local pizza place. Since Becks and Cash went to a Red Sox game, they've been almost as inseparable as Becks and me. So, Nori and I decided that a double date was necessary before Beckett leaves.

And tonight just so happens to be Beckett's last official night here.

He leaves tomorrow evening. Which I've put off thinking about.

A selfish part of me whispers that I have so little time left with Beckett, I don't want to share him during these precious moments.

A more grown-up, sensible part of me knows I can't think that way or I'll be devastated when he leaves, despite the conclusion I came to in my article and all the measures I've taken to protect myself on that front.

I remind myself that I wouldn't do anything differently on the road to get here. I'm glad I jumped in headfirst, went all in this summer, because to know Beckett is to love him, and this time together has been a privilege.

"I'll come get you in about an hour?" Beckett stands and grabs his phone from the coffee table.

"Sounds perfect," I reply, trying not to think about the fact that the drool stain on his chest is likely the reason he needs a shower.

My phone rings not long after he leaves, and I reach for it, assuming that he's calling to say something dumb or funny or intended to make me blush.

"Miss me already?" I ask as I swipe to answer without looking at the Caller ID.

I'm shocked when Freya's laugh bubbles from the phone speaker. "I miss you every day, my dear. Every single day that I walk into the OneWorld offices and sit at my desk, I think *wow, work would be so much better if Keeley were here, too.*"

"Ahh, sorry!" I cover my eyes with my free hand. "I thought you were someone else."

"I figured. But my declaration still stands." My boss laughs. "I do miss you."

I smile. I haven't chatted much with Freya lately—aside from her laughing at the horoscopes I submitted last week for the Serendipity Springs website and a quick call we had to go over her notes on a town council segment I was adding to the site.

At that point, she let me know Nisha had received my article submission, but I haven't heard anything about the Evoke position since. Which I figured might happen. These things can take time.

And no matter if I get the job or not, I'm comfortable with what I submitted.

"Miss you too, Freya," I say with a laugh. "One of these days, I'll drive up to Boston for the day and write my horoscopes and traffic reports from the comfort of your cushy office. Deal?"

"Orrrrr," Freya says coyly, drawing out the word so it has three syllables instead of one. "You and I could do lunch. Every day."

"What?" I ask dumbly.

Freya laughs in delight. "I'm putting you on speakerphone here, Keels. I have someone with me who'd love to deliver this news herself."

"Hi, Keeley, it's Nisha!"

I gasp. Like, audibly.

And promptly attempt to turn said gasp into a cough so I don't come across as a rabid stalker-slash-fan. I'm sure that's not the best look in a potential new employee.

Luckily for me, Nisha laughs. "I loved your article."

"You did?" I ask dumbly.

"I did. It was a great take on the legend, super unexpected —it took me by surprise, then made me think. Which is what we always aim to do with our content here: *evoke* something in people. You're a talented writer, Keeley. And the story earned you a job as the new full-time staff writer at Evoke. If you'd like it, that is."

"If I'd like it?" I repeat—but in a much more yell-y, overexcited tone.

"I'll take that as a yes?"

"Yes!" My stomach is in a knot of anticipation.

"I'll send you an email with an official offer and all the details. But for now, consider this an unofficial welcome to the Evoke team!"

It's all I can do not to squeal.

I did it!

I landed the job.

I can't wait to tell Beckett.

"One thing I am curious about, though," Nisha says, cutting through my mental celebratory breakdance of excitement. "For my own knowledge, what happened?"

"What happened?" Jeez, I'm literally parroting everything this woman says right back at her.

"With your grandfather and the handsome Irish guy's grandmother?"

I pause for a beat, wracking my brain. "I never said he was handsome in the article!"

"Oh, please, Keeley." Nisha laughs. "As writers, we all know the importance of subtext. It was clear you thought so."

I can't help but laugh, too. "We never actually found out what happened. But like I said in the article, the ending wasn't the important part."

"And what about you and the aforementioned handsome grandson?" Freya asks, and I can hear the wicked smile in her voice. "Are *you* together?"

I shift uncomfortably. "For now."

"Until he goes back to Ireland?"

I swallow a little thickly. "Yup. He's moving back to Ireland, and I guess I'm moving to Boston. Like for Noeleen and Douglas, our time will come to an end."

And the ending doesn't matter, because we've had this summer, I remind myself internally.

"Plenty more manfish in the sea!" Freya declares without missing a beat.

I laugh, just like I laughed when she said this exact thing about Andrew. But this time, the laughter is so forced, it sticks in my throat and brings tears to my eyes.

As I say my final thank yous and hang up, I feel an overwhelming rush of bittersweet emotions.

I'm delighted. Proud. Happy.

But I'm also sad, because the inevitable that's been shadowing me all summer, hanging over me like an insistent raincloud, is now about to pour: *Beckett's leaving tomorrow.*

I thought that if I could put this in a "summer romance" box, I could put a lid on that box after he leaves, and keep myself from getting hurt. But I can no longer deny that my already achy heart gets sadder with every second that ticks by until his inevitable departure.

And while I know, in my heart, that the hurt is worth it, it doesn't make it hurt any less.

Chapter Thirty-Seven
Beckett

"To Keeley!" we cheer as we hold our glasses up and clink them together.

"Thank you so much, you guys," she says, smiling.

Cash has a beer, Keeley and Nori have wine, but tonight, I'm sticking with Coke, because I want to be entirely lucid for our date.

Well, double date. But at least I'll get Keeley alone at the fair later.

I smile at the memory of her sleeping on my chest earlier, making little snuffling sounds as she dreamt, and I etch it into my mind so I can remember it forever.

I'm beyond proud of her for getting the job—I knew she would—but it also hits me viscerally. I knew the end was coming, but the confirmation that she has the job in Boston makes me realize our time is running out.

When she came running into my—*Mr. Prenchenko's*—apartment to tell me that she'd just gotten off the phone with her current boss and new boss-to-be, I gathered her in my arms and swung her around before kissing her forehead and telling her she's amazing and I'm beyond happy for her.

It was a half truth. I *am* happy for her. But I'm also sad for *us*.

I felt like a scumbag, a total hypocrite, for having those mixed emotions over something so important to her. I guess maybe a part of me thought that we could keep pretending summer would last forever.

But it won't.

So we can't.

Despite my hidden mixed emotions, dinner goes well. The pizza is incredible. Cash and Nori are a really fun couple. And Keeley and I hold hands under the table like we're teenagers on a first date.

A pretty perfect evening, once I successfully redirect my mind and focus on the here and now.

Roisin and I never really had couple friends. We hung out with Aoife and her husband Declan a few times over the years, but Aoife's (admittedly) slightly abrasive personality bugged Roisin.

As Cash tells me about the kids' baseball camp he's starting, I find myself thinking about how Keeley would probably love Aoife. Find her rough edges funny and appreciate how real she is.

"That sounds incredible," I tell Cash honestly. "If I were staying longer, I'd totally offer to help out."

Cash smirks. "At coaching baseball?"

I blanch. "Hell, no. But I'd make a mean administrator, I'm sure."

The girls laugh at this, and I squeeze Keeley's hand under the table.

"If someone had told me a few months ago that I'd be on a double date with Nori and Keeley and Keeley's new man, I would've laughed in their face," Cash says as he takes a swig of his beer.

Keeley wrinkles her nose at him. "Why's that so hard to believe?"

Cash smiles and slings an arm around his girlfriend. "Because a relationship was the last thing I was looking for, but then, I found the woman of my dreams."

"Hush!" Nori swats his arm playfully, but it's impossible to miss the pleased glow that flushes over her cheeks. "And found isn't the word I'd use," she says with a giggle.

"How did you two get together?" I ask.

Nori's eyes swipe across to Keeley and she props her elbows on the table. "You know what's crazy?"

"How Cash is so obsessed with you that he'd probably buy you a unicorn if you asked, but you're still settling for pizza?" Keeley fires back with a grin.

Nori pokes her tongue out at her. "My unicorn is in the mail, I'll have you know. And no, what I was going to say was that I've never told you the entire story, Keeley."

"Oh?" Keeley tilts her head.

"I thought you'd think I was crazy, at the time. Man, I thought I was going crazy at first, too. But now that you're with Beckett, I think you'll understand."

"Understand what?" she asks.

"You know when I was going on all those dates from that dating app? Well, when I got back to The Serendipity after every date, I'd see myself in the mirror holding hands with Cash. At first, I thought I was seeing things because I was so stressed with buying Serendipi-Tea at the time." Nori shakes her head in wonder, her eyes a little glazed. "But actually, it was like the building was telling me I should be with him. Like it *knew*, somehow."

Under the table, Keeley suddenly squeezes my hand. Tight. I swallow, squeezing back.

Meanwhile, Nori looks from Keeley, to me, and back to

Keeley again. "I was going to tell you, but I thought you'd take me to the doctor to get my head examined."

Keeley laughs, and to most people, it might sound genuine, but I sense the strained note to her laughter. "You're right. I probably would have."

Nori gives her a quizzical look. "But you and Beckett got locked in the elevator together and on the fire escape together this summer..."

"Not to mention the library," I say.

Cash grins. "Hey, we didn't know about that one."

And we certainly won't be telling you about when the building locked us outside in the rain, I think with a smile.

"Maybe the building was telling you guys something, too," Nori says, her voice tinged with something akin to hope.

Keeley screws up her eyes for a second before she smiles. "A few months ago, I *would* have told you that you were crazy, you're right about that. But honestly, I've opened myself up to the idea of something bigger than us playing a part in shaping our lives. Maybe the building, maybe fate, I don't know... all I know is that it gave Becks and me the best summer together." She looks at me, her blue eyes luminous as she adds, "It was life-changing."

Life-changing, indeed.

Because there's no denying that I've fallen head-over-heels in love with this incredible woman who has changed my life.

My mind suddenly jumps back to something Cash said after the baseball game last week—how being in Serendipity Springs and falling for Nori changed him.

I get it.

For way too long, I've used the job security of a career that doesn't inspire me as a crutch, a security blanket I relied on because I refused to acknowledge how I really felt, what I really wanted.

But being here this summer has changed me, too. Made

254

me think about how I can take control and change my life, like Cash did.

Like Keeley's currently doing by taking this new position.

In many ways, I can see myself staying here. A fantasy part of my mind has already quit my job back home and asked Ezra to take on full-time lessons. Has started apartment hunting. Has told Keeley how I really feel about her and has asked her to be my girlfriend and is planning trips to visit her in Boston...

I shake my head, pushing the fantasy away as a waitress deposits what appears to be an entire pan's worth of tiramisu in front of me.

I will never get used to the portion sizes in this country.

"Thank you," I tell her, staring at the seven pounds of dessert.

"Yum!" Keeley says, unfazed as she digs her spoon straight into the Everest of whipped cream.

I can literally feel my eyes soften as I look at her. I never considered staying here in Serendipity Springs as a potential option before, and I find that the thought is still turning over in my head, marinating there, as Cash and I split the bill and we all walk outside.

It's a pleasant night. Cool and crisp and with a hint of lingering warmth from the day. Keeley and I walked to the restaurant together earlier, her happily chattering about the logistics of moving and renting a U-Haul and apartment hunting, and me watching her as she spoke, soaking her in.

When we get to Cash's vehicle, he gestures towards it. "You sure you guys don't want us to drop you off at the fairgrounds?"

"No, thanks," I say at the exact same time as Keeley says, "Nope! We're good."

We smile at each other. I get the feeling she wants to be alone with me almost as much as I want to be alone with her.

Nori hugs Keeley as Cash and I shake hands, and then Nori gives me a hug, too.

"You make her happy. Remember that," she says softly in my ear as she pulls away.

The words wash over me.

Keeley makes me happy, too. Beyond compare. So much so that I'm considering literally changing my life for her. And the thought doesn't scare me.

As Cash and Nori jump in his vehicle and drive off, I take Keeley into my arms. Kiss the top of her head. Finally alone together.

"Ready?" I ask, my hand reaching for hers.

"Born ready."

We walk down the darkened street, hand in hand. A sprinkling of stars glow above us, and though the night is warm, she shivers.

I quickly shrug off my jacket and drape it over her shoulders, putting my arm around her and pulling her close in an attempt to share my body heat. "If you're cold, I can order us a rideshare."

"No, I'm fine. Just thinking."

She's smiling, but she really is uncharacteristically quiet right now, so I ask, "Penny for your thoughts?"

She hesitates for a moment. "Don't you think it's weird what Nori said, about the building kind of... bringing her and Cash together?"

"Not really."

The Serendipity threw Keeley and me into numerous moments of forced proximity that ultimately led to love. It helped us discover that our grandparents had been brought together by the building, too.

I smile at her teasingly. "I mean, you did just write an article about how that kind of lore surrounds the building, and that it's steeped in legends about love... right?"

"Right." She nods, her expression slightly frustrated, like she's struggling to articulate her thoughts. I give her space, and after a beat she adds, "After writing the article and all the exploration on the legend we've done this summer, it's undeniable that there's some kind of truth to it. The building somehow plays some kind of role, helping fate or meddling in matchmaking or whatever. I just mean..." she stops. Swallows. Winces.

For a moment, I think she's going to leave her thought unfinished.

But then, in a voice so small, I can barely make it out, she says, "I just mean, I'm sad that what the building did for *us* was temporary."

I look at her, really look at her, soaking in her earnest blue eyes and messy black hair and flushed cheeks. The wrinkle in her brow and downturn to her lips.

And the only thought that jumps to the forefront of my mind as my eyes meet hers is: *what if it didn't have to be?*

Chapter Thirty-Eight
Keeley

I'M FINE.

I'm totally, completely, utterly fine.

The last moments of lingering twilight fade just as the fairground lights up the night with a million glowing, flashing bulbs that twinkle through the darkness.

The sounds of canned music and the delighted squeals of children high on sugar and adrenaline mingle with the scent of fried dough and cotton candy as Beckett and I go through the motions of a great final date night together.

An *excellent* date night, in fact.

Beckett pulls me from food stand to food stand, exclaiming over offerings that are strange and wonderful in his eyes, but regular fair food in mine: Funnel cakes, Dole Whip, giant corn dogs on sticks, giant soft serves with jimmies, and of course, deep-fried Oreos.

"Come on." Becks tugs my hand and pulls us into the lengthy Oreo line-up, wrapping his arm around me and pulling my back against his chest while we wait. His chin comes to rest on my head, and I smile.

"Are you using me as a headrest?"

"I can't help it that you're the perfect tiny height to do so." He chuckles, and I feel the sound reverberate through his chest. "In fact, are they even going to allow you to ride the tilt-a-whirl?"

"Since I was twelve, I'll have you know," I squawk indignantly. He kisses the top of my head, and I soak in the sensation of his lips brushing my hair, his body heat warming mine. *I'm fine.*

When we finally get the prized Oreo in hand, Becks takes one bite and proclaims it "an atrocity" and "a crime against mankind."

I laugh and declare him "tastebud challenged" as I eat the rest.

He watches me, wiping a smudge of sugar from the edge of my lip with his thumb.

We play carnival games—Beckett proves to have an excellent arm despite his claims earlier tonight that he'd make for a terrible baseball player—and he wins me a giant stuffed elephant by knocking down a stack of cans. I name him Ernie and declare he's to be best friends with Bert the capybara.

Beckett threads his fingers through mine. "Wanna ride the Ferris wheel?" He grins at me. "I hear it's very romantic and cozy and hardly anyone has thrown up on it this year."

"Dream date, right here," I tell him, but my heart clenches a little behind my smile.

I'm totally fine.

We board the ride, and as Beckett's arm tightens around me and the wheel begins to move, the soundtrack in my head switches. *I'm fine* dissolves into *I love him.*

I love him I love him I love him I love him.

Those three little words are on a loop, playing on repeat in my mind as we go around.

When the wheel stops at the top, Beckett kisses me softly.

So sweetly and tenderly and carefully that, for some morti-fying reason, I start to cry.

And, like, not a pretty, dainty cry. This is floodgates opening.

"I never cry," I tell Beckett, furiously swiping away the tears. "Not even when I have terrible PMS."

"It's okay to cry," he replies, gently placing his thumbs under my eyes to swipe away my mascara stains. He smiles. "Even when you're PMSing."

"I'm kind of a more wanting to burn the world down PMSer," I confess.

Beckett smiles at me like I'm the center of the entire universe. "Why doesn't that surprise me for a second?"

"Because you know me," I say with a snort-hiccup-cry-laugh, and he draws me close.

He doesn't ask me whether I'm okay, or what's wrong, like he can somehow sense what I need in this moment—not to talk, to just feel what I'm feeling. He lets me snuggle into his chest and cover him in snot and tears and mascara for the rest of the rotation of the wheel.

I feel a mixture of mortification and absolutely not caring what people think when we exit the ride, me with red eyes and black tracks all down my face, him holding Ernie. Which earns us a very strange look from the ride operator.

"Everything okay there, Miss?" he asks me, frowning at Beckett.

No.

I sniffle. "Yes."

The guy leans forward, dropping his voice. "You need me to call someone for you?"

"Huh?" I stare at him blankly. "Who? And why?"

Beckett, beside me, balks.

"Keels," he says gently. "I think this guy thinks *I'm* the reason you're crying."

"But you *are* the rea... oh my gosh no, he didn't make me cry by being mean to me or something!" I exclaim as the penny finally drops. "I'm crying because tonight is our last date, not because he's a man-jerk."

"Oh!" The ride operator looks beyond relieved. "Good. Good."

"But thank you for being so concerned and willing to help a woman out if she needs it." Beckett shakes the guy's hand, then winks at him. "Luckily, in this case, Keeley here is a bit of a... how do you say it... *riot grrrl* who could probably take me in a fight."

"Hey!" I swat Becks's arm, laughing in spite of myself.

"Ah, I see," the guy says, looking bemused as Beckett waggles his eyebrows at me, eyes glinting.

I know what he's doing.

He's trying to make me smile. Make me laugh. Balm my tears with stupid humor and inside jokes.

It's working, somewhat.

I slip my hand into his as we walk away. "Shall we get another fair snack?" My tone is forced in its brightness.

"Do you want to go home?" he asks gently in response.

In such a short time, he knows me so well. "I do. Do you?"

That lopsided dimpled grin moves slowly over his face. "I do. Frankly, I've had enough of sharing you with other people, and I'm thinking it's high time for the fire escape."

Last time for the fire escape, I correct mentally.

Tears prick my eyes for the second time tonight. I'm a mess. "Nowhere else I'd rather be."

Chapter Thirty-Nine
Keeley

W HEN WE GET BACK to The Serendipity, I unlock the door to my apartment and head straight to the window so I can unlock it and climb out, knowing Becks is right next door doing the exact same thing.

Quick as a cat, I maneuver onto my desk and grip under the window. I tug at it, pulling it upwards.

It doesn't budge.

I tug again.

Stuck.

What on earth?

For a moment, I wonder if The Serendipity has a sick sense of humor because, all summer, it's been locking me places with Beckett. But tonight, of all nights, it decides to try to stop me from getting to him?

No. No way.

I pull again, and this time, the window flies open. So suddenly and with such force that I stumble backwards and knock the box of Gramps's things from where it sits on my desk.

"Oh, come on!" I say in exasperation as papers and records go tumbling every which way.

Beckett's form appears outside the window.

"Everything okay in here?" he asks, ducking to poke his head inside. Before waiting for my answer though, he easily vaults through my open window—way more cat-like and graceful than I will ever be—and kneels to start cleaning the mess.

"It is now," I say with a goofy grin. This man, I tell you.

As Beckett and I stack everything neatly back in the box, his fingers linger on a faded LP cover.

I peer over his shoulder at the record, which is called "Moondance" by some old guy named Van Morrison.

He smiles fondly at it, nostalgia sweeping over his features. "This was one of my Gran's favorites. She used to play it all the time when we were kids."

"No way," I say. "Gramps used to play this all the time, too. In fact, I'll maybe bring it with me tomorrow when I go see him. It might cheer him up."

Gramps hasn't been too well lately, so Ez and I decided to go see him in the morning. I kind of wanted to ask Becks to come with us, too, but I know he'll need to pack.

Pack.

The word hits me like a punch to the gut.

"Definitely," Beckett replies. "You should do that."

He passes me the record and then pops the lid back on the box. The two of us then climb out to the fire escape.

I don't prop my window open like I usually do. In fact, once I'm out, I shut it almost defiantly, like I'm volleying a metaphorical ball into The Serendipity's metaphorical court.

Your move, building. I dare you.

Outside, we sit down, and I rest my head on Beckett's shoulder, as I've done so many times over the past few weeks.

I'm still clad in his jacket, and I savor the feel of his warm presence and comforting smell.

"You feeling a little better now?" he asks me softly.

I nod and shake my head at once. "Mmpf."

"I get that," he says.

"It was a good idea to come home instead of staying at the fair. I was about to flood the place," I joke, trying to lighten the mood.

He matches my tone. "Jeez, Keeley, after that Ferris wheel ride, there was a second when I thought I might have to spend the remainder of my time in America in jail."

"If they locked you up, you wouldn't be able to get on a plane tomorrow night," I say.

This is also meant to sound jokey. Light.

It doesn't.

"If it helps, I kind of wanted to cry, too." Beckett smiles at me softly, his eyes indeed a little misty. "Can't believe tonight's our last night. I wish I could stay."

"I wish you could too." I look at my hands. "People leaving always makes me feel a bit messy inside, and I feel extra messy tonight."

"I understand."

Embarrassed, I look away. I hate being vulnerable like this, showing my emotional cards.

But Becks reaches over and puts a gentle hand on my chin, tilting my head so I'm looking straight into those amazing hazel-green eyes. "Tell me what's going on in that beautiful head of yours, Keeley."

My chest tightens. "I don't think you even want to begin to know."

"Try me," Beckett says lightly. "You can always tell me anything, Keeley."

I hesitate again—my eyes still fixed on his—and I realize I

really can trust him, really can bare all my vulnerability. All my inner ugly.

"Remember I mentioned that my parents had a messy divorce?" I begin hesitantly.

"I do."

"After the divorce, my mom was so hurt, so cut up, that she didn't want to be around my dad anymore. *Couldn't* be around him, in fact. Even the risk of running into him around town was too much for her. So she left."

I hesitate, my breath a little shaky. I hate this story and never tell it, but Beckett's silence, giving me space to talk and share, helps me continue with the next, most painful part.

"She gave up Ezra and me willingly. Handed full custody to my dad and walked away."

Beside me, Beckett stills, statue-like, as he absorbs this.

The admission hurts to speak aloud—that the one person who was meant to love me most, love me unconditionally, left me.

Chose to retreat to her hometown three states away over staying with her kids. Her only son and daughter. Removed herself from our lives entirely.

I know now that my mother was going through some depression and anxiety issues at the time. I understand that, logically. But my heart still squeezes every time I think about the fact that she begged my dad not to leave her. And then, when he was no longer part of the equation, I was in turn easy to leave. Or at least, easier to leave than I should have been.

And that fact has become like a root buried so deep in me, so ensconced in shame and unworthiness, that I've never tried to dig it out, but simply tried to bury it deeper.

"I guess she didn't really want us, when it came down to it."

My eyes burn as I pick at my fingernails, the remnants of my shameful admission still ringing in my ears.

265

When Beckett finally speaks, his voice is rough. "I'm so sorry, Keeley."

I shrug. "It is what it is. But when she left, she broke my heart."

"That's awful, Keeley. Truly awful. I'm so sorry you went through that."

"It was a long time ago, but I guess I still get triggered when people leave—it was a huge step for me to let that lie in my article about Noeleen and Douglas, to not focus on her leaving, but on the good times they had. Because that's what I wanted—*want*—to do with you, now. Don't cry because it's over, smile because it happened, right?"

"Like I said earlier, it's okay to cry. What you went through was awful." He pauses. Swallows. Clears his throat. "But I've been thinking about what you said earlier tonight—and what if this didn't have to be temporary? What if I didn't have to leave?"

I smile sadly. "But you do. You've got your job. Your home. Your family. A niece or nephew on the way. You've even got a demo to bring back home to kickstart the crazy successful music career I want you to have."

"But I've got you, here in Serendipity Springs. And what *I* want is to try to make this thing between us into something more. Something that goes beyond the summer."

These are words I simultaneously ache to hear and ache because I hear them.

Because it's not enough. *I'm* not enough to make a person change their entire life plans.

History has shown me that. And even though this summer has taught me not to focus on the ending, I know the ending is still inevitable.

If Beckett stayed here and we stayed together, I'd live in fear. That dark ugly root in me would twist as it reminded me, over and over, that I was the wrong choice, and one day he'd realize that, and he'd leave.

That's why it had to be just for the summer. Temporary. Neatly in its own little box.

Because, that way, we can never break each other's hearts, like Noeleen and Douglas. Like my dad broke my mom's. Like my mom shattered mine.

"It has to be this way," I say softly, and the ugly words stick in my throat uncomfortably even after I speak them aloud. Festering there, like a chokehold. "I'm moving to Boston for my job, and you're going home to Ireland."

He nods, and in the darkness, his hand finds mine. He squeezes.

"I love you," he says.

My heart flips over. It's both too soon and too late for these words, and I don't want this to go any deeper between us than it already has when I know that it has to end here and now, but I can't hold back the words as I say, "I love you, too."

That much will never change.

"C'mere," he says, pulling me towards him. And then, he gathers me into his arms and holds me tight.

Like he's never going to let go.

But I know he is, because I've told him this is what we have to do.

Because he's Beckett.

I lean into his embrace, silent tears streaming down my face as I let him hold me, one last time.

Chapter Forty
Beckett

"Okay Beckett, I've got an important question for you," Callan says, his dead serious expression over my laptop screen, where I've got FaceTime open.

"Fire away," I say, assuming he's going to ask about my flight details so he can pick me up from the airport tomorrow.

Tomorrow. As in, I'm supposed to get on a flight tonight.

It came so fast.

Way too fast.

"When you get back on Irish soil, will you be getting yerself a spice bag or a fry first?"

Eoin rolls his eyes spectacularly at Callan, like he's been mortally offended. "Forget spice bags, you dose, he's clearly going for a Supermac's."

"I'd get a wee gravy chip from Grainne's, so I would." Aoife licks her lips.

"Wise up, all of you," Niamh says, hand on her chest like she's clutching imaginary pearls. "He'll be wanting a fish supper."

"Spice bag," Callan insists staunchly.

They all stop bickering long enough to swivel their heads to peer at me like an expectant line of meerkats.

"Well?" Aoife demands.

"Honestly, all I really want is a proper cup of tea. The tea here is shocking."

It's the wrong thing to say, and I realize it the second it leaves my mouth, as chaos inevitably ensues, all four of my siblings yelling over each other about the "disgrace" of America having bad tea, and how they could have shipped my poor, deprived self an extra-large box of Barry's Gold Blend if I'd only asked.

If there's one rule for the entire island of Ireland, it's that a cup of tea is appropriate in all circumstances and can cure most ailments, up to (and sometimes including) murder.

Cold? Warm up with some tea.

Heartbroken? Sure, tea will cheer you up.

Committed a heinous crime against humanity? Whack the kettle on.

So, the thought of not having tea as a magic catch-all is beyond comprehension to the rest of the McCarthys. Although right now, I'm painfully aware that no amount of proper Irish tea could soothe my aching heart at the thought of leaving Keeley.

Last night on the fire escape was painful. It physically hurt me to hear about her mom leaving her as a child. After she went through that—and then having her long-term boyfriend leave her for another woman—I can totally understand why she was so upset.

I can even understand why she says it has to be this way between us. Why she shut me down when I told her I want to make our relationship last past the summer.

Not that it makes it sting any less.

269

Or makes it feel any less wrong that I'm just supposed to walk away after that.

This morning, she's going to see her Gramps at Silver Springs with Ezra—he apparently hasn't been well for a couple of days. I wanted to come with them, but it felt a little inappropriate to ask. So, I told her I'd meet her later, after I'm done packing, to say goodbye.

I paste on a smile and address Niamh, "I'll have all the Barry's tea I want in a couple days."

Aoife narrows her eyes at me. "Will you, though?"

"Well, seeing that I'm due to get on a plane and fly home, I'm going to go with yes," I say patiently, pointing to my neatly packed suitcase and guitar case on the couch beside me.

"Ach don't tell me that's still happening," Callan groans.

"Glad to hear you missed your big brother so much that you're over the moon excited for his homecoming," I reply, all sarcasm in an attempt to veil the fact that I am trying (and failing) not to be offended.

"Course we miss you, you big eejit," Eoin says. "We just thought you weren't coming back."

"We assumed you were calling us today to tell us that," Niamh adds, wagging a finger at me. "I told this lot when you refused to get me that Oprah signature that you were too busy kissing on that American girl next door. But I forgive you because I'm happy you finally found someone who's willing to kiss your sorry self."

"I'm not sure how to respond to that," I say.

Niamh shrugs. "'Thank you' would do nicely."

"Also, what makes you think I've been kissing the girl next door?"

"Because you light up like a bloody blowtorch every time you talk about her," Callan says.

"I haven't told you *that* much about her."

Every time I've caught up with my family, I've merely filled them in on the things I've been doing. Keeley just happened to be a big part of many of those things.

"Catch yourself on!" Aoife cries. "You've been walking around for the past two years with a face like a slapped arse on you, and the second you met this girl, you're suddenly grinning from ear to ear like the Joker."

"Keeley and I spent a lot of the summer together," I say slowly. "But we're from opposite sides of the Atlantic. I have a job and a family back home, and she has a job coming up here in Boston. We're both leaving."

I'm just repeating the facts of why it apparently has to be this way. Maybe if I speak them aloud, they'll seem more believable.

It doesn't work.

"Beckett Patrick McCarthy," Mam interrupts, striding into the frame out of nowhere.

"Hi, Mam."

"Hello, son," she practically harrumphs. "Now, I have just one thing to ask you."

Finally, someone who wants my flight information so I'm not stuck taking sixteen buses back to Mayo from Dublin airport.

"Yes Mam?"

"With all due respect, my dear boy, have you lost your ever-loving mind?"

"I—" I stare at the screen as Mam claps her hands and orders my siblings to skedaddle.

"It's my house, Mam!" Aoife protests.

Mam puts her hands on her hips and stands to her full Irish Mammy height of about five foot nothing, looking scarier and more intimidating than a six foot five Viking in

271

the process. "Do I look like someone who gives a flying rat's behind about whose house this is? Out with you, the lot of you!"

My siblings make a hasty retreat, which is smart of them.

I'm smug for about half a millisecond before the wrath is directed at me.

"So?" Mam demands, hands still planted firmly on her round hips.

"Mam, I have no idea what you're talking about."

"I'm talking about the fact that we've been over the moon to see you happy after watching you miserable for so long. And now, you're planning to walk right back into your miserable life as if this summer has taught you nothing!"

"Miserable's a harsh word," I say with a forced smile.

Mam doesn't return it. Instead, she levels me with a *look*. "It's true. I know how close you were to your gran, but after she passed, you retreated into yourself where nobody could reach you. Since you've been there in Serendipity Springs, it's like you've been brought back to life."

"I know, Mam," I say with a nod. "I have been. And I'm sorry I was so closed off. I should have been more present. When I get back, I promise things will be different."

"Would you ever quit, Becks! Sheesh. For the love of all that is holy, I'm not asking for an apology. I'm asking you to see that it's a good thing to choose *yourself* sometimes. To do what's best for you. Your whole life, you've done nothing but put us first, sacrifice your own desires to help your family. And son, I appreciate that more than you could ever know." She pauses, gives her head a shake. "But I wasn't kidding when I said you needed to take some time this summer to get away and see how different life could be for you if you'd only just let yourself live it. You've been rotting away doing nothing for far too long."

"I have a job you know, Mam."

"You hate that crusty old job!"

She's right. I do.

"You're totally wasted at that school, and you know it."

I hate to admit it, but she's right again.

"When I get home, I'll quit," I promise, realizing as I say it that it's true. I will. I think I already knew it was something I needed to do when I got back.

"Or, you could just not come home at all."

I frown. "But... I need to be there."

"Why?" she demands. "If you're quitting the hoity-toity job, then what's your reasoning here, son? Because I'm all ears."

"Aoife's baby's on the way," I say, but even to my ears, it sounds like I'm grasping at straws.

"PLANES EXIST, YOU UTTER EEJIT!" Aoife's yell comes from offscreen, confirming that my siblings may have left the room, but they've absolutely been eavesdropping this entire time.

"Wow, tell me how you really feel, Aoife," I say, but I can't help it—I'm smiling.

"We don't need you to take care of us, Becks." Mam's eyes soften. "For a long time, I know that you focused on putting us first, put your own happiness aside to look after everyone else. But guess what? You've been gone half the summer and we're all still standing."

"Barely," I joke.

Mam glares at me. "Hush with that. We don't need you to be here to take care of us, Beckett. We just need you to be happy. And this Keeley clearly makes you happy."

Mam's words are sweet. Sincere. And they remind me that my family loves me. No matter where I am or what I do, they want the best for me.

"She makes me very happy."

"Are you in love with her?"

"I am." I nod again. "And I know she loves me. But I don't know if that's enough."

"I swear, sometimes I feel like I've raised a bunch of halfwits!" Mam's voice changes to match her fiery eyes. "Of course that's not enough! Love isn't just a feeling, it's a commitment. A decision. Something you need to fight for. You can't just sit there on your laurels, you need to fight for her, son! Don't run away. Stand strong and fight for what fate has put in your path. The gift of love that's been given to you. Don't let history repeat itself."

"What do you mean?" I frown at her slightly blurry image on the computer screen.

She gives me a pointed look. "I think your Gran spun you wee 'uns fairy tales and superstitious stories and folklore galore because it was easier, sometimes, for her to live in fiction than it was in fact. It's my belief that your Gran had a good and happy life, but that she didn't face up to some hard realities, and this caused her some regrets."

Hearing this surprises me. I always thought that my gran lived with no regrets, always wore her heart on her sleeve... but knowing that she and Douglas broke each other's hearts when she left, Mam's words make me realize that Gran made a choice, and that choice had consequences.

"I don't want that for you, son. While I totally understand that we all have to do what we have to do to get by, I encourage you to live your truth, Beckett. Fight for whatever makes you feel something real."

"Thanks, Mam," I say—the most sincere thank you I've ever uttered. Because she's right.

I love Keeley.

I want to be with Keeley.

I *choose* Keeley.

And I'm going to do everything in my power to show her that. To fight for what I know we have.

"We love you, Beckett," Mam replies. "And I know you always like to quote your Gran saying *what's for you won't pass you*, but I came up with a new version for you to consider."

"Oh yeah?" I ask.

Mam smiles. "When fate gives you what's for you... don't let it slip away."

Chapter Forty-One
Keeley

"You look tired," Ezra tells me when he pulls up outside The Serendipity to pick me up so we can head to Silver Springs.

This again.

But I know he's not wrong—I saw a bit of a resemblance to the Swamp Monster when I looked in the mirror this morning. I didn't sleep a wink last night, tossing and turning while my own sour words—*it has to be this way*—burned in my brain.

"Thanks, bro," I reply sarcastically as I climb into his SUV.

"Seriously, though. Are you okay?"

I grimace. "Beckett leaves today."

"Yeah, I know. Did you two have a fight or something?"

"No." I exhale sharply before admitting, "I'm just really sad it's over."

"It is? I just figured..." Ezra trails off, shooting me a slightly bemused look.

"Figured what?" I ask, my smile humorless.

My brother shrugs. We're close, but we don't really have

heart-to-heart type conversations, well... ever. "I don't know. Part of me figured that he might stay. That you might go there. That you'd do long distance." He winces a little, like he senses that he's overstepped our usual conversational boundaries. He adds a smile and shrug while saying, "But what do I know?"

Grateful for the shift in tone, I laugh and give him a little punch in the arm. "You know nothing, my dear brother."

"Honestly, I don't disagree. So let's hope Ev gets Mae's brains, because I am empty of all knowledge." Ezra laughs, and I relax into my seat, glad that some kind of equilibrium is restored, for now, and that our conversation is back in safer territory, for now.

Talking about Beckett hurts too badly at the moment.

By the time we're entering the Silver Springs lobby, I'm still trying to push away my swirling thoughts of last night at the fair and the fact that Becks is currently back at Mr. P's apartment, packing the last of his stuff. I need to focus on Gramps right now.

Lainey, the receptionist, gives us a wave as we walk by. "Your grandfather is in much higher spirits today."

"I'm so glad," I reply. I have the old "Moondance" record tucked under one arm, and a box of chocolate-covered cherries—Gramps's favorite—tucked under the other.

Ezra and I head towards the back porch, where Gramps is apparently relishing the fresh air after a couple of days in bed.

And Lainey's not wrong. We find him in a rocking chair, tucked under a woolen blanket and cheerfully sipping coffee as he admires a group of birds hopping across a path that intersects the flowerbeds in the pretty gardens.

"Magpies," Gramps tells us. "Four of them."

I slide into the seat beside him, and Ezra sits across the table.

"Are there often birds in the garden here?" Ez asks conversationally. "Do they put out feed?"

"Never." Gramps shakes his head in mild irritation. "Antonella who lives here is terrified of birds. Lets out an awful shriek if she sees one. So they never put out food. But these magpies have been in the garden since I came out." He smiles affectionately at them, his eyes a little misty.

"Maybe they're paying you a morning visit, too," I say.

Gramps's eyes—the same deep blue color that we share with Ezra and my father—fix on me, and for a moment, they're startlingly clear. "Or, maybe they're here to visit you."

"That's a nice thought." I smile at him. "Hey Gramps, I brought something for you."

I place the cherries and the record on the table in front of him.

He completely ignores the candy as he zeroes in on the record.

"Oh, I love this one." He runs a wrinkled hand across the front of the record sleeve, and then begins humming the tune to himself, tapping out a rhythm with his fingertips.

"Oh, it's a marvelous night for a moondance..." he sings softly to himself. Then stops. Looks from the record to the magpies. They've stopped hopping now. In fact, it almost seems like they're looking at us.

Which is weird. Obviously, my lack of sleep is making itself known.

"Strange that the magpies are here today of all days. Four was for... what was it? A boy? Yes. *Four for a boy*."

Ezra and I share a concerned look before my brother reaches over and gently pats Gramps's hand. "Is there a record player here, Gramps? I can ask Lainey to play it for you later. Or maybe we could go inside now and you could rest up while it plays. If there's no record player, I could play it for you on my phone..."

Gramps isn't listening. He's sliding the record out of its sleeve.

"Oh, well the player's not out here, Gramps," I start, but I stop short when he pulls an old, yellowed envelope out of the sleeve next.

He holds it in his hand for a moment. Ezra and I share another look.

"What's that, Gramps?" Ez asks gently.

"A letter from back when I was still a boy, in so many ways." Gramps sets the envelope on the table. It's addressed to him, his name written in a loopy, swirly script. He looks at it for a beat, then turns to me. "Do you have a boy in your life?"

"Um," I say. Swallow a little painfully.

"A boy you love?" Gramps prompts.

"Yes." The word tumbles out of me before I can stop it. Ezra's eyes widen almost comically at my response.

Gramps looks at me for a long, long moment. His eyes are lucid again, but his brow is deeply furrowed.

And then, he surprises me by sliding the letter towards me. "This is for you, my sweet girl."

My sweet girl.

He used to call me that all the time when I was growing up. I haven't heard the endearment in ages, and it makes me smile as Gramps presses the letter into my hand. Unsure what else to do—and more than a little curious—I tuck it into my purse.

At that moment, the magpies in the garden fly off.

Gramps watches them go. "I was a very stubborn, head-strong boy back in my day," he continues, his tone a little remorseful. He smiles down at the envelope. "Always thought I knew everything about the world when I knew nothing at all. I hope your boy isn't too stubborn and proud to keep him from following his heart."

279

"No, Beckett is..."

Incredible.

"Are you the same, Ben?" Gramps turns his eyes to my brother. "Stubborn?"

"I'm Ezra, Gramps," my brother says, gently as could be. "Ben's my dad, your son."

"Ah. Yes." Gramps nods, his eyes a little dull again. "Of course."

"But in answer to your question... yes, I can be way too stubborn sometimes." He grins at me. "Keeley here's the same. It must run in the family."

We spend the rest of the visit chatting on lighter topics, drinking coffee, and even playing a round of Gin Rummy.

When Gramps begins to tire, we make our leave. And as we say our goodbyes and give him hugs, Gramps says: "Remember, don't let your circumstances dictate your heart, my sweet girl."

The words hit me like an arrow to the heart. Bullseye.

Chapter Forty-Two
Keeley

MY BROTHER ROUNDS on me as we walk towards his SUV.

"You're in love?" he demands.

"Shh," I tell him, digging in my purse.

I finally pull out the letter and stare at it for a moment, taking in the foreign stamp that says "Eire."

The Gaelic word for Ireland. Beckett taught me that this summer.

My stomach flips. The letter's from Noeleen. It has to be. I just *know* it, in the very depths of me.

"What is it, Keels?" Ezra asks with a frown.

"I think it's from Beckett's grandmother."

His eyes flicker with interest, but he seems to read the room remarkably well, because he points down the street at Serendipi-Tea. "I'll get us coffees, give you a moment."

"Thanks."

I sink down on a bench and flip over the envelope to examine the postmark. It's dated 1970—a few years after Noeleen left town. With trembling fingers, I carefully take a piece of paper out of the envelope.

It's thin, worn where it folds.

My dearest Douglas,

It's been a few years since we've spoken, but I hope you know that I still think of you fondly. I have your ring tucked in the back of a drawer, as a memory of you.

The time we spent with each other was nothing short of magical, and I truly believe it was ordained by fate. Our time together is a cherished memory I will carry with me forever—close to my heart, for only myself, because speaking aloud about what we had would never do it justice.

Leaving you was one of the hardest things I've ever had to do. But your father made it clear that there was no future for us together, and I would have never wanted to put you in an uncomfortable position with your family...

I gasp in horror at the words I've just read.

This was not, in any world, an ending I could have imagined.

Reading on is no easier, as Noeleen's words communicate that my great-grandfather did not view an Irishwoman from a working-class family to be a suitable wife for his only son, whom he intended to be the future mayor of our town.

So, Noeleen left. She couldn't bear to cause any fuss with the Roberts family. And that way, my grandfather would never be forced to choose between love and duty to his family.

She mentioned that she heard from Sissy that Gramps had, indeed, eventually been elected mayor, and was loved by the people of our town. She said she was happy to hear he had married. And that she had married too.

She concluded by saying that she sent this letter as closure. To let him know that she was happy, and now that she'd had word he was happy too, she knew that all's well that ends well, essentially.

Although the phrase Noeleen used was "what's for you won't pass you."

By the time I'm finished reading the letter, tears are streaming down my face.

It's a lot to process, and when Ezra comes back, he takes one look at me and my tear-stained expression, then drops to a seat beside me. Hands me a takeout cup. "Two pumps of caramel syrup and a splash of heavy cream."

"You're the best, Ez. Thanks," I say through a sniffle.

He smiles at me. Nods towards the letter. "Was it from Noeleen?"

"It was. Sent in 1970, a few years after she lived here."

"Whoa. That's crazy. I don't think Dad was even born yet." My brother hesitates, his tattooed forearms flexing as he grips his coffee cup. "Do you... want to talk about it?"

"According to this," I say as I hold up the letter, "she left because our great-grandfather didn't approve of her as a potential wife for his son."

"What? That's insane."

"I know, right?" I finger the letter. "I guess it was a different time back then, but still... I can't believe that our great-grandfather got involved to that extent. All to apparently help Gramps's chances at being voted mayor." I shake my head. "In the letter, Noeleen said that she didn't want Gramps to have to choose between her and the life he had in front of him. She thought that wouldn't be fair, so she left."

"She didn't give him a choice in the matter?"

I shake my head. "Don't think so."

"Can I read it?"

"Sure." Noeleen and Douglas are as much a part of Ezra's history as mine.

My brother skims the letter quickly, then turns to me with an incredulous look on his face. "And you say *I'm* the one who knows nothing."

"Pardon?"

Ezra's still staring at me like I've metamorphosed into the literal swamp monster. "Did you and I read the same letter?"

"I believe so."

"Because what *I* got from that was that Noeleen was scared she wouldn't be enough for Gramps. That he'd regret his choice if he stayed with her." Ezra grimaces at me.

My heart picks up speed as his words hit shockingly close to home. "I didn't think of it that way..."

"Because you were so focused on her leaving."

"I guess." My heart is truly pounding now.

Ezra pauses. "Maybe that drew your attention because of a certain someone else who's leaving later today..."

It's my turn to grimace.

"What happened with you and Becks, Keels?" Ez asks as he studies my face.

"Sometimes, love's meant to be temporary." I say aloud the spiel I've been repeating in my head all night. Swallow thickly before I continue. "And while it might not have been meant to be between Gramps and Noeleen, it all worked out for everyone in the end. And things will work out for me and Becks, too. We'll each go back to our separate lives, and this hurt will be a happy memory one day."

"Okay, that's one take." Ezra gives his head a shake, looking a little baffled. "But sometimes it's meant to *be*, period. Forget all the circumstances surrounding it. Look at Mae and me. When I met her, I had no idea it would lead to her being my wife and the mother of my child. I was on vacation in Seoul, for goodness sakes, I wasn't searching for a wife. But there she was. And because it was meant to be, we worked to get ourselves to where we are today. We knew we were meant to be together, against all odds."

"But how did you know that? How did you know she'd love you and never leave?"

He stares at me for a minute, and a flicker shoots through his eyes that I've never seen before. He looks... pained.

"Jeez, Keels. When you said earlier that you and Beckett were over, I thought it had to do with you and Andrew breaking up so recently and you being gun-shy to jump into a new relationship, especially one with complications given where you both live. But this is about Mom, isn't it?"

I don't answer his question directly. Instead, I say, "Beckett told me he was thinking about staying here. But if he *did* stay, he would eventually leave. Just like Mom. Just like Noeleen. Hell, even Andrew left and he's *from* here. Lives in the same building as me."

There it is. My darkest shame: *I'm fundamentally leaveable.*

"Stop it!"

"Stop what?"

"Wallowing like that," Ezra says. Firmly. "Andrew didn't leave you, and you know it. You guys grew apart because you weren't meant to be together. You had no future together. And Mom... well, you can't let the past dictate the future. Mom did a terrible thing when she left us. But she made her choice, and now, she has to live with the consequences."

"What do you mean?"

"I mean she doesn't have me, or you, or Mae, or Everett in her life. And man, is she ever missing out by not having Everett around."

"Big time," I agree as Ezra's words sink in.

"Keels," he says, grabbing my hand and squeezing it. "Mom made a bad choice. And Noeleen made a choice, too.

285

And sure, it worked out in the end for everyone, but it didn't have to work out that way. Fate brought her and our Gramps together for a time, or whatever it was she said in the letter. But to make it work past that, they both had to choose each other."

"You make it sound so simple."

"Simple. But not easy," he corrects. "It sounds to me like Noeleen didn't let herself choose Gramps in case the circumstances around their relationship ended up crushing it. And it sounds like Gramps was too proud to go after her when she took that worst-case scenario and ran with it."

Don't let your circumstances dictate your heart.

I stare at Ezra as he continues, "If Beckett is telling you that he's choosing you, you have the option to choose him back, instead of just leaving him before he can leave you. Because if you live your whole life that way, sure you might have a bunch of happy memories at the end of it... but you'll be remembering them alone. Like Mom. It's not about leaving or not leaving, it's about running away or else choosing to stay and fight for what—*who*—you love."

His words sting like a slap to the face.

I'm a total hypocrite.

I've let my circumstances dictate my heart in every way, putting up protective barriers to try and control the narrative. I've tried to shape my situation so I don't get hurt again.

This summer, I came up with the idea that the ending doesn't matter as a shield. An attempt to live in the moment and not worry about the potential of getting hurt. To *control* the potential of getting hurt.

But what I've effectively done is placed conditions on my feelings for Beckett. And that's just not the truth of how I feel about him at all.

I still stand by what I wrote in my article—that sometimes with love, the beginning or end doesn't matter, but the journey—but I no longer stand by that being mine and Beckett's love story.

Because what we've got? I never want it to end.

"I don't want to run away from love," I say miserably. "I'm just so scared of having to live through that feeling, that rejection again. And the fear is so strong, it's been overshadowing all my choices."

Ezra pauses. And then, he smiles. "You asked me a moment ago how I know that Mae will never leave me, and the simple answer is: I don't. I don't know what the future holds. But I wake up every single day and choose her, and will continue to choose her, even when the going gets tough—because it does—because I love her. And when you really love someone, they will always be worth choosing. To the point that your fears of what you could lose in the process will come second to making that choice. So, make the right choice, Keeley."

"There's only one choice," I reply, jumping up from the bench. There's no time to waste.

It's Beckett.

I choose Beckett.

And I choose him knowing that I can't control how it looks or where we live or what tomorrow might bring.

I'm going to cut that lifeline and let myself truly fall. And instead of constantly bracing for impact, I'll live in the knowledge that whatever the cost, I've made the right decision for me.

For *us*.

Beckett deserves no less in life than to be loved unconditionally.

And you know what? Neither do I.

Chapter Forty-Three
Keeley

THE TWO-MILE DRIVE BACK to The Serendipity takes approximately seven hundred and fifty-nine years.

First of all, Ezra insists on driving no more than five over the speed limit. Which is preposterous, given our circumstances. You'd think a shaven-headed, tatted-up dude who's just been directed to "drive as fast as your Toyota can manage!" would have a little *Fast and Furious* in him.

But no.

Ezra drives like a half-blind octogenarian who forgot to wear his glasses.

And as if that wasn't enough, we hit every red on every single traffic light along the route and stop no less than three times for pedestrians on crosswalks. One of those pedestrians, of course, has a puppy who decides to lay down mid-crossing for a little rest.

I roll down my window, half considering sticking my head out and yelling at the guy to pick up his dog and *move it!*

Ez, from the driver's seat, grabs my arm and yanks me back down. "Dude, chill. Isn't his flight later tonight?"

"Yes, but..." I cross my arms and glare. "That's not the point."

Ezra's lips tick up. "What is the point, then?"

"I'm trying to make a statement! Profess my undying love!" I throw my arms out to accentuate my point.

Which, in combination with my current under-eye bags and bedhead, makes me look not unlike Becks's beloved banshee.

Ezra snickers. "Becks is a lucky guy."

"Drive faster, grandma!" I retort.

When we finally get to my building, Ez hardly stops the car before I'm flinging the door open, calling, "Love you, byeeee" as I race inside The Serendipity.

The sound of his laughter follows me, which makes me smile. I'll buy him a burrito or something later to make up for being such a brat this morning (and also to thank him for all of his infinite wisdom). But right now, I am a woman on a mission.

Inside the lobby, I run for the stairs, racing up the grand staircase to the second floor and veering towards the hallway that leads to our apartments.

Ping!

The elevator chimes, and I turn my head to see the doors slowly closing on Beckett.

Without giving a single fraction of a thought as to what I'm doing, I one-eighty and bolt for the elevator.

Throw myself through the doors... and promptly run into something hard.

Not again, I think as I fall forward, weightless for a moment before—

"I've got you, Keeley," comes Beckett's achingly familiar and comforting voice as his arms circle around me, catching me mid-fall.

I look up into my favorite hazel-green eyes in the entire

world, which belong to my favorite person in the entire world, as the elevator lurches to life and starts moving. Smile as I relish the feeling of being in his arms again.

Safe. Cared for. Cherished. Totally at ease and comfortable and at home.

Home.

The word has me crashing back to reality as I see the guitar case I just tripped on (again) sitting next to a backpack and a suitcase.

Panic builds in me.

He's on his way to the airport already.

"Beckett!" I cry, scurrying to a stand before leaning over and jamming the emergency stop button.

The elevator shudders to a rickety, shaky stop, and Becks peers at me, his expression halfway between quizzical and amused.

"Keeley!" he replies, matching my tone. His eyes are twinkling. "Want to tell me why you just did that?"

"Because fate can only do so much! The building can only do so much!" I'm yelling. Probably sound half-frantic. And I don't care. "But I can choose to do the rest. To make the right choice. And I choose *you*, Becks. I choose to stick with you. *Get* stuck with you. Over everything, I pick you. Whatever that looks like. Wherever this goes or whatever ends up happening, I'm not going to run away. I'm going to face my fears."

I'm out of breath, talking in half-garbled, quick, gibberish-adjacent riddles.

"I just want to be with you. Maybe I could buy a plane ticket and come with you while we work out what's next? Or even just ride with you to the airport or..."

I trail off.

Because he's laughing at me. The jerk is laughing at me... *again.*

290

"It's not funny! I love you!"

He smiles a smile brighter than a thousand burning suns. "I love you too, Keeley, but I think we can pump the brakes for a second on all your grand plans. I'm not leaving for the airport. I was just going upstairs."

I blink at him. "I... I... what?"

He indicates the elevator panel, where the "up" arrow is indeed flashing as we stay stuck. We're somewhere between floors two and three, I now realize.

"Why are you bringing your guitar and bags upstairs?"

"Because Mr. Prenchenko is coming back later today, so I can't stay at his place anymore."

"You're making even less sense than I was a second ago, Becks."

"Nah," he says with a shrug, but his eyes are dancing. "Nothing has ever made more sense. I'm taking my stuff to Cash's place so I can crash on his couch for a bit until apartment 2C officially becomes available."

My feet feel glued to the floor, yet my legs feel precariously wobbly, all at once. "But... that's where I live."

"Yes. Until you find and move into your new place in Boston, and then, 2C will be where *I* live." He smiles. "And where you come visit on your days off."

I shake my head. "I don't have to take the job, Beckett. I don't want to leave you."

He puts a hand on each of my arms and looks me dead in the eye. "You're taking the job, Keeley. And I'll be right here in Serendipity Springs, teaching lessons and recording more music with Ezra and helping Cash with baseball, which will be a learning curve to say the least." He chuckles. "I want the best for you always, and this job is going to bring you joy and help you grow—so I think you should take it. With the reassurance that you're not leaving, you're moving forward. With me. Because we'll continue to be together, still spend every moment we can together... if that's what you want, that is."

"Is this real?" I ask dumbly, my heart picking up so much speed that it's in danger of imploding. "You're actually moving here? Into my apartment?"

Beckett looks down at me like I am the center of the entire universe. "I wouldn't want to be anywhere else."

Chapter Forty-Four
Beckett

AFTER WE DEPOSIT my bags in Cash's living room, Keeley and I make our way back down to the second floor. Almost as if by default, we walk through her—*my!*—apartment and climb out to the fire escape.

We sit side by side, upper arms and thighs touching, and Keeley rests her head on my shoulder.

I take a moment to soak in the fact that she's here with me. That I'm staying here, too. And nothing has ever felt more right.

My heart is full.

"I have so many questions, but first, I have to say... I'm so sorry about last night, Becks. Sorry for panicking. Sorry for running. Sorry that, in that moment, I couldn't let myself believe in you, or in me, or in us." Her voice is laden with remorse, and I put my arm around her, drawing her close.

"You don't need to be sorry," I tell her. "I totally understand. But I am curious, what happened between then and now to change your mind?"

She looks up at me, blue eyes big and round. "I found something this morning."

From her pocket, she extracts an envelope, and when she hands it to me, my stomach turns over.

Gran's handwriting.

"What?" I turn to stare at her. "How?"

"It was tucked into the sleeve of that record I brought Gramps." She gently nudges my arm. "I think you should read it."

With trembling fingers, I extract a wrinkled, weathered letter. It's from Gran, addressed to Douglas.

As I read, my heart goes through a whole series of gymnastics—pain for Gran being rejected by Douglas's family, sorrow for her feeling like she had no choice but to leave, relief for reading her detailing that, even though it was painful, everything had turned out okay in the end.

I swallow thickly, my eyes a little glazed as I reach the end of the letter. And then, I turn back to Keeley, feeling a little raw. "This is what made you reconsider?"

"Noeleen left because she thought she wasn't enough for Douglas." Keeley sinks her teeth into her bottom lip. "And I realized that's what I did last night. I left because I thought you'd eventually regret it if you stayed, and that would be my fault. I realize now that I was projecting onto you what my mom put me through."

"I get it," I say gently. "But I need you to understand something. Nothing about this could ever be your fault, because my decision to stay here is just that—*mine*. I've decided to stay of my own accord. Not because I felt obligated, and not because of anything you could or would potentially do. I'm staying because *I* want to be here with you. Forget fate, forget what's meant to be or not meant to be... because I *choose* you, no strings, no conditions. Just love for you."

What I've realized during my time in Serendipity Springs is that when Gran died, the magic didn't die with her.

No, that magic has always been here, because I see now that magic is what we make it.

Gran made decisions that shaped the course of her life —*her destiny*—but she also decided to find joy and contentment in the little things in life. In the people around her who loved her. In the highs and the lows, she chose to always believe in better... and that belief starts in believing in yourself.

Just like Keeley and I both learned this summer. We had to believe in ourselves before we could truly believe in *us*. In the magic we've found together.

"I love you, Beckett." Keeley's voice cracks on the words, and my heart expands impossibly more for her.

"You were never going to be easy to leave, Keeley," I tell her with conviction. "In fact, you were never going to be *possible* to leave. You're my home now."

She swallows thickly, and when she tilts her head so her eyes can meet mine, they're shining with tears. "All I want is to be yours, Beckett... wherever this life takes us, wherever we might end up, I'm all yours." She smiles. "And I know you're mine."

And if that isn't the sweetest, most magical music to my ears.

Epilogue
Keeley

One Year Later...

THE ROOFTOP GARDEN of The Serendipity is beautiful in July. It's blooming with a million fiery, bright colors and sweet floral smells that carry on the gentle breeze, mingling with the chatter and laughter that fill the summer air.

And I mean *fill*. This place is bursting to capacity, which briefly makes me think about fire code, which makes me smile as I remember all of my nights on the fire escape with Beckett last summer.

I smooth down my favorite ripped jeans as I look at the huge crowd that has gathered to celebrate the amazing talent that is Beckett McCarthy.

My heart couldn't be more full.

Beckett's entire rowdy family are front and center, happily (and loudly) excited to be on their first trip to America, although Niamh is still coming to terms with the fact that she may not meet Oprah. Aoife bounces baby Keira on her knee as she talks to Mr. Prenchenko, who appears to be asking her a million questions. Mr. P is quite the self-proclaimed Hibernophile these days.

Hibernophile meaning person obsessed with Irish culture, for the record. I had to Google it after Mr. Prenchenko used it in conversation a few times and I finally caught on to the fact that he wasn't talking about herbs.

Now, the word "faerie tree" gets thrown into the conversation, and I smile at the now-familiar lore. When Beckett and I went to Mayo for a very chaotic Christmas last year, we did a driving tour of the country's top sights, navigating a million twisty-turny backroads lined with stone wall fences as he took me to see a famous faerie tree in Cork.

I wanted to go and kiss the Blarney stone, but Beckett said that it was a germ-infested tourist trap and that he would kiss me instead. Which, of course, I readily agreed to.

So, instead of lining up to kiss a rock, we went to see the Cliffs of Moher and the Ring of Kerry and drove all the way to the North of the island to take in the Giant's Causeway. We went to Irish bars to drink pints of fresh Guinness— which Becks claimed again was superior to the canned variety we can buy in the States, but honestly I still couldn't tolerate the stuff. We also checked out Irish trad music performances in Temple Bar and Galway town.

On all these outings, Beckett wore a baseball cap to hide his face from the ever-growing crowd of people who recognize him since "Love and Serendipity" went viral on SoundCloud.

Now, several months later, we're gathered in Serendipity Springs—where it all started—for the launch party of best-selling international artist Beckett McCarthy's debut album. Made up of a collection of songs he wrote back in Ireland, mixed with several tracks about falling in love when he least expected it, and even a country-esque song—"Riot Grrrl"— that he wrote just to make me smile.

Because if there's one thing Beckett never fails to do, it's make me smile.

"Isn't this amazing?" Nori asks as we watch Cash, Ezra, and Becks set up the equipment.

"Unreal," I agree with a grin. Becks and I often hang out with Cash and Nori, who both still live in the building. Serendipi-Tea continues to grow and flourish under Nori's ownership, and we visit the shop often—especially now that she is importing and stocking Becks's beloved Irish Barry's tea. He may have shed a tear when he drank his first cup.

Cash and Nori are also engaged now and make for super fun couple friends. We've even formed a beer league baseball team.

We're terrible.

Cash can barely play due to his injury, Nori shrieks and closes her eyes every time the ball comes near her, and Beckett can never remember any of the rules. Or which way to run when he hits the ball.

It's chaotic and hilarious and a totally perfect pastime for us.

"I don't think I've ever even met a celebrity, nevermind known one," breathes Mae from my other side, her hand cradling the belly that currently holds Everett's little-sister-to-be.

Everett is dancing and putting on quite the performance for the Hathaways, who are sitting on a bench near the back, holding hands and as in love as ever. They're the original elevator meet-cute of the building, and I'm happy Beckett and I share a similar origin story as a couple.

If I have one wish, it's that we're as happy and content and as in love as they are in generations to come.

Somehow, I have no doubt that that will be the case.

"Don't catch Becks hearing you call him that. He hates that word," I tell Mae with a smile. And it's true. My boyfriend, forever humble and gracious, seems a bit baffled with his success, but I like that he's the sort of guy who will never let it go to his head.

All he wants is to live the small-town life here in Serendipity Springs, and make music in Ezra's studio in his spare time between teaching kiddos guitar. He's made enough money from signing with a label to teach all of his lessons on a purely volunteer basis. He even utilizes the local community center—and occasionally one of the quiet rooms in the library (with Sissy's lavish blessing)—to reach more kids.

I glance at Sissy through the crowd. With her hair a foot high and her smile a foot wide, she's earning a lot of surreptitious, confused glances from Beckett's younger brothers.

"He'll have to get used to it," Mae throws back at me, smiling indulgently. "Especially after your write-up on today's event!"

"I'm not sure I'll have quite that much reach," I say with a giggle.

Becks and I decided that this party today was the perfect opportunity to celebrate his album launch and welcome his family to the USA. And I'm thrilled to be doing a write-up about it for Evoke Serendipity Springs—the new sister site to Boston-based Evoke that I now run.

Yes, that's right. You're looking at the head writer for the first regional Evoke website. Nisha has plans to roll out many more over the next year, but Serendipity Springs got to be the pilot location.

After I took the job in Boston last summer, I moved out there, as planned, and Beckett moved into my apartment at The Serendipity.

It was a great arrangement for a few months. We Face-Timed daily, drove to see each other on weekends, and Beckett would come up frequently during the week through the late fall and winter so we could go to Bruins games (which he loved) and Celtics games (he was baffled to discover that the team has no Irish players despite the name).

We ate our way through all the foodie goodies on offer at Faneuil Hall, and one weekend, Beckett brought Gramps to visit me. We wheeled him around the aquarium so he could look at the penguins.

It was fun.

And as it turned out, good for both of us. Beckett put down roots in Serendipity Springs with his work and friends and music, and it put me in the drivers' seat of the situation in a much healthier way than what I'd been doing before, when I was trying to stuff my love for Beckett in a box.

I'm no longer living in fear and making reactionary choices. Instead, I'm choosing to face my fears head on. And when your fears have nowhere to hide, nowhere to fester in the dark, they're no longer as scary or difficult to conquer.

Our time doing long distance taught me that my love for Beckett would overflow out of any vessel in which I tried to contain it, and seeing how strong it is—how strong we are together—has allowed me to deepen both my trust in him as a partner and my trust in myself.

What I've realized is that, when you're with the right person, you make things work. You let your heart shape your circumstances.

Of course, when Nisha approached me earlier this spring about heading up a regional chapter of the brand, I was ecstatic to bring my dream job to my hometown, where my dream boyfriend now resides.

What's for you won't pass you, Beckett's Gran used to say. But we also work hard not to let it pass us. Because that's what real love does—it holds on, holds tight, and holds true.

"This turned out to be quite the event," the building's owner, Archer, says to me with a nod and some semblance of a smile. He and his wife Willa stand near us, his arm around her slender waist. "Although I'm a little worried we are over capacity right now."

"I won't tell if you don't," I reply, which transforms his normally serious disposition into a smiling one.

Archer was gracious enough to let us use the rooftop garden for today's album launch, and when I got to chatting to him about planning this party, it transpired that The Serendipity meddled to bring him and Willa together, too.

And that wasn't all. Archer informed me that Willa's friend Sophie, who used to tend to the garden on this rooftop, fell in love up here and moved with her former best friend Peter—now the love of her life—to North Carolina.

In fact, the more Beckett and I have gotten to chatting with the residents of The Serendipity, the more these types of stories emerged: Olivia and Logan on the other side of the hall fell in love when they became next-door neighbors; Matteo, who owns Aria (which I need to try again as a date location) and Iris from upstairs met when the building started delivering her his newspapers; Scarlett, the nice girl who lives in the basement, fell in love with her brother's best friend shortly after moving in; and my new friend Phoebe got together with her boyfriend, Jay, in a similar fashion.

In fact, everywhere I look at The Serendipity, the magic of love is all around me.

The more I fought against falling in love, the harder I fell. There was no escaping the plans it had for me... and I'm so glad I faced my fears and let myself get swept away in love's journey, because it brought me here.

I wouldn't want to be anywhere else.

"Hello, everyone!" The speakers set up on either side of the makeshift stage squeak as Beckett's lilting voice echoes across the rooftop. "Thank you for being here for this exciting day—a day which, if I'm being honest, I never thought would happen."

301

Everyone claps and cheers. Cash puts two fingers in his mouth and whistles.

Then, Beckett begins to strum his guitar. The crowd dies down as he says, "And while there are many people to thank for making this happen, there's one person in particular that I want to acknowledge."

His hazel-green eyes zero in on me. Hold me captive.

"Keeley Roberts," Beckett says, his lips curling into the dimpled smile I know and love. "You're my muse, my inspiration, the love of my life. The only one for me, now and always, and I love you more than you could ever know."

He then starts to play the opening chords of my favorite track.

The one with the hauntingly beautiful melody I first heard coming from the library.

The one he sang for me at the recording studio that made me rush in to kiss him.

A song he named "Stay."

Only Magic in the Building

a whimsical romance series

The Serendipity

Emma St. Clair

The Cupid Chronicles

Courtney Walsh

Petals and Plot Twists

Jenny Proctor

Misfortune and Mr. Right

Savannah Scott

Clean Out of Luck

Carina Taylor

Off the Wall

Julie Christianson

Signed, Sealed, and Smitten

Melanie Jacobson

The Escape Plan

Katie Bailey

A Note From Katie

Sláinte, everyone, and cheers to book number eight!

If you're seeing this, a huge thank you for being along for this wild ride with me and for reading Beckett and Keeley's story.

I grew up in Ireland. Not too far from Mayo, actually. And though I've lived in Canada for over a decade now, I still maintain dual citizenship with Ireland, and this book was a super fun way for me to reconnect with my roots. Writing it made me feel homesick in all the best ways. It also made me really crave a good cup of tea.

Anyhow, without further ado, on to the many, many thank yous necessary for this book's existence...

To all of the wonderful ladies in this group project, it's been such a pleasure to work with you all and get to know many of you better. Special thanks to Kiki and Courtney for all of the tireless work you both put in to make The Serendipity such a magical place to be. I cannot believe how much behind the scenes coordination goes into a project like this!

Julie - Thank you for bearing with my twenty five million

questions about everything, and for working so closely with me to make our characters such good friends. I loved seeing the four of them happy at the end, and it was so much fun to put our heads together to make this happen. Love you always.

Another special thanks to Alex, who held my hand (as usual) through every tiny step of this book and endlessly encouraged me. Your wisdom is incredible, and you're such an amazing friend. I'm so happy to have you in my corner. For this one, an extra special thank you for using your own experiences to help me sensitively and authentically address the topic of dementia.

Leah, for the hundreds of voicenotes and memes per day that are fuel to my soul, for all the writing sprints we hyped each other up to do, and for a friendship that means the world to me. You're one in a million.

To Emily, for an exceedingly helpful edit, and also to Madi, for helping my book take shape in critical places (as always, you have your finger perfectly placed on every plot-hole and problem, and I'm in awe of it).

Thank you Megan for your unbelievably helpful beta read, and to Abby, Suzan, and Jody for catching all the straggling typos at the eleventh hour—as always, I'm so appreciative of you all.

To my main girls, the Emilys, who are the most fantastic dream team any author could ever hope to have in their corner. You two keep me sane in so many ways, and I hope we can work together for a long, long time. So much love to you both.

Thank you to Melody, for the gorgeous cover and incredible group cover concept. I loved working with you!

To my street team and ARC readers, and to my loyal readers who've come on this rollercoaster of an author journey with me—THANK YOU ALL! I am endlessly grateful to have the honor of people hyping, supporting, and reading my books. I'm so lucky to have each and every one of you.

And last but certainly not least, to my family: my husband and kiddos, who are my entire world, and also the entire Hanna clan across the Atlantic who love to talk excitedly over each other at any given opportunity and gave me endless inspiration for the McCarthy family.

And with that, a special shoutout to my little brother Jenson, who's been absolutely "lethal" in helping me get up to date with today's Irishisms from afar—I definitely owe you a spice bag next time I'm home.

Tons of love,

Katie B x

Also by Katie Bailey

The Quit List

Donovan Family

So That Happened

I Think He Knows

Only in Atlanta

The Roommate Situation

The Neighbor War

Cyclones Christmas

Season's Schemings

Holiday Hostilities

About the Author

Katie Bailey is an Amazon top 25 bestselling author of rom coms with relatable characters and tons of chemistry. Her aim with every new love story she writes is to give readers a good laugh, maybe even a bit of a cry, but definitely leave them with a new book boyfriend.

When she's not busy writing, Katie spends her time chasing twin tornado littles, cursing the cold Canadian winters she endures each year, chugging coffee by the bucketload, and crushing on her husband, who's the real life inspiration behind all of the fictional men she's written.

You can connect with Katie on Instagram @authorkatiebailey

Made in the USA
Coppell, TX
25 April 2025

48702207R00187